THE FISHERMAN'S RING

By: James E. Joyce

Printed in the United States of America

Library of Congress in Publication Data:

Joyce, THE FISHERMAN'S RING
ISBN 148-3-939-03-0

CONTENTS

I. IL PAPA 'E MORTO

"Your Holy Eminence . . . coffee is ready in the sitting room. Mass Begins shortly in Chapel."

Sister Vencenza had checked a few moments before, and the Pope's coffee hadn't been touched. It wasn't like him to be late. She would have to return to the commissary to brew more if his holiness was to have a cup of hot coffee this morning.

"Your Eminence, are you awake? Your coffee is ready." For a month now she had followed the same routine.

She could always hear him moving quietly about the nearby bedchambers. The nun recalled their first meeting when his secretary, Father 0'Brien had introduced her to the Pope.

"Sister, I shall be lost if I can't get a good cup of coffee each morning. Would it be too much trouble for you to have someone place it in my sitting room? Unfortunately, I'm completely adrift in the Papal Palace. I can't seem to find anything. I rise before dawn and say mass in chapel at 5:30. Is the hour too indecent to warrant such a service?"

His eyes twinkled when she had quickly and intelligently responded to his overly condescending request.

Sister Vencenza was a perceptive woman. She had been around the Vatican a long time. She had never seen anyone as alert and as relaxed as this new Pope, John Paul I. His concern for the individual was unquestioned. His intelligence was obvious. In a less scrupulous person, the combination of simple austerity and the ability to intelligently communicate with throngs of faithful followers could be very dangerous weapons. This Pope would be fooled by no one.

Sister Vencenza knocked three more times. Each rap was more intense, indicating her growing concern. A hush came from beyond the door. She pressed an ear to one of the massive panels, but could hear no sound. She decided to call upon Father 0'Brien. He usually met with the Pope at 7AM to brief him on the daily itinerary. Then the priest would return to his apartment to sort out any changes suggested by his Eminence before 9AM.

Sister Vencenza hurried along the papal corridors. They had changed since Pope Paul VI had cleared out the moneylenders. Father 0'Brien's apartment had been made over from vacated offices of the Special Administration, the financial group that had been on the same floor as the private papal chambers. The group was reorganized by Paul VI in 1968. Thirteen staff members, four of them accountants, had been transferred to the new finance office, The Prefecture of Economic Affairs of the Holy See.

Lord, thought the nun, *The Pope's personal secretary certainly is housed a long way from his Eminence, even if it is on the same floor.*

She finally reached Father 0'Brien's door and knocked. The priest was already awake. Clad in a bed shirt, he rose from an easy chair and reached the door in several long strides. Their early morning confrontation was quite amusing. Father 0'Brien, startled by the sharp raps, yanked open the door. His hazel eyes blazed from his unshaven face. The middle-aged nun stood clutching a crucifix in her left hand. The right was poised for another assault on his door. This time it would be Father 0'Brien's chest that would be rapped and not the door that had been solidly anchored and now was suddenly removed from in front of Sister Vencenza.

"Sister! What do you want at this ungodly hour?"

"Father, please come quickly. I believe his Holiness may be ill. He didn't awaken at the usual time. My knocking on his door was of no use."

The priest's manner softened instantly as he read the concern in the nun's voice. Noting his own attire, he forced a smile and excused himself, explaining he would dress and accompany her. As he put on the black clerical garb and white Roman collar, he began from habit to mentally rearrange the day's schedule. By the time he had finished dressing and had scratched an electric razor across his stubble, a number of alternatives took shape in his mind. Perhaps audiences with the Pope should be cancelled, at least for today. Father 0'Brien had been through all of it before and was prepared for any emergency.

Closing the door to his apartment, he waved a hand for the Sister to follow as he hurried briskly down the hall. He thought fleetingly of the 109-acre Vatican City complex, an entity in itself, which surrounded him.

The Vatican is a miniature city, employing 3,000 people and permanently housing some 700 residents. Inside its walls are the Papal Palace, Audience Hall, the Vatican museums, the Sistine Chapel and St. Peter's Basilica. There is also the main civil administration building and some 20 to 30 other buildings, including a hospital, railway station, generating plant, radio broadcasting building, bank, telephone exchange, expansive kitchens and a warehouse.

The Vatican is recognized as a sovereign state under the temporal jurisdiction of his Holy Eminence, the Pope. Diplomatic relations are maintained with many countries. Foreign governments have had established relations and emissaries here since the fourth century. The exchange of permanent diplomatic ambassadors dates to the sixteenth century. Outside is Rome. Most of its facilities, controlled by business, government and church interests, were at Father 0'Brien's command in any Papal emergency. Until 1870, the Pope had actually been the temporal ruler of Rome itself. And, Father 0'Brien knew that century-old relationships between Roman families did not change, even when governments came and went.

Suddenly Father 0'Brien, with Sister Vencenza in tow, rounded the corner to the Pope's chambers and thought he caught a glimpse of a bishop at the chapel door. The Pope must have scheduled a private mass. It was almost 5:30. Sister Vencenza stood back, gasping for breath. Her concern was obvious. Father 0'Brien, not yet so concerned, rapped several times on the bedchamber door. After no response, he knocked more urgently and called to his Eminence through the closed door.

Sister Vencenza scurried to check the sitting room again, hoping the Pope was having his coffee. She opened the door and peeked inside. Her heart sank. The silver coffee tray appeared untouched.

Father 0'Brien decided to phone Cardinal Jean Villot, the Vatican Secretary of State. On rare occasions, due to the illness of a Pope, he becomes caretaker of the Vatican. Before retreating from the closed door, Father 0'Brien absentmindedly placed his hand on the doorknob. As he turned to leave, he twisted the knob. Noiselessly, swinging on its massive, well-oiled hinges, the door slowly opened.

The priest, having taken one step in the opposite direction, realized he had access to the Papal bedroom. Spinning around, he crossed the threshold. Several hurried steps placed him at the foot of the canopied bed. There sat Albino Luciani, better known these last thirty-four days as Pope John Paul I. Reposed as in life, his back was propped up by pillows, but his gray head was slumped forward, resting on a reading table. Across one edge lay a chubby palm, its fingers clutching a sheaf of personal papers. The Pope's eyes were closed. The thin rimmed glasses resting on his nose would no longer serve as windows to this world.

Moving to the side of the bed, Father O'Brien probed for any sign of a pulse. There wasn't any. Haltingly, in a high-pitched voice, he shouted for the nun. Sister Vencenza crossed the sitting room and entered the Pope's bedroom through the opposite door. Father O'Brien jumped, startled by her entry from that unexpected direction.

One look at the priest's face, and the slumped figure on the bed told Sister Vencenza that the Pope was gone. Sadness swept her fragile body. Tears washed her trembling fingers as she covered her face. She began murmuring, over and over again, as she rocked back and forth on her unsteady legs.

"Il Papa 'e Morto!!!"
"Il Papa 'e Morto!!!"

By late afternoon, the entire world knew that the Pope had died. Vatican sources described the cause of death as a coronary stroke. The news media was told the Pope had a history of medical ills. Apparently, after only one month in office, the strain on his frail constitution had been too much.

It seemed only yesterday that he had taken the oath of office. September had been a time of inspiration for the Catholic laity. Seven hundred and thirty-two million strong, they had welcomed him as their spiritual leader, hoping he could unite the Catholic Church, which had been wracked with dissent and unbridled rebellion since Vatican II.

His predecessor, Pope Paul VI had been unable to bring about the reformation of the Church, the intended purpose of Vatican II as envisioned by its originator, Pope John XXIII. Pope John had not lived long enough to see his cherished vision come true. It had been left to Paul XI to infuse the Catholic Church with the Holy Spirit. But, Paul had proven himself an old guard member of the entrenched Italian Curia; an administrative genius temperamentally unsuited to meeting the spiritual needs of the Catholic layman.

It was to Pope John Paul I that the international community of Catholics had turned, desperate in their need for pastoral guidance. His brief reign, a little over a month, had infused millions of disheartened believers with a new sense of purpose. He was a kind and fatherly leader. Perhaps this was the Church's last chance to fulfill its responsibilities as the originally ordained ministry of Jesus Christ.

What the Catholic laymen failed to understand were the political and financial realities of their beloved Holy Mother Church. Before this day was out, the leaders of the world's most powerful governments and the presidents of multi-national corporations would be requesting re-evaluation of various projects and commitments affected by the death of

Pope John Paul I. Intelligence agencies and financial analysts around the world wondered, who had the most to gain from the death of this particular Pope?

The same thought had occurred to Franco Antico, Secretary General of Italy's traditionalist conservative organization, the Civilita Christiana. Its membership was comprised of fifty thousand Catholics in forty-one countries. A call was placed from the headquarters of Civilita Christiana to the offices of the National Catholic Register in the United States.

"Could the Register recommend anyone who could assist in a private investigation of a very delicate nature?"

Requests of this kind were not uncommon between such like-minded entities around the world. The editor of the Register asked why the caller simply didn't use local talent. The voice on the other end shot back a list of qualifications, making it obvious that the Register's help was needed. Putting the caller on hold, the person on the other end asked the Register staff members for suggestions.

Returning to the phone, the caller was informed that the best recommendation was a Mr. Jamie Bolin, who at that moment was in Rome on vacation. Mr. Bolin was staying at the Cavalieri Hilton. Complete details on Mr. Bolin's background would be sent Air Express and should arrive in Rome tomorrow morning. The usual professional courtesies were exchanged and the caller hung up.

Later that night, the telephone rang in the apartments of Cardinal Jean Villot. An aide to the cardinal took the call.

"Yes, the Cardinal was in but can not be disturbed, The day's frantic activities, precipitated by the Pope's death have exhausted him".

The voice on the phone was a familiar one. The Cardinal's aide was very courteous and gave assurances that would be reconfirmed by Cardinal Villot tomorrow morning. It was agreed that when a Mr. Jamie Bolin contacted the offices of Cardinal Villot and mentioned a certain code word, he could expect full cooperation from the Vatican. What's more, Mr. Bolin would be provided with the services of a very knowledgeable and discreet Jesuit.

At 8:30 a.m., Saturday, September 30, Cardinal Jean Villot, Secretary of State, the Pope's postituto, interim administrator, Camerlengo of the Holy See, reluctantly spoke with the caller of the previous evening.

"Preposterous, absolutely ridiculous! Of course I understand the significance of such a possibility. NO! I don't wish any unsubstantiated disclosures to the world's leading newspapers. Or for that matter to anyone else."

A bargain was struck. Mr. Bolin would receive full cooperation when and if it was necessary. Only Cardinal Villot would receive a written copy of all information contained in a finalized report by Mr. Bolin. One more thing . . . the entire affair had to be concluded by October 13th. Later, the new Pope would decide what, if any, action would be taken. Any and all such action would be forthcoming only from the office of the Vatican Prosecutor. If necessary, at the appropriate time, one "leak" might be permitted to the press to forestall anyone from taking action on the preposterous supposition proposed by the caller. Furthermore, the Cardinal wanted no more direct contact with the project.

The Cardinal had no sooner hung up than the phone began to ring again, establishing a pattern of incessant calls that would continue for some time.

Rising from the straight-backed cane chair, the Cardinal waved to an assistant who dutifully sat down and began taking the calls. Shaking his head, the Cardinal remembered a theologically provocative question put forth by harried members of the Curia. *Did telephones lead lives of their own?*

Moving to the dining room, he seated himself in an overstuffed chair. Hunching forward, the Cardinal picked up a silver butter knife from the table. Listlessly, he transferred butter and marmalade from dish and jar to several pieces of lightly browned toast. As the toast touched his small, pursed lips, he absentmindedly stared at the poached egg being served on a china plate, delicately inscribed with the Vatican crest.

Lingering over his breakfast and sipping coffee, the old Cardinal sat back and gave a worried sigh. Seventy-two years old, and for the second time in less than 60 days, he had to bury a Pope. It was also his responsibility to take complete charge of the Vatican and make preparations for the election of a new Pope. Once more he had to prepare for the arrival and accommodation of 120 Cardinals from around the globe. In preparation for their arrival, this weekend he would stay in seclusion with the defacto members of the Curia, directing his personal staff in their assigned tasks.

The first priority was the security of the Cardinals and foreign dignitaries. Plans for the conclave would be set aside until after the Papal funeral.

On Saturday afternoon, the first of the daily "congregations" was held. Twenty-nine Cardinals were already in attendance, and by voice vote agreed to hold the funeral of Pope John Paul I on October 4th. By similar acclamation, the conclave was designated to begin on October 14th. Between now, September 30th, and the 14th of October, the number of Cardinals and their entourages would be multiplying like rabbits within Vatican City and Rome.

Three thoughts were uppermost in the mind of each Cardinal:

Could the discomfort of a conclave in the Sistine Chapel be once more endured? Would this conclave be as expensive as the last one? Could a new Pope be selected who could achieve the same popular acclaim as had Pope John Paul?

It had previously been fifteen years between conclaves. During the last years of Pope Paul XI, each Cardinal had time to develop politically acceptable alliances. But, the newly elected Pope had just died, allowing no time for the Cardinals to realign Church politics.

Deals, compromises and promises had been made to keep the Vatican in Italian hands. No one had dreamed that payments would become due so quickly on bargains struck at the last conclave. Or had they? Was it possible that there had been a conspiracy in the College of Cardinals?

John Paul I had been a very special man. The Cardinals might already be captives of their own creation. In this election, the Cardinals would be wheeling and dealing as best they could; but perhaps one group had already counted the votes, based on favors owed, and knew who the next Pope would be. Anything could happen! For the first time in more than 400 years, there could be a non-Italian Pope. Power could be shifted away from the Italian dominated Curia.

It was such a possibility that prompted the Civilita Christiana to employ Jamie Bolin. Italy was on the road to Communism. Parliament was becoming less friendly with Holy Mother Church. Time was running out. If the Church turned eastward toward Russia, it could change the balance of world power for the next 100 years. It had been necessary to act quickly. The confidential file on Jamie Bolin reached the desk of an administrator of the organization. After careful review, it was determined that Bolin was the man for the job. A simple plan was developed to obtain his services without revealing the identity of his employer.

A cashier's check for $10,000 U.S. was made out in his name. A subsequent bookkeeping entry credited organization cash and debited advertising and public relations expenses. A letter of explanation and the cashier's check were sealed in a manila envelope. It was to be delivered to Jamie Bolin by an attractive female courier. The courier was not to know the true identity of the administrator. A blind advertisement was placed in the early Sunday edition of the newspaper.

Female Model Wanted

26-30 yrs. of age, blond, 5' 7", slender build, 117 to 123 lbs. College educated must speak English language. One day assignment, fee 180,000 Lira. Interviews 4-6 p.m. today, room 326 Cavalieri Hilton. Call on house phone for appointment.

The administrator would choose the first attractive applicant. She would deliver the envelope to Bolin. The woman would be followed to insure delivery. The 180,000 Lira would be written off against part-time secretarial help for the month of October. Disbursement would be made from petty cash

The decision to use a female courier had obvious advantages over a phone call and money drop. She could prove useful later. The dossier on Jamie Bolin indicated his susceptibility to beautiful young women. What the courier did after delivery of the envelope was her own affair.

By tomorrow evening, the organization's plan would be in motion. The bizarre circumstances surrounding the death of Pope John Paul I would be thoroughly investigated. The audacious scheme was dangerous. The business and political intrigues, jealously protected by the Church, might be exposed to the faithful. The world might get a peek inside Pandora's Box. A great deal was at stake, but such a risk had to be taken.

Jamie Bolin was being offered the opportunity of a lifetime. He was ideally suited for the assignment. He had an uncanny ability to correlate random pieces of information into hard factual evidence and he possessed a charming disregard for authority; a combination that would bring him into conflict with the secret guardians of the Church. There was no doubt that he would accept the assignment.

He would have complete access to the Vatican. The Curia, administrative body of the Church, temporarily ceases to exist upon the death of a Pope. All its members are suspended from duty. Cardinal Villot is an absolute stickler for obedience to this regulation.

When Paul VI had died, a Cardinal returned to his office to retrieve some personal papers. He was severely reprimanded and left immediately. Beginning today, Saturday, September 30th, no member of the Curia would return to his office until a new Pope had been elected.

The offices would be dark and accessible for at least 10 days. As a member of the press accompanied by a Jesuit priest, he would be free to go anywhere in Vatican City;. privy to the intimate gossip of returning Cardinals. More importantly, the personal staff of the dead Pope would be anxious to share remembrances with a sympathetic listener.

Sunday afternoon, October 1st, Cardinals and political dignitaries from around the globe were arriving at the airport outside of Rome. At the same time, a slender green-eyed blond was strolling casually down the sixth floor hallway of the Cavalieri Hilton. Her destination was room 617. In her shoulder bag were a small manila envelope and 180,000 Lira.

II. JAMIE BOLIN

Casually responding to a number of soft knocks on his door, Jamie allowed access to the apartment. A beautiful, leggy blond with captivating emerald green eyes stood in the open doorway; so close he could feel the body heat. An absolute stunner, he thought!

"Are you Mr. Bolin?", came the mellow throaty query; spoken with a studied composure that masked the nervousness of the mysterious caller. "Yes, I'm Jamie Bolin, but I'm afraid you have the advantage, "Miss --- Miss?" His lean, muscular frame stepped back from the entrance as his question begged a reciprocal introduction.

"Oh: I'm sorry, my name is Livingston, Carol Livingston. I've been instructed to deliver a packet to you." May I come in?"

Jamie reached out, taking hold of her hand, and lead her inside. "Why not make yourself comfortable, and tell me what this is all about?"

Her lithe figure gracefully moved in the direction of' a nearby couch, one hand clasped femininely on the shoulder strap of her tooled leather bag. The loose, smooth-swinging arc of her other arm accentuated the languorous fluidity of her ample breasts. The multi-hued filmy hemline of her fawn silk dress floated just below the bend of her knee. His eyes lingered on the shapeliness of her firm, curvaceously sloping calves malingering into slender ankles with a hint of athletic muscularity.

"Please bear with me, Mr. Bolin. I have a bizarre little story to tell."

Her moist parting lips in sync with her sensuous catlike form husbanded amidst luxurious brocade cushions. The strikingly attractive young woman began relating her strange encounter with her temporary employer.

"You see, . ." she began hesitantly, "well, the truth of the matter is, I was becoming painfully bored here in Rome on holiday. So bored, in fact, that I answered this silly advertisement in the morning newspaper."

Her head moved laterally in self-admonishment as she continued, "Hope you under stand that from time to time we English tend to do odd things. I assure you, Mr. Bolin, this is definitely my odd thing:"

Bolin knew well of mad dogs and Englishmen. Perhaps it was those very British eccentricities that caused London to be his favorite city. Although, being Irish, he was cognizant of the Englishs' perfidy in regard to his own countrymen. A sentiment that did not spill over into his conversation.

Carol, regaining her composure, began again, "Following the instructions in the advertisement, I came to this hotel and called room 326. Invited up, I was met by a gracious Italian gentleman. The man explained the ad was really for a courier and not a model as I had presumed. It seems a letter had to be discreetly delivered to an American journalist staying right here in the same hotel."

"You mean me?" Came the interruption, punctuated by the force of his resonant voice. The harmonic effect on her nodding affirmation prompted her to continue.

"The man told me the fee as advertised would be paid in advance. It would only require ten minutes of my time just long enough to take the lift from the third to the sixth floor. Was I interested? Who wouldn't be, I thought, remembering my outstanding bank overdraft in London? I asked him if drugs or anything illegal were involved. After convincing me such was not the case, he gave me your name, physical description and room number. I was paid 180,000 lira and given an envelope addressed to you. Then he rode the lift with me to the sixth floor. When I walked down the hall a few minutes ago, he stood watching . . ."

Before she could finish, Bolin bolted from the room. Gaining the hallway in several quick strides, he adopted the wary stance of a professional fighter, a counterpuncher. His hard eyes pierced the otherwise placid atmosphere of the long corridor. No one was in sight. Jamie's demeanor instantly softened, and he rejoined his startled guest.

A tight knot twisted his gut; sinewy muscles again sucked up in-rushing adrenaline provoked by the seemingly sinister hand movement of his enigmatic visitor. Only when she withdrew the envelope from the folds of her handbag did his renewed apprehension subside. Nonchalantly, she tossed the sealed white packet atop the coffee table and stood up as if to leave.

A firm declination of his hand waved her back onto the couch. Bolin picked up the packet and dropped heavily into a nearby chair. Tearing off one corner of the envelope, he ran his index finger the entire length and then removed the contents. Unfolding a neatly typed one-page letter, a piece of sky blue paper drifted into his lap. Only years of practiced detachment concealed his amazement. The cashier's check payable to him was in the amount of $10,000 American. Whistling to himself, Jamie's attention focused on the letter.

Dear Mr. Bolin:

Please excuse the rather bizarre manner in which we have chosen to contact you. We simply have no desire to be directly connected with the subject we would have you investigate. In any case, the money is yours. You have been highly recommended, and we believe you will more than willingly accept this assignment.

We have every reason to believe that Pope John Paul I was murdered. Furthermore, we are very concerned about the involvement of the Roman Catholic Church in international secular affairs, and we anticipate a growing confrontation between Catholics and Communists.

If you accept this assignment, you will have complete access to Vatican City and many of its files. Contact Father Rene, an assistant to the Vatican Secretary, Cardinal Jean Villot. Father Rene can be reached at the number written at the bottom of this letter. To further identify yourself, simply mention the word "bicycle." Father Rene will arrange for a Jesuit priest to accompany you; and if at any time you need further assistance, call upon Father Rene.

As for your assignment, find out all you can about the last 34 days of Pope John Paul I. Research and critique the various relationships and changes in relationships between the Vatican and foreign governments in which the Pope might have been involved. Your investigation must be completed by the evening of October 11. We require a single typewritten report mailed to us the same day in care of General Delivery, Box 458, Rome. You are perfectly free to do as you wish with the information you uncover. The $10,000 is for your services through the next ten days and for the single copy report. Kindly destroy this letter after reading it.

The girl knows nothing about this letter or The cashier's check.

Phone 62-754

A helleva way to spend my vacation, he thought. Refolding the letter, he tapped its sharp edge several times upon his outstretched thigh and sought confirmation of its contents from her.

"Tell me, Miss Livingston, is all this really on the level?"

"Believe me, Mr. Bolin, I have told you the absolute Truth." Her upper body leaned forward, tension interlaced the fingers of her meandering hands; letting them come to rest on the calf of her bare leg. "As for the contents of the letter, I haven't the foggiest."

He accepted the sincerity in her voice and body language, encouraged her to relax, suggesting she begin by dropping the Mr. Bolin. After all, her task had been accomplished. Casually, he invited her to join him for dinner. She accepted, thinking it might be fun getting to know him. More importantly, she was dying to know the contents of the letter.

"Would you care for a drink?" solicited Jamie, removing himself from the confines of the richly upholstered, plush chair. Several quick steps took him to the portable Cherrywood bar in the corner of the room.

"Do you by any chance have Harvey's Bristol Cream?" Having made the inquiry, she moved to the side of the bar nearest him.

"Fresh out of sherry, I'm afraid. Let me fix you something with a little more sting in it:" His reply was rhetorical, having already made her a drink of similar name.

"Anything alcoholic will do nicely, thank you." Her fingertips brushed his as the seemingly innocuous libation changed hands.

"Make yourself right at home. I'll be back shortly."

There was a certain air of closeness as he passed her. More like a sharing of space than an intrusion. Carol moved to the window and stared out at the crowded piazza below. She restlessly twisted the stem of the cocktail glass between thumb and forefinger. Some time elapsed before she returned to the couch and finished her drink.

Jamie put his Trac II on the wash basin, rinsed his face and ran his hand over its smoothness. A glance at his Seiko told him it was 5:10 p.m. Plenty of time to take her to dinner before beginning to look into the death of Pope John Paul I. He had already made up his mind to accept the assignment-what a challenge! He wasn't at all surprised by the allegations in the letter. He was surprised by the amount of the cashier's check. And he was absolutely delighted with her. Bolin's anonymous employer had chosen well; his professional qualifications were precisely suited for the assignment ahead.

Wrapped in a dark blue bath towel, Jamie opened the door and saw her relaxing on the divan. Her legs crossed at the thighs. Her head lay tilted back on the cushions. She was indeed a very beautiful woman.

Her exquisite breasts were provocatively thrust skyward. The curves of her body accentuated the tightness of her hard belly. Instinctively, he committed to memory the slenderness of her hips and the fantasy provocation of her thighs.

Aborting his voyeuristic journey, Jamie moved noiselessly to the bedroom. Dressing quickly, he splashed a dash of Yardley's musk on his freshly shaven face. Retracing his steps, he closed the bedroom door just loudly enough to alert her to his reappearance.

Sitting upright, both arms outstretched, she pressed her palms outwardly. Relaxed and alert, her interest once again centered on him, all six feet of him weighing in at 185 pounds of solid muscle as he stood looking down on her. Jamie wore a tweed wool sportscoat, tailored gray slacks and a European-fitted blue silk shirt open at the neck. Attracted to older men, she later found out he was 41, fourteen years her senior.

"I'd like to freshen up a bit, if you don't mind. It will only take a minute." Her tight buttocks held his appreciative gaze as she disappeared behind a closing door.

Jamie became more seriously preoccupied. Withdrawing a notepad from his inside coat pocket, intending to transcribe pertinent information contained within the letter. He wrote down the priest's name, the phone number and the general delivery address. Copying the word "bicycle," he underlined it and committed the Cardinal's name to memory.

The envelope and letter were torn into tiny pieces and tossed into a nearby wastebasket. The cashier's check was safely tucked inside his wallet. Now he could relax and enjoy the pleasure of her company.

He looked up just as she re-entered the room. Her long blond hair flowed over her bare back and wafted round her angular cheekbones.

She took hold of his hand, urging, "I'm famished. What about you?" Her uncomplicated directness was masculinity captivating. Tactually she led him into the hallway and on to a waiting elevator.

"Any place special you'd like to dine while you're here in Rome?"

Carol appreciated his solicitousness, replying, "You pick the spot. Good food and quiet decor are all I ask. Okay?"

He had thought about taking her to the Giggi Fozzi, a very cosmopolitan restaurant, always bursting with activity, where he was acquainted with the regulars and waiters alike. It was his favorite eatery in all of Rome - had been for as long as he could remember.

On research holiday from Oxford one year, he had stumbled across Giggi's. Its patrons took to his easy conviviality, and he had been introduced to a number of old Roman families. His graduate work relating to church politics after the fall of the Roman Empire had been well received by his Oxford Don. Principally because of the information he had gleaned from the archives of those same Roman families.

Remembrances faded as he felt a tug of encouragement on his hand. Carol began running down the wide expanse of steps leading from the hotel to the piazza. She urged him on to a waiting taxi. Entering the cab, he was aware of the warmth emanating from her grasp. At that moment he thought of the perfect place to take her.

"Drop us at the Cafe Greco, will you please? And take the Via Condotti. The restaurant is just opposite the Piazza Di Spogna."

It was by all accounts an indecently early hour to dine in Rome. There were, however, certain advantages. No reservations would be needed. Few patrons would be there at 6:30 on a Sunday evening, except for an occasional businessman and his mistress; thereby insuring quiet, excellent and unhurried service.

The cafe was only several miles distant, but because of the usual weekend tourist traffic, the taxi crawled along at a snail's pace. Carol caught her breath from the headlong dash down the steps. Her facial features were very animated as she placed her hand on his forearm and pressed her body close to his.

Jamie had come to Rome hoping for just such an encounter. No time was going to be wasted being coy. He very much wanted to enjoy every minute of their anomalous rendezvous. Jamie's fingers toyed with the back of her hand. The two of them, lost in the privacy of their own thoughts, sat in silence for the remainder of the ride.

"How very lovely," she breathlessly sighed upon entering the Old World atmosphere of the cafe.

The expensive little restaurant oozed with charm. Jamie requested a table in the rear, far removed from the kitchen noise. Italian males are known for their demonstrable appreciation of beautiful women. The patrons of the Cafe Greco were no exception. Carol loved the admiring glances bestowed on her.

Passing one occupied booth, a gregarious tippler raised his glass and shouted, "Salute!" expressing his approval of Jamie's choice of companion.

Each table in the cafe had its own exquisite arrangement. In perfect symmetry stood crystal water and wine goblets, a decanter of Perrier, ornate sterling silverware, and bone china place settings on a damask tablecloth. Discreetly, Alfredo the wine steward awaited their pleasure. Jamie, ignoring the proffered wine list, requested the very best.

"A bottle of Classico Vecchio Reservas Chianti, please, preferably a Borghese."

The look of eternal boredom disappeared from Alfredo's face. In Jamie he recognized a true aficionado of the grape. Such a superior Italian wine fermented in the cask for three years before bottling, and once bottled, aged five more years before quenching one's thirst. Produced by only four vineyards in all of Italy, those of Pasolini Dal Onda Borghese were the best of best. The Cafe Greco had exactly one bottle in its cellars.

Alfredo's demeanor of cool disdain changed to that of affable host. Their meal, he assured Jamie, would be prepared to absolute perfection. He would alert both the chef and the table waiter. Jamie conveyed his thanks in flawless Italian.

Carol, uncertain of just what had transpired, nevertheless acknowledged that her dinner companion was very much at home in Italy. She desperately wanted to turn his attention to the matter uppermost in her own mind.

"Jamie, it should be obvious to you by now how interested I am in both you and your activities. If it's not too confidential, what was the substance of the letter I delivered to you this afternoon?"

She remained somewhat bemused when he did not rise to the bait. Biting her tongue for having started the evening badly, she berated herself for being a woman of both British and Scandinavian descent. *Too Goddamn direct.* She chastised herself. Such brashness is threatening to most men, especially Americans. She hoped it might be different in his case. Irishmen were usually oblivious to the machinations of women. Her entreaty had not fallen on deaf ears. It was simply poor timing.

Jamie saw her as a very sensual, unknown variable in a yet-to-be-determined conspiracy equation. Despite the inherent danger of beginning an affair under such tenuous circumstances, he could hardly resist the challenge. Romantic entanglements always swept the cobwebs from his brain and kept ever-present ice-cold cynicism from his heart. Second echelon recompense was indulgence of his Irish penchant for lively conversation and blatant exaggeration.

Without the slightest reference to the contents of the letter, he began to reveal something of himself to her--how he had become through trial, error and misadventure, an investigative reporter. His subject matter was dictated by insatiable curiosity or handsome advances that compensated for the boredom of a particular assignment.

His wife had been killed in a private plane crash four years ago. Her death left him sole care of three children who now attend various universities in the States. Reappearance of Alfredo cut short further comment on his family situation.

A neat two fingers of the velvet liquid was liberated after eight years' captivity for Jamie's approbation. Dismissing the affectation of inspecting the cork and inhalation of the bouquet, Jamie's palate attested to the hardy, full-bodied flavor of the vintage.

His raised stemware served as an appropriate gesture of approval. Here was a wine to be truly enjoyed rather than enhance the ego, a simile reflected in his preference for women as well. Alfredo rimmed their glasses with fluid smoothness. Jamie solicited her agreement with his selection and turned his attention to dinner.

She suggested he choose the entire meal. Their raised crystal reflected rays of warm ruby richness in acknowledgement of mutual agreement. It also hinted at their anticipation of a more erotic convoluted relationship.

The table waiter scribbled away as Jamie scanned the menu.

"The Tuscan pâté, and sprinkle it with a bit of finely-chopped onion and a small amount of garlic. Would you also bring us a side dish of freshly-cut prociutto in creme sauce?" The unusual combination made a not-too-filling antipasto ala Bolin.

Perhaps, thought Jamie, *she might enjoy a Suppo Di Verdura.* Recalling her ass-tight trim figure, he decided to forego the simmering fresh vegetable soup.

"Ah, for the entree, let me see. Tre turkey fillets basted in Possito Di Mascota. Uno for the Signora and due for me, per favore, and as for the vegetable, asparagus Piedmont is excellente."

To satisfy their Anglophile origins, tea would be served with the entree. The waiter filled their water goblets from the decanter of Perrier, no ice, and returned to the kitchen.

Carol inquired about Jamie's children. "The kids are very self-reliant. We're a close-knit family. Time spent together is measured in terms of quality rather than quantity. That reminds me, my daughter Katherine is joining me here in Rome for a few days beginning next Wednesday. Enough about the children, once I get started . . . anything else you'd care to know about me?"

"Everything:" was her enthusiastic response, the contents of the letter never far from her thoughts.

"Lady, you're an Irishman's dream come true. There are of course my parents. My father's Irish and mom is mostly German. The old man is a fun-loving Mick, a dreamer and a very, very heavy drinker. I suppose an occupational hazard of third generation, hard-bitten immigrants chasing the American buck. It was he who insisted I have a Catholic education.

Grade school was taught by the Sisters of Loretto. High school was a paradox, scholastics compliments of the Christian Brothers and military indoctrination courtesy of the United 5tates 5th Army. I went on to get an undergraduate degree in electronics and an MBA from the University of Michigan. Through a lucky set of circumstances, I received a Rhodes scholarship and did post-grad work at Oxford."

Jamie regaled her with tales of his non-academic lifestyle, capping that part of his conversation with his escapades in England. Carol through feminine fantasy vicariously joined in his adventures. Subconsciously, she began falling in love with him. Educated at Oxford, Irish and somewhat bent on mayhem, he represented in her mind's eye a quixotic combination. Had an Englishman so well educated introduced himself in the same manner, it would have projected imaginary impressions of a cold and withdrawn intellectual personality.

Jamie's self-description, embellished as only an Irishman can, had just the opposite effect. It represented a conflict in reality; a whimsical Gaelic mind capable of Germanic discipline; educated in the staid halls of Oxford, bastion of British intellectualism. His grandiloquence was specifically designed to stir the heartstrings of any woman who struck his fancy.

Carol, anything but an ice lady with a beguiling sense of humor and an earthy sensuality, correspondingly exhibited her rising desire for him. Her animalistic directness, a decidedly English trait, assured her of Jamie's continued infatuation. *Bed and board or bored in bed?* She laughed in silence.

He considered revealing more of himself to her, including his years of frustration in the world of big business and the amoral conflicts that had shaped his emotional maturity.

The waiter returned with the appetizers and large chunks of hot Italian bread. The antipasto was delicious. Pouring more vino, Jamie created an intentional lull in the conversation.

The candlelight cast delicate shadows upon her exquisite features. Lovely high cheekbones and white creamy skin glowed from the warmth of the Chianti and her emerging affection for him. Diaphanous guardians of long, light lashes shuttered her eyes audaciously, daring him to explore hidden caverns of loveliness in expectation of extracting their emerald green wealth.

Her mouth was sensuously inviting. She nibbled a morsel of bread and raised the wine to her lips. Should he place in jeopardy the fragile amorous mood of the evening by dredging up his corporate past?

Mulling over the question, his thoughts drifted in retrospect. Financially strapped after Oxford, he needed to replenish his coffers. He plied his trade as a business major and electronics engineer. Reaching the top quickly, he fortunately or unfortunately got what he wanted. At age 37 he was Vice President and General Manager of the electronics division of a large conglomerate. He had moved frequently and changed corporations several times to achieve rapid success. Regretting his choice of occupations, he became disenchanted with corporate lifestyle and most everything that kept western civilization afloat.

He was not so naive as to believe the myth perpetuated on some juvenile western minds that other cultures were less driven to similar forms of self-destruction. Immersing himself in the lost art of self-reliance, he learned in a spasmodic groping fashion how to develop essence. What the hell was man doing on the planet, and how did he, Bolin, fit into the scheme of things?

Curiosity led him to test the waters of diversified philosophical thought and mystical practices. A confrontation over corporate policy brought his resignation. He chose a world more suited to his disposition, doing as he pleased and living well. No purpose could be served telling her of his past frustration. He cleared thoughts of the old days from his mind, reached across the table and touched her fingertips.

"I'm having a marvelous time. You are a very beautiful woman. I'd like to get to know you better. Tell me more about yourself."

She took feminine delight in the opportunity to bargain. "I promise not to bore you if you tell me about the letter I delivered to you. Deal?"

"Deal!" he laughed, knowing full well he would tell her only what suited his purpose. Pouring more wine, he leaned forward in his chair and encouraged her to begin.

"My father is an official in the British National Health Service. Mother was Swedish. She came to London during the blitz, a model and companion to a Swedish entrepreneur. At war's end, she married my father. Several years ago, mother passed away and dad buried himself in his work as manager of a government-owned medical complex in London." Carol's eyes sparkled when she longingly spoke of her parents.

"When I was eighteen, they sent me abroad to study at the Sorbonne. I majored in foreign languages and photography. After graduation, I became a freelance photographer. Constant travel and loneliness prompted my return to England. I'm happily employed as a staff photographer for Smithe and Bowers and love every minute of it The agency is located on Queen's street in London, a hop, skip and jump from dad's place, and my own flat is nearby."

Carol stopped talking and reached for her handbag. Flipping it open, she handed Jamie her calling card. How typically English, he mused

<u>Carol Livingston</u>
Photographer

Smithe and Bower International

Office 21 Queen St.	**Residence 116 Hartford Rd.**
London 71-6486	**Picdilly 53-9842**

She thought nothing of giving her card to anyone who might interest her or who could further her career.

Jamie asked where she was staying in Rome. He recorded the name of her hotel and room number on the back of the card, tucking it away in his wallet.

The entree was served, and the waiter emptied the contents of the wine bottle into their glasses while clearing away the appetizers. Jamie nodded his thanks and urged Carol to continue. She broke off a small piece of bread and began eating with relish, pausing momentarily, fork in midair, to remind Jamie about the letter. She caught his eyes shamelessly observing the swell of her breasts.

A wave of her fork interrupted his salacious daydream. He laughed at the obvious delight she took in his appreciation of her physical assets.

"The letter," she teasingly admonished, "You promised, remember. And besides, I'm dying of curiosity."

His explanation proved less than gospel as he fabricated, "A conservative group of businessmen has an investment in a popular but rather scandalous rag. Occasionally they break an important news story to enhance the magazine's seamy image."

He continued to embellish the white lie, "I heard about them from other journalists. Although very secretive, their fees are quite generous. No one bothers to trace their identities. No reason to kill the goose that lays the golden eggs. I've been asked to write an imaginative article on the sudden death of the Pope."

"Bloody gopher! Is that what you think I am? Shame on you for taking advantage of me this way, just because I'm attracted to you."

Not knowing the real extent of her own consternation, Carol held herself in check.

"Bloody gopher? Hardly an endearing self-description. Would you mind translating?", Jamie responded in mock consternation. He knew that he had patronized her with his contrived explanation.

"You throw a red herring of a story like that at me and expect I'll go for it. No wonder the Irish and the English don't get along. Look, damn it. I was paid almost two hundred American for ten minutes' work this afternoon, and you tell me a cock-and-bull story about some non-existent dirty old men. More likely, the poor old Pope was murdered. No doubt with your penchant for grand malarkey, a sensational expose is in the offing. Am I getting warm?"

Her napkin sailed across the table and plopped right in Jamie's lap. Carol really didn't give a damn. Her righteous indignation only served to stimulate their interest in each other; as laughter prevailed when Jamie feinted rebuff. He was more than annoyed by the ease at which through luck or intuition she came perilously close to the truth.

"Enough shop talk. Look, I apologize. But after all, heart attack, murder, and suicide, so what. I've been paid a sizeable retainer, and with the exception of meeting you, it's screwed up my vacation plans, if you'll pardon the obscenity, royally. More importantly, I'd like to see you again before you leave for London, but I'm going to be very busy and surely you have friends here. Men friends, that is."

Carol sensed she had the diplomatic advantage, and it would only rub salt in the wounds to pursue further full disclosure of the letter's contents

"You're a better fisherman than a storyteller," she playfully chided.

"I'm all alone here in Italy. Don't know a bloomin' soul. Came here on holiday to break off an affair with a married man in London."

The lightness of sweet sarcastic banter removed itself from her demeanor. A note of sadness crept into her conversation as she described her present situation.

"As a photographer, I have numerous opportunities to meet men, as you can well imagine. Such encounters always end on a sour note. No one takes my work seriously. One look at my body and the man always wants an affair, not a commitment."

Backing off from herself induced verbal therapy, Carol asked Jamie if he really wanted her to continue. Without waiting for his reply, she unburdened herself.

"My friend in London is a wealthy industrialist. We first met when I was a student in Paris. At the time, I ran the whole gambit of young protege routine. Until six months ago, I hadn't seen him in five years. Apparently he moved his family to London because he believes the communists are gaining control of France through a coalition government with the socialists. Afraid his fortune would eventually be confiscated; he surreptitiously sold his French holdings and smuggled the cash into England. I accidentally ran into him while shopping in Herrod's. Our relationship simply progressed on a day-by-day basis."

Carol then went on to elaborate on the genuine shortcomings of French lovers.

"He wants to buy me a place outside of London, insisting that I quit my job. Although he does adore me, I'm afraid he wants to hide me safely away and eventually I will become just another one of his possessions."

In her university days, Carol had plenty of opportunity to observe Frenchmen in action. Her insight was gained from sad experience through the first plush of euphoria to the last tear of loneliness. Jamie knew all about Frenchies' games. They were past masters at softball-hardball love affairs.

"I know how you must feel. Some of my best friends are Frenchmen and their conquests of English and American women are legendary. In reality, it's the game of love that fascinates them, not the women. If the truth were known, they view Englishwomen as cold and unimaginative."

"American women fare even worse, considered childish, lacking in worldly intelligence, hell to live with, over-organized and silly champions of every crackpot bandwagon that comes along. An opinion I might add that is held by more than Frenchmen:"

"This is silly," she admitted. "'Here we are having a lovely evening, and I babble on like a schoolgirl. Let's change the subject as of right now. I'll even go along with your continued escapades of the dirty old rich men. What do you think of that?"

For the next hour their conversation was that of two emerging lovers exploring each other's compatibilities and similarities. Jamie, aware of the time slippage, flagged the waiter's attention and ordered dessert. "Cheese pie, crostata di Ricotta for two please, a Brandy Alexander for the lady, a Drambui for me."

The pie, a specialty of the house, was two inches thick. Its pasta crust consisted of egg yolk, dry Marsala wine and lemon peel filled with Ricotta cheese, egg white, raisins and blanched almonds. Unable to do justice to the sumptuous dessert, Jamie and Carol agreed it was time to leave. Jamie settled the bill with generous tips for Alfredo and the table waiter. Outside the restaurant, Carol in hand, he hailed a taxi, directing it to the Minerva Hotel on the piazza near the Pantheon.

"I'm due at the Vatican early in the morning, and I need to burn the midnight oil in preparation for tomorrow. Do you mind terribly if I drop you at the door?" Quickly adding, "Would you spend Saturday afternoon and evening with me before you leave for London?"

Carol was pleased he hadn't insisted on spending the night, although she might have enjoyed it. "I'd like very much to see you on Saturday. Ring me in a day or two, luv?"

"That's a promise," he happily acknowledged as the taxi pulled up to the hotel entrance.

Instinctively, they kissed each other on parting. Carol waved as the cab receded into the night. Jamie turned in his seat to observe her entering the hotel lobby. They would think of each other often in the coming week.

Neither had been aware of the sleek dark blue sedan that had followed them from the restaurant. Its engine idled hotly in the driveway of the Minerva Hotel. A light rain began to fall as cigarette smoke drifted pugnaciously through the half-open window on the driver's side. The door sprang open, and a blurred figure hooded by a rain-splotched fedora hurried to the hotel entrance.

III.VATICAN CITY, MONDAY, OCTOBER 2ND

Bolin reluctantly rolled over and shut off the alarm. Groping for a compilation of pillows, he propped himself upright in an effort to stay awake. Momentarily his thoughts drifted back to last night and her rock hard nipples. Then, through sleepy eyes, tiny, blurred, red digits took shape 6:45. It was too early to ring the Vatican, but not room service.

The steam from the shower hung on the mirrored cabinet as Jamie rummaged a dulling twin blade over his stubble. Toweling off, he dressed inconspicuously in gray gabardine slacks, Black English loafers, and an oxford blue shirt with button down collar, open at the neck. Time slipped by while he leisurely ate a hearty breakfast. Consuming his coffee on the run, he grabbed a lightweight cardigan on his way out; deciding to call Father Rene when he reached the grounds of the Vatican.

The streets of Rome were bustling with activity as he hailed down a cab, instructing the driver to let him off on the east bank of the Tiber. From there, he crossed the bridge on foot and walked purposefully in the direction of St. Peter's Square. The walls and buildings within Vatican City rose to greet him from their hilltop enclave.

Almost before it began, his ascent of the Via della Conciliazione was over. The square lay directly in his path. Its enormous scope swallowed up thousands of tourists crisscrossing its centuries old surface. People, diminutive in size, like red ants on the move in the jungles of Brazil, were swarming over the steps leading to St. Peter's Basilica. The prodigious square, which had required eleven years to construct, could easily accommodate a Papal audience of over 400,000 of the faithful.

Bernini's famous colonnade, four spectacular rows of marble pillars that stand sixty feet high on both elliptical, open space boundaries of the square. The front row of pillars is capped with a balustrade, supporting the chalk white statues of 140 great saints of Mother Church guarding the multitudes below. Bolin's intended destination is the gate of St. Ann near the Swiss Guard barracks, deceptively concealed by the staggered rows of Bernini's towering columns.

The guard at the gatehouse moves from a position of parade rest, to an at-ease, military posture upon Bolin's approach. The grip on his gleaming petard relaxes at the mention of Father Rene's name. Jamie is directed to a phone cubical suspended on the wall of the arched portico encapsulating a massive, black, wrought iron gate.

On the third ring a crisp, youthful voice inquires as to the caller's purpose. After a brief explanation, Bolin hears the click of the extension followed by the baritone voice of Rather Rene.

"Ah, Mr. Bolin, I've been expecting your call. I believe you have some news for me. Do you not?"

News? Thought Bolin. *What God damn news?*

"Oh of course, Father, I almost forget - your cousin's 'bicycle' trip across Europe this summer. Yes, very exciting. I'm sure you'll want to hear all the details. How do I reach your offices?"

Father Rene directed Jamie to the Belvedere Palace. "Walk west past the Vatican Press building, turn north at the corner. The post office will be on your left. The very next building is the Belvedere Palace; come to room 231. I'm looking forward to our visit."

At the further instruction of Father Rene, Bolin handed the phone to the guard, who then issued Jamie a one-day pass authorized by the priest. The pass required Jamie to leave the premises through the same gate before 5:00 p.m. Proper credentials for repeated visits and overnight accommodations would be provided when Jamie met with the priest.

Biting his tongue, Jamie refrained from asking if heaven requires one-day passes. Instead, he thanked the guard for his assistance and walked on, in the direction of the Belvedere Palace. Recalling his brief conversation with the priest, two things struck him as very odd. He didn't recall hearing a second click. That would have meant that the first person answering the phone had hung up when Father Rene picked up his receiver. And what about Father Rene's explicit directions? He had told Jamie exactly how to reach his office on the second floor of the Belvedere Palace. Neither Jamie nor the Swiss Guard had mentioned from where the call had originated.

Concern over these disturbing observations was set aside as Bolin was approached by two very attractive young women. He chastised himself for what he was thinking, especially about the tall, curvy redhead. At first glance, he had not seen the daily missals and rosary beads. The women were nuns in street attire.

"My, how times have changed." He laughed aloud.

Upon entering room 231, Bolin studied the young man who greeted him. Father Rene appeared and Jamie was ushered into his private office. Moving to the priest's desk, Bolin glanced at the phone console, doing a leisurely about-face, he extended his hand to Father Rene.

"It's a pleasure to meet you, Father. As you know, I've been placed in your care to compile an exclusive story on the short reign of this pope"

The priest gingerly accepted the proffered handshake.

"I'm aware of your assignment and will cooperate as best I can. Are you familiar with the rites and teachings of the Catholic Church? By any chance, could you, in a pinch, utter a few innocuous Latin words?"

"Father, I was raised a Roman Catholic, and in fact have written a doctoral dissertation, 'The Church During The Middle Ages.' I can, if necessary, carry on a stilted conversation in Latin. Why, may I ask, are you pursuing this line of questioning?"

"Because," said the priest, "it will be simpler for all concerned if you assume the role of a visiting American priest. You're here on special assignment from Santa Clara University on a Stanford grant. Your assignment is to historically document the transfer of power through three Popes in less than ninety days. A monumental task for any organization."

Whewee! Thought Jamie. *Frenchmen certainly could indulge their propensity for intrigue over the simplest of assignments.* On second thought, Jamie realized how artful was the cover prepared for him by the priest. Santa Clara University is a Jesuit school. Stanford University, one of the world's most prestigious. With these credentials, impersonating a Jesuit priest, Jamie would have ready access to everyone in Vatican City.

Father Rene judiciously seated himself behind his large oval desk and pressed a concealed buzzer. The young novitiate, Laurent, came from the outer office. Father Rene, speaking in French, requested that a routine cover letter be prepared for Father Bolin. The bearer was to have overnight accommodations during his stay in Vatican City; access to all buildings and records and could go and come as he pleased.

As was customary in such scholarly pursuits, Father Bolin would be shown every courtesy until his departure on Wednesday, October 11th. The letter was to be typed on official Vatican stationery and stamped with the facsimile of Father Rene's signature. Laurent returned to the outer office to prepare the document.

Father Rene explained, "Such a letter is standard procedure for dignitaries and priests on special assignments and will provide you with excellent credentials."

How clever of the priest, damned clever: thought Jamie. According to its wording, his privileges terminated in 10 days. When he left the Vatican on the tenth day, a Swiss Guard would destroy the letter, no matter which gate he exited. He no longer would have access to the interior Vatican grounds,

Father Rene informed Jamie, "There will be a slight delay ín continuation of our meeting, your Jesuit guide, Father Joseph Gault, is enroute to the office. I'm expecting him at any moment. Personally, I prefer not to know anything about the real purpose of your visit. In an extreme emergency, I can be reached at another number, 73-641. I hope, however, that further direct contact will not be necessary. I am very busy with the burial preparations and internal security matters brought about by the death of the Pope."

Jamie received the distinct impression that Cardinal Villot, Father Rene's direct superior, knew nothing of the details of this particular matter and likewise didn't want to know. While waiting for Father Gault, Jamie, rather, Father James Bolin, casually questioned Father Rene.

"How did you know I was telephoning from the guard house adjacent to St. Anne's gate?"

The priest motioned for Jamie to come around the side of the desk. Touching a large drawer-like panel, it rotated on an invisible hinge-like mechanism. An array of brightly-lit LEDs (Light Emitting Diodes) was displayed on separate registers. Each register contained a series of three numerical positions. In all, there were five rows. Each row corresponded to five telephone lines connected to the phone console on top of the desk.

Father Rene, pleased with Jamie's inquiry, launched into a long dissertation on the new electronic age.

"Marvelous, isn't it," exclaimed the priest. "The devices were installed in the offices of Curia Cardinals and their assistants. Nicknamed 'ANGEL,' the system displays the extension number of a caller's phone. Pressing a button over a particular array activates an on-line memory bank in the Vatican's central computer. The building location number of any call made within the Vatican is automatically displayed on this small, rectangular faced oscilloscope on the console."

Before Jamie could respond, the intercom buzzed. Laurent's voice came over the speaker, announcing the arrival of Father Joseph Gault. With a touch of his hand, Father Rene activated a mechanism that opened the door to his office. Father Gault strode into the room.

Walking up to Jamie he introduced himself and then jested, "I'm looking forward to assisting a fellow Jesuit from America."

Jamie didn't acknowledge the greeting; his eyes were still glued to the LED console.

Father Gault's thumb pointed in a mockingly accusatory manner in the direction of Father Rene, "The Curia staff members cannot refrain from demonstrating their toys for visitors. Those devices have been installed with the understanding that they were to remain secret. Within a month, they became a personal status symbol, and everyone knows of their installation. So much for our vaunted Vatican secrets."

Bolin appreciated the nuances of the electronic technology thus far demonstrated. If Vatican technicians and Vatican purchasing power could develop such gadgets, what else went on behind these massive walls? He immediately thought about the Vatican broadcasting station. He made a mental note to investigate it. No wonder his mysterious employer had paid him so well. Someone knew how useful his electronics background would be.

"Father Bolin, why don't you and Father Gault tour the nearby grounds and get acquainted?" suggested Father Rene as Laurent came in and handed Bolin his letter of authority. The noviate also gave Jamie a key to a suite in the Villa Pius IV. The suite number is stamped on an oblong plate embedded in the shaft of the key. Laurent then handed over a small metallic card. "Father Gault will explain its purpose."

"Where shall we start, Father Gault?" asked Bolin as the two of them left the Belvedere Palace. "Please call me Joe," requested the priest.

Jamie returned the courtesy, preferring to be called Jamie rather than Jim. As the two men stroll, Jamie tried to size up Father Joe. The Teutonic priest was six feet tall, stockily built, his coarse black hair flecked with gray. His powerful demeanor and lack of intimidation in the presence of Father Rene had been very impressive. Bolin made a mental note of the fact that Father Joe is a very stubborn man and no one to tangle with in a physical dispute.

The German priest initiated an attempt to familiarize Jamie with the Vatican. He quickly learned that Jamie needed no such help. The two men strolled down the via del Pellegrino, a short cut from the Belvedere Palace back to St. Anne's gate. Traveling but a short distance, they stopped in the back of the Vatican Press building.

"Jamie, take the small metallic card and place it in the slot near the door set flush in the wall," instructed the priest.

When the card was inserted a small door swung open. Inside the exposed cubicle are a number of mini-bikes hooked to a battery charger system. Bolin and the priest removed two bikes and Joe produced a card similar to Jamie's and shoved it into a receptacle on the bike that started up its little electric motor. Removing his card from the slot by the door,

Jamie followed Father Joe's example and observed that the small door swung shut automatically.

Father Joe briefed him on the novel transportation system, "Such facilities exist in every major Vatican building. The mini-bikes provide convenient conveyance around the 108-acre city. You will find a drawer under the seat containing a small map of the Vatican and the bikes can be kept as long as necessary. If a unit is parked outside a recharger station, it means there is no room inside. A Swiss Guard will move it to another location."

Jamie thought it was a very simple and ingenious transport system.

While Joe continued his explanation, "Bicycles had previously been used. Someone had come up with the idea of storing them and then had come the mini-bikes, followed by the electronic card lock and ignition system, a very orderly, technological progression."

The mini-bikes twisted and turned in their route to the Villa of Pius IV; turning upon the via Del Pellegrino.

Father Joe told Jamie, "I can arrange any interviews you might wish to conduct. I can also advise you where to obtain any necessary documents or historical records. It will not be necessary for me to remain with you all the time."

Circling behind the Belvedere Palace, they passed the parking lot across from the via S. Pio X, the road which led to the Belvedere courtyard. Jamie was told to remember the way through the vast maze. There was only one entrance on the east side and only one exit on the west side. The exit was reached by maneuvering along a narrow walled-in portico, a precarious and bumpy passageway.

Once outside the courtyard, they rode along the right branch of the road leading them to the Villa of Pius IV .The left fork branched off toward St. Peter's Basilica. The center road continued on to St. Peter's monument. Parking their bikes, Father Joe led the way to Bolin's suite. The rooms were ornate and spacious, a very comfortable place to interview people, and it provided an ideal respite for Bolin to collect his thoughts and take a break from time to time.

It was almost noon when the priest inquired, "Would you prefer lunch in your rooms?"

Someone, thought Jamie, *has a great deal of influence with the Church to get me such lavish accommodations. Getting the story on Pope John Paul I might not be too difficult, but would it make any sense? Would he really uncover a plot to murder the Pope? Or, did the prelate simply succumb to the pressures of his new office?*

"A good idea, Father, will you join me?" responded Jamie, adding "Might it also be possible on such short notice to get Father 0'Brien to join us?"

"I believe I can arrange to have him join us for lunch. Yesterday, when Father Rene talked to me about you it was decided that one of the first persons with whom you should have an interview would be Father O'Brien. So I called the Pope's secretary and asked him to stand by for a meeting sometime late this morning or early afternoon. He has no duties and is simply idling away his time awaiting the election of a new Pope. After that, he will either be secretary to the new Pope, or he will be reassigned."

"Why don't I place a call to him now?" suggested Father Joe. "After lunch you and he can chat a bit, and I'll get caught up on some of my other duties."

Jamie thought the last suggestion was an excellent idea. Father Joe placed the call to Father John 0'Brien. Already, thought Jamie, the Jesuit was one step ahead of me.

While he had Father 0'Brien on the phone, Joe asked his preference for lunch and gave him Jamie's building and room number. Father O'Brien replied and stated he was looking forward to meeting Father Bolin and was pleased someone in the Church is interested in documenting as quickly as possible his remembrance of the late Pope.

Father Joe called the commissary and ordered lunch. "Would you care for some wine, Jamie?"

"No, thank you, Father." The priest nodded and ordered a bottle of Heinekin's for himself.

Father O'Brien arrived 20 minutes later. As the two men introduced themselves to one another, Jamie noticed a decided tremor in the priest's hand. Father O'Brien had the flushed and veined cheeks of a good Irish drinker. His light blue eyes and cheerful smile spread a warm glow across his face. Hesitantly, he offered Jamie and Joe cigarettes which they declined. It seemed the secretary kept one going at all times and the nicotine stains between his index and third fingers identified him as a lifelong chain smoker. Jamie took an instant liking to this vulnerable, open and friendly man.

The three of them stood chatting near the oval, Italian Provincial table in the corner of the room adjacent to a large window overlooking the papal gardens. Father Gault signed the luncheon chit upon arrival and thanked the elderly Italian waiter. Graciously the German priest asked Father 0'Brien and Jamie to join him at the table.

Jamie observed the contrasting personalities of the two priests. On one side of him was seated a cheery faced Irishman belonging to the order of St. Vincent de Paul. On his left sat the tall, formidable, physically impressive, German Jesuit. Having already consumed a large breakfast Jamie settled for an avocado salad, a glass of milk and a small dish of ice cream.

The Irish priest had a stacked ham sandwich on rye, apple pie and a Bloody Mary. Father Joe was a meat and potatoes man, roast beef au jus, baked potato and no dessert. His burly hand wrapped around a raised glass as he filled it from the bottle of Heinekin's.

The discussion at lunch centered around the preparations for the Pope's funeral, two days away. From the conversation, Jamie gathered that Father Gault was connected with Vatican public relations. He changed his mind when Joe started talking about the security preparations for the funeral. The priest spoke with the authority of someone who had long experience in such matters.

Joe talked about Aldo Moro, the former Prime Minister of the Italian government, leader of the Christian Democratic Party. Moro had recently been murdered. His bullet-ridden body was found stuffed in the trunk of a car at a busy intersection in Rome. Five shots at close range had snuffed out his life. His kidnappers, the notorious left wing, Italian red brigade, had been responsible for the brutal slaying.

The Pope's death would again bring hundreds of dignitaries to Rome from all over the world. Father Gault was part of the Vatican security organization responsible for their safety while in Vatican City. At the funeral, 40,000 to 60,000 people would be assembled in St. Peter's Square. The main function of the Swiss Guard was the protection of Vatican property. Three hundred strong, they also served as honor guard to the Pope and the Cardinals.

The main security force for the funeral consisted of 5,000 Italian soldiers and policemen. Their function and assignments must be cleared individually through the Vatican Council for Public Affairs. Its head was Archbishop Agostino Casaroli. Joe mentioned that Casaroli was indirectly his boss.

Jamie registered a distinct impression of the Vatican as a city and a church under great psychological stress. The Church, employing an outmoded system of thought, was fighting for its last breath. He could feel the tension. His assignment would not be as simple as he had earlier assumed. An eerie feeling that he could not explain permeated his bones.

His attention began to refocus on Father Joe just as the priest excused himself. He was going to leave Jamie and Father O'Brien alone.

Before rising from the table, he inquired, "Jamie, who would you like to see next?" Jamie's response came as a surprise.

"Could a meeting be arranged tomorrow with someone knowledgeable in Vatican financial matters?"

With a quizzical expression, Joe told Jamie to meet him for breakfast, after which he would take him to the offices of the Prefecture of Economic Affairs of the Holy See. Noting the Jesuit's look of surprise, Jamie now scored his encounter with the priest as all tied up. Score one for Jamie and one for the Jesuits. He was becoming apprehensive about the game remaining a friendly one.

As Father Gault left the room, Jamie and Father O'Brien move to the divan, where they could continue their discussion more comfortably. Jamie knew he had better invent a cover story plausible to the priest.

"Father," Jamie began, "I had originally planned to come to Rome to document the transition of papal powers from the hands of Pope Paul VI to John Paul I. It seems American Catholics wanted to know all about the new Pope. Now, because of his untimely death, I will be more interested in the historical aspects of his short reign."

Jamie asked the priest for his impressions of the Pope. "What events stood out that might be of historical significance? Did you maintain a record of the Pope's daily itinerary? Could you possibly provide information that would serve as a 34-day historical road map?"

Father O'Brien was well aware of the significance of Pope John Paul's appointment calendar. He had, after all, been secretary to Pope Paul VI. Historians were already calling him to inquire about both deceased Popes. Therefore in his appointment book Father O'Brien kept a brief daily record of his own impressions of each audience or meeting involving Pope John Paul I. Under a separate system, he filed memos and letters relating to those audiences with the copies filed by date and time of day. Everything was meticulously recorded in his appointment book.

The priest momentarily got up from the divan and retrieved his briefcase. Walking over to Jamie, Father O'Brien handed over twenty-seven neatly typed ll x 14 Xerox copies, all bound in a leather folder.

"Jamie, please sign this receipt for these documents, and don't make any copies of the information. When you're finished with the material, the folder should be returned to me."

Jamie flipped through the pages, astounded at the amount of information. Father O'Brien was a master recordskeeper.

"Excuse me, Father, but could I ask why there are only twenty-seven days recorded, beginning with September 3rd? Didn't the Pope reign for thirty-four days?"

"No, Father Bolin. That is a popular misconception. Pope John Paul had been elected during the conclave in late August, but he did not assume the powers of office until the Rites of Investiture were performed. In the case of His Excellency, this took place on September 3rd. His reign lasted 27 days, not 34, as quoted in the newspapers."

The priest continued to talk about the Pope, but became physically upset as he did so. It was apparent that Father O'Brien felt the Pope had been an extraordinary man. Jamie listened attentively, as Father 0'Brien discoursed, and made copious notes, stopping the conversation from time to time to clarify various points.

Jamie would later reconstruct all the information in the form of sequential events, hoping it would lead him to uncover any conspiracy which might have been plotted to murder this particular Pope.

As an investigative reporter, he had an uncanny ability to separate a grain of truth from the chaff of rumor. Father O'Brien's information would be invaluable in crosschecking and verifying conversations and dates throughout the investigation. Father 0'Brien's recall during the interview had been beyond reproach.

Jamie relentlessly questioned the priest very closely on the details of finding the Pope's body, "What kind of papers had the Pope been holding in his hand?"

"I hadn't thought to look at them at the time, but when I later returned to straighten up the effects in the Pope's chambers, I remembered the papers and searched for them. It was then I discovered that the last page had been left behind, lying near the side of the bed. Apparently the page had fluttered to the floor and remained partially hidden under the bed during the confusion that was created by the removal of the Pope's body. I read the page. It contained only one paragraph. Then I returned it to a file basket in the Pope's office on the floor below."

Fortunately, Father 0'Brien committed to memory what he had read, because when he later returned to the Pope's office the page was not in the file basket. His recollection of the contents on that last page were:

"In summary: the monasteries are lacking appropriate screening procedures for the selection of novitiates. Diocesan priests show reluctance toward maintaining weekly collections at mass. Church properties are not being maintained. The young priests are becoming politically involved in organized radical movements. The Church in this region must regain its authority or grave consequences will prevail."

Father 0'Brien explained that he had paraphrased the paragraph but was certain that he had retained its meaning. It had not known whether it was the last page of a report to the Pope or a speech written for the Pope.

Jamie wondered if it was an indictment of a district, diocese, country, or a general comment concerning the attitude of many young priests. At this turn in the conversation, Jamie suggested they call it a day. He needed time to review the 27-day itinerary. Could he meet Father 0'Brien again, later that week?

"Perhaps for dinner and a few drinks?"

The priest replied affirmatively and inquired of Jamie, "Can I arrange for a Vatican limousine to take you back to your hotel, or will you be staying here tonight?"

"Thanks for the offer, Father, but I prefer to return the mini-bike to St. Anne's Gate and walk part way back to Rome before hailing a taxi."

Jamie locked the door as the two men exited the suite. Once outside the building Jamie headed for the mini-bike, withdrawing from his pocket the metallic card. It would be of no use to him now. The mini-bike was gone:

"Apparently, Father 0'Brien, the streets of Vatican City were no different than the streets of Rome." laughed Jamie as the two men walked together as far as the turnoff to St. Peter's.

They exchanged goodbyes, and Jamie entered the portico leading to the Belvedere Courtyard. It was still a considerable walk to St. Anne's Gate and he could not escape the feeling that he was being watched. At the guardhouse, he turned in his one-day pass and left the confines of Vatican City.

Turning to his right, Jamie came to the via Della Conciliazione. Heading east away from St. Peter's Square, he walked towards the bridge spanning the Tlber River. No one was on the street when Jamie came down the hill and crossed the bridge. At the next intersection, he hailed a taxi. The traffic on this side of the Tiber was heavy. Carelessly, Jamie stood in the street, near the curb, along the Corso Vittorio Manuele.

Suddenly, out of the corner of his eye, he saw a car not 100 yards away coming straight at him. Jumping back on the curb he stepped behind a lamppost as the car sped past; moderated its speed and rejoined the flow of traffic. Jamie lost sight of it as a taxi pulled over to the curb. Had someone deliberately tried to run him down? For what? The idea didn't make any sense. The hell with it, thought Jamie probably just a coincidence.

"The Hilton and hurry!" he nervously instructed the cabby.

IV.
STRANGE BEDFELLOWS

Sinking into a lethargic state, while soaking in a tub of hot water, Jamie was jolted back to reality by several loud raps on the foyer door. "Damn it!" he muttered, feeling most unhappy about being awakened from his musings.

"All right!" he shouted. "Be right with you."

Jamie had forgotten all about his call to room service. Splashing around, he regained his equilibrium. Hurriedly, he wrapped a towel around his warm, dripping wet body.

He called out, "Come in, the door isn't locked."

The waiter stood by patiently, ignoring Jamie's appearance. Jamie managed to sign for the meal with water running down his hand and perspiration clinging to his face. A few minutes later, after showering off in ice cold water, with his teeth chattering and skin icy blue, he briskly toweled down and wrapped himself in a short, scruffy, rust colored robe. Food tray in hand, he retired to the bedroom where he set about turning it into a makeshift research center. Brief case, pencils and notepads were placed on his right. His dinner and the Pope's twenty-seven page itinerary lay to his left. Jamie sat propped up in bed with all the dignity of a Hoboken wineo.

Fingering the stubble of his whiskers, he began the tedious task of reviewing the information supplied by Father 0'Brien. Apparently, the Pope's day began around 9:15 with his first audience. He averaged five audiences a day, the last one usually ending around 5:30. Father 0'Brien had also meticulously noted miscellaneous interruptions such as phone calls or urgent, unscheduled visits.

Each evening after supper the Pope continued working and frequently held private discussions with archbishops and cardinals. At one point, Jamie put aside his notes. While rubbing his hands across weary eyes, he spoke aloud as if admonishing someone.

"Hell! Ten people couldn't handle the Pope's workload, let alone one old man."

By 10:00 that evening, Jamie had spent three hours scrupulously pouring over the Pope's log. In all, there had been 250 audiences. Saturdays were reserved for staff meetings and on Sundays, with rare exception, the Pope rested. Methodically eliminating those audiences concerned with Church rituals and perfunctory diplomatic courtesies, Jamie managed to cull the number of significant events to nine audiences, four evening conferences and three staff meetings. With his knowledge of the Church and Father 0'Brien's excellent notations, the process had been tediously time-consuming but not difficult.

Sixteen items were listed separately on his notepad. A vague pattern of correlation began to emerge, and Jamie made an entry to that effect. The first item on his list corresponded to the meeting he had arranged for tomorrow morning. It concerned a review of Vatican finances and was entered as such in Father 0'Brien's log.

5/9 Tuesday, 9-12 noon - Finances

Location: Office of Prefecture of Economic Affairs

Subject: General review, balance sheet and income statement

Presiding: Cardinal Egidio Vagnazzi, followed by the Manager of Administration. of Patrimony and then Bishop Mar of the Vatican Bank

---

Jamie reached for the phone and called Father Joe.

"Hello, Father Gault? Is that you, Joe? Jamie Bolin here." Sorry to call so late. Where shall we meet in the morning? Yes, I'll look for you there. By the way, Father, will Cardinal Vagnazzi or Bishop Mar be available?"

The priest, with a note of sarcasm, laughed out loud.

"Not likely, Jamie. Have you heard of the Swiss gnomes? By comparison, the Cardinal and Bishop Mar are considered recluses."

Without waiting for a response, he rang off with, "Good night, Jamie see you in the morning."

Jamie was taken back by Father Joe's remark. What did the Church have to conceal that forced her financial officers to be so obscure and secretive? The gnomes of Switzerland were the most conservative and difficult-to-reach bankers in the world. Europeans note the day and then the month.

Jamie climbed out of bed and went into the next room. Drawing aside the ornate drapes, he stared pensively down into the streets of Rome.

Carol Livingston heard the phone ringing as she entered her room. Hoping it was Jamie, she caught it on the third ring.

"Hello?" "Click." *Damn it, wrong exchange. I do wish he'd call.* In dismay, she slammed down the receiver.

A solitary figure came out of the Vatican telephone exchange. Passing under a street lamp, he tossed a cigarette butt into the night air with a flip of his thumb and index finger. He watched the dying embers fall as he stuffed his hands deep down inside his cassock. A worrisome frown imprinted the otherwise unblemished surface of his forehead. After a brisk walk, he reached the parking lot behind the Belvedere Palace. A few minutes later, a blue Citroen disappeared across one of the bridges into Rome. A determined cluster of fingers massaged the knob of the gearshift as the car accelerated into the night.

The covers felt warm and inviting. Carol's naked body snuggled into bed. Her nipples tingled as the coolness of the sheet touched her breasts. If he didn't call by tomorrow evening, then she would call him.

"So much for men!"

Her voice filled with equal amounts of frustration and longing. Pulling the covers tightly around her, she dreamed of what might have been last night. Her mouth parted in a half-smile as she teased herself to sleep.

Jamie flipped the TV to an innocuous Italian movie. Clearing the mess of papers from the bed, he rearranged the pillows and left a wake-up call for 6:30 a.m. With the noise still blaring from the tube, he nodded off to sleep.

At 8:30 the next morning, Father Gault stood on the steps leading to the Palace of the Holy Office. The building located outside the Vatican walls lay to the south of St. Peter's Square and just to the left of Bernini's famous colonnade. The eyes of the priest restlessly swept the wide expanse of lawn. Father Gault recalled yesterday's conversation with Bishop Mar. Joe had suggested to the Bishop that Cardinal Vagnazzi make available several key financial personnel for today's meeting. The personnel should not withhold any information but should be very discreet in their disclosures especially if Father Bolin probed too deeply into certain sensitive areas.

"Bishop, inform his Excellency we are dealing potentially with a very dangerous man. He is a professional in his line of work. We cannot be too careful."

A taxi circled the plaza lawn and stopped near the steps. Jamie alighted as Father Gault came to greet him. The heavyset priest moved with agile quickness. His arms hung loosely by his side, but. . . How strange, thought Jamie, I hadn't noticed that yesterday. His attention was drawn to the priest's slightly cupped hands. Each finger was in perfect register with its companion. Jamie searched his memory, trying to recall where he had last seen that kind of precise, effortless movement. No matter, he shrugged, probably athletic by nature.

"Morning, Joe."

"Good morning, Jamie . . .sleep well? Hope you don't mind if we move right along. I have scheduled the meeting in forty-five minutes at the Teutonic College. If we hurry, we can grab a bite to eat in the basement cafeteria."

With Jamie in tow, the priest circled behind the Palace and headed west. Walking quickly for five minutes, they found themselves negotiating a long descent of stairs leading to the cafeteria below. Once inside, Joe located a table while Jamie took in the bright, cheery atmosphere. He found himself surrounded by a myriad of chattering Vatican employees, tourists, Swiss guardsmen in their swirled pantaloons and ruffled shirts, while nearby, sat monastically clad clergy.

"Did your visit with Father O'Brien go well?" the priest inquired.

"Yes," replied Jamie.

"He's an interesting man. I hope the next Pope recognizes his value."

Jamie and Joe spoke amiably as they ate. When it was time to go, Joe urged Jamie to hurry. *God! These Germans are efficient*, thought Jamie, as he stood up and drank the dregs from his coffee cup. Joe was already halfway out the cafeteria, heading for the second-floor conference room.

Monsignor Anton was the first to greet Jamie as he entered. Joe introduced the priest as the Manager of the Budget for the Holy See. Next came Bishop Caesarinni from the Office of the Administration of the Patrimony of The Holy See. The third gentleman was introduced as Nicholas Zapato, a representative of the Vatican Bank. The five men informally sat in a tight horseshoe-shaped arrangement at one end of a block-long mahogany table. Monsignor Anton comfortably ensconced himself at the head of the table. Seated to his right, Father Gault briefly outlined the purpose of the meeting.

Turning to Jamie, Monsignor Anton inquired, "Where shall we begin, Father Bolin?"

Pausing just long enough to retrieve a yellow pad from his attaché case, Jamie flipped the pages until he came to the appropriate item on his agenda. Focusing his attention on the priest, he said, "Monsignor could you perhaps give me a brief rundown on the history of the Vatican's financial setup?"

"Father Bolin, your question is a difficult one. Although in 1968 Pope Paul VI reorganized the financial offices of the Vatican, the problems of administration go back more than one hundred years. You see; the Papal States were dissolved completely by 1870. The Church suffered heavy financial losses and by the early 1920's, except for its properties and art treasures, the Church was insolvent. Miraculously, the Italian government chose at just that time to reimburse the Vatican for the annexation of the Papal States. The settlement provided badly needed operating cash. Much later, during the latter stages of the Second World War, money came pouring in from the United States. By 1960, the Catholic Church was exceedingly wealthy."

"If the Church was wealthy, why did the reorganization occur?" solicited Jamie.

"We had grown rich despite ourselves, Father Bolin. Church revenues were collected and dispatched by fourteen different offices and commissions, all with varying degrees of autonomy. No one office understood the entire financial situation. In fact, no single group within the Vatican controlled the purse strings. Without warning, the cash flow from the United States dwindled in the middle sixties. The causes were many and not likely to be cured. The American youth were rebelling, and conservative American Catholics were disheartened by the changes wrought by Vatican II."

Monsignor Anton further elaborated.

"The Church had committed itself to a program of tremendous expansion throughout Africa, Central and South America. Once again She wanted to minister to Her flock in the name of the Holy Spirit."

Jamie realized this kind of general information was getting him nowhere. The other four men shifted uncomfortably in their seats. Without warning, Jamie interrupted. "Is it true Monsignor that the Vatican desperately needed to improve its image because of past Fascist associations and accumulations of vast amounts of wealth?"

The Monsignor's face reddened as he answered.

"If you're referring to our fraternization with the Axis governments during the Second World War, I'm inclined to agree with you, Father

Bolin. The Church is still being criticized for not saving more European Jews during the war. That gigantic error in judgement haunts many of us, including myself, even today. Regarding her wealth, the Church has been unable to stifle rumors of its diversity and amount."

Jamie decided upon another tact.

"Are you trying to tell me that in some extraordinary and subtle way the year 1968 represents a watershed in Church history?"

"Actually, Father Bolin, the change occurred much earlier-shall we say 1929? Although, it was not until Paul VI reorganized the financial structure of the Church in 1968 that the Vatican fully appreciated its new role in the world. The reorganization eliminated the old offices and commissions. Strict budgetary controls replaced discretionary spending habits. Three financial offices were created, modeling their operations after successful businesses. The centerpiece of the new system is the Office of Prefecture for Economic Affairs, headed presently by Cardinal Egidio Vagnazzi. The Cardinal reports directly to His Holy Eminence. His office controls the implementation of all Church financial policies."

"Like the executive finance committee of a large industrial organization, Father?"

"Yes, that's correct," the Monsignor answered as he continued.

"The second office is the Administration of the Patrimony of the Holy See. It administers the Vatican payroll, which includes 3,000 employees and manages the Church's investments in securities and real estate. The third office in our financial trinity is the Vatican Bank."

Modeling their operations after successful business enterprises, Jamie turned the phrase over in his mind, and then he made the connection. The Office of Economic Affairs is the equivalent of a corporation's executive finance committee. The Patrimony of the Holy See is the same as the office of Controller, the corporate accounting function. But what about the Vatican Bank? Then an article he had once written for the Wall Street Journal flashed into his mind. *Oh, my God!* thought Jamie. *What a brilliant planner Pope Paul VI must have been. No wonder he was chosen by the College of Cardinals.*

Dead silence pervaded the room. Jamie realized everyone was awaiting his response to Monsignor Anton's explanation of the Vatican's financial organization. Buying himself a little time, Jamie jotted down several notes before dropping his next bombshell question. With several sharp strokes of his pencil, he dramatically underlined the analogy drawn between Vatican and corporate financial organizations.

Jamie doodled on his notepad while he sat back in a slouched position, smiling disarmingly. He raised himself to an upright posture. His thumbnail rested on his clenched teeth, and the pencil was now poised in a determined fist. Jamie launched his next inquiry, jabbing his pencil, like an errant missile, in the direction of Monsignor Anton.

"Tell me, Father, has the Vatican deliberately engineered the demise of the parochial school system in the United States?"

Before Anton could reply, Joe jumped up. "Hold on, Father Bolin; what kind of a question is that? It has no place in this discussion."

"I think it does," retorted Jamie, "and I'm sure the Monsignor knows why I asked it."

Anton, with a gentle wave of his hand, dismissed Father Joe's concern.

"Tell me, Monsignor, is the Church experiencing a diminishing positive cash flow from the States? Are the schools draining general funds that much?" continued Jamie.

"Yes," intoned a reluctant Monsignor, giving vent to a brief sigh as he tried to explain the Church's dilemma. "We are spending enormous sums to expand the Church's Christian ministries in Africa, South and Central America. In these areas, the young parish priests are exceedingly close to the poor. Filled with the ideals of Vatican II, the young priests rush with headstrong enthusiasm to embrace the rudimentary doctrines of socialism and finally communism. And, after all, Father Bolin, Christian communism is the idyllic state for mankind according to the teaching of Jesus Christ."

Jamie could not help sensing the sarcasm in the Monsignor's voice. The Vatican was still controlled by the conservative Italian Curia. Although sympathetic to the philosophical tenets of socialism, the Curia was vehemently anti-Communist. Monsignor Anton's sarcasm reflected the views of his superiors.

Anton spoke about many of the Church's problems in the Western world. "It seems, Father Bolin, that both European and American Catholics are demanding more voice in parish administration. Vocal and liberal theologians are flagrantly denouncing basic precepts of the Roman Catholic Church. The women's liberation movement is enticing Catholic women to abandon the rhythm method of birth control in wholesale lots."

Jamie's thoughts wandered back to the early days of his own marriage. The rhythm method was a half-baked scheme of the Vatican to lull women into a false sense of security while eliminating all spontaneity from the act of sex. Named Vatican Roulette by its knowledgeable detractors, the rhythm method inspired many a liberal priest to jokingly suggest aspirin as an additional precautionary measure to their male parishioners.

"Yes, aspirin:' replied one jovial Irish Jesuit while playing stud poker after a local Knights of Columbus meeting. "Not ingested, you idiots," he laughingly told the men seated at the table. "Firmly held between your wife's knees, should you be seized with a sudden urge of affection."

It had been difficult that night to separate the hilarious roar of laughter from the groans of repressed passion.

Jamie was beginning to understand, as Anton droned on, that he had stumbled onto a chilling new doctrine adopted by the Vatican. No wonder Joe had violently objected to his question. The one thing no religion can tolerate is an ever-increasingly well-educated group of laypersons exposed to an ever-expanding technological base. This can turn thousands of years of dogma into old wives' tales overnight.

The Church had taken a calculated risk, slowly closing American parochial schools. If parents could bring pressure to bear on politicians, then aid would be granted to private schools, and the diminishing cash flow would be halted. Had the original scheme worked, the Church could have its cake and eaten it too. Jamie caught the flat tone once again as Anton continued.

"Public aid to private schools would have succeeded except for two factors--the United States Supreme Court: and," sighed the priest, "the disenchantment of American Catholics with Vatican II. Conservatives lost respect for nuns and priests. Liberals had pleaded for the Pill and divorce and received approval for neither. Many fled the Church. Some took up the newly popular born-again Christian movement. The Catholic Church in the United States functions in name only."

The Monsignor then belittled the Europeans.

"In Western Europe, things are only marginally better.The Church is still a symbol of authority, but Europeans are frugal in their contributions. European theologians make Luther seem ultra-conservative by comparison. These men toy with such ideas as, 'Did Christ really exist? "Were the Gospels only an allegorical representation of a set of principles dating back to the Essenes, a mystical Jewish sect known to have existed from 200 BC until 75 AD? And is there really such a place as Heaven or Hell?"

Monsignor Anton had become completely absorbed in his own subject matter. No amount of silent gestures by Father Gault could shut him up. You could cut the air with a carving knife as the priest continued to empty himself before the small group of men sitting around the conference table.

"Yes, Father Bolin, we are faced with a theological rebellion in Western Europe and shrinking revenues from the United States. By the year 2050, the earth's population will be at least twelve billion. There will be a billion and a half in China, two in India. Another one billion total in the U.S., Western Europe, Canada, Australia and Japan. Our projection shows the remaining seven and a half-billion people will inhabit Eastern Europe, Russia, Africa, South and Central America. Those seven-and-a-half-billion represent a population ten times the present size of the Catholic Church. Think of it, Father, the enormous number of uneducated humanity, already favorably disposed towards the Christian religion, just waiting for the redemption of their souls by Holy Mother Church. The Church's ecclesiastical duty is clear. We have no other viable alternative."

The Monsignor's eyes seemed to momentarily glaze over. The timbre in his voice reminded Jamie of Billy Graham. The Monsignor was preaching a sermon with all the gestures of an evangelist.

"Just what might that clear-cut duty be, Monsignor?" Jamie intoned so as not to break the spell.

Father Joe reached across the table, about to say something. He rested his hand on the Monsignor's arm to calm him.

"That's all right, Joe, I'm certain Father Bolin will be discreet with this information. After all, he comes to us with the blessing of Cardinal Villot."

Father Joe shook his head and sat back while the Monsignor concluded his oratory.

"We must reach an accommodation with the Russians"

Jamie was so startled by the remark. He almost fell off his chair!

"At the same time, we will lend our support to socialism and self-determination in Africa, Central and South America. We will need assistance from the capitalist countries, the multi-national corporations and the international banking community. Does my frankness surprise you, Father Bolin?"

Jamie was astounded by the candor of the priest. Why was he being given all this information? Was it because of the death of the Pope? Had all the presumed strategies become obsolete? Had the Holy Roman Catholic Church written off Western civilization as beyond redemption? Just what the hell was going on? Jamie's mind raced on as the questions piled up in his head.

He had learned from his post-graduate studies what few people in the secular world understood. Even seasoned politicians and astute academics failed to recognize what he had discovered. The Roman Catholic hierarchy consisted of the largest single body of knowledgeable, powerful, intelligent and superbly educated men in the world. Such an abundance of human resources enabled "the Church" to not only survive but to prosper throughout it's nearly 2,000 years of existence.

Jamie did not believe Monsignor Anton's touch of the theatre was anything but intentional, but why? To allay any suspicions of those present, Jamie decided to simply ask several more innocuous questions.

It occurred to Jamie that he was being allowed to unlock Pandora's Box. What more surprises lie ahead?

Bishop Caesarinni chided Anton on his rambling oratory and suggested a coffee break before continuing. Father Joe called the cafeteria, glad to have something to occupy his mind while he continued to worry over what Jamie might yet learn.

"Order me a Coke, would you please," asked the portly banker, Zapato.

Turning to Jamie, he remarked, "I understand you're from California, Father. Do you know anyone from the Bank of America?"

"No sir," responded Jamie. "I'm afraid not."

"Santa Clara used to have a fine basketball team, didn't it, Father?"

"Yes, but that was quite some time ago," recalled Jamie, thankful he had always been a rabid college fan.

The priests sat around the table swapping stories. During a lull in the conversation, Monsignor Anton took his leave.

"I'm afraid I have another engagement yet this morning, Father Bolin. Please excuse me. I'm sure you can get any additional information you require from the good Bishop or Mr. Zapato."

"Certainly Monsignor. I deeply appreciate the time you have given me this morning. I hope to see you again before leaving Rome."

"Perhaps?" the priest replied rhetorically as he got up to leave.

Father Joe leaned over to Jamie. "Would you mind if I didn't stay?"

"Not at all, Joe; but could you meet me at the Vatican library this afternoon? I need you to find someone to accompany me to the Pope's funeral tomorrow."

"I'll see what I can do, Jamie."

"How about 4:30 this afternoon, Father?"

"Yes, Jamie, that will be fine. See you then."

Father Joe raised his voice as he looked in the direction of the departing Monsignor.

"Anton, just a minute please. I'd like a word with you."

Jamie imagined the lively conversation between the two priests would be hot and heavy.

Before leaving the room, Monsignor Anton had a brief, private conversation with Bishop Caesarinni and Mr. Zapato.

When the two men returned to the conference table, the Bishop inquired, "Father Bolin would you like an overview of the Church's financial condition? We are not as secretive about such things as we have been in the past. Because of the complexity of managing Her financial wealth, the Church now prepares annual budgets, income statements and balance sheets as well as investment portfolio analyses. A great amount of this information leaks to various curious outsiders anyway."

"It would be very helpful, Bishop, if you could preface that information with a brief historical account, starting perhaps with the early 1800's?"

Jamie sat back as Bishop Caesarinni began to reveal the fabulous financial history of the Vatican. Such information, although known to a small group of scholars and financial analysts, would shock the average lay Catholic.

"The Papal States were restored to the Pope by the degree of the Congress of Vienna in 1815. All Church properties confiscated by Napoleon were returned to the Church. The lands had originally been given to the Papacy by wealthy noblemen prior to the ninth century or were territories conquered by Cesare Borgia in the sixteenth century."

"Just a moment, Father, why should a Borgia donate land to the Vatican?" Jamie asked, as if he didn't already know what the answer would be.

Bishop Caesarinni didn't flinch as he answered.

"I'm afraid, Father Bolin, the Borgia family at that time was the Catholic Church."

"I beg your pardon, Bishop?" Jamie feinted confusion as the priest replied, "Cesare Borgia was the son of Pope Alexander VI!"

"How extraordinary! Who would believe it?" intoned Jamie as he continued.

"Are you speaking of a considerable amount of territory?"

Jamie thought he caught a look of grandeur in the Bishop's eyes when the priest replied.

"Would you call 16,000 square miles and three million Italians a lot, Father Bolin? I prefer to think of it as the temporal kingdom of Holy Mother Church! The people were very poor and were governed by the priests. There wasn't much left after the French had bled them to death. Church-imposed taxes were minimal. In fact, many of the citizens were beggars. Forty-five years later, in 1860, during the reign of Pius II, Italian noblemen rebelled and formed the modern Italian nation."

"The Church's temporal domain was reduced to 5,000 square miles and 700,000 subjects. In 1870, during the Prussian-French conflict, Italy annexed the remaining Papal States. The French, who strangely enough were protecting the Vatican land, departed; and the Italian army moved in, thus ending our temporal kingdom here on earth. The greatest loss, of course, was the city of Rome, itself. Pius II took refuge on these very grounds, here, inside the Vatican walls."

"I've heard it said, Bishop, that after the loss of the Vatican States, the Church had a very difficult transition period. Can you elaborate on that?"

Jamie continued to urge the Bishop to disclose the forgotten modern-day events leading up to World War II.

"Very difficult indeed," continued the Bishop. "For fifty years from the reign of Pope Pius IX to Pius XI, each succeeding Pope made himself a voluntary prisoner of Vatican City. Church records from 1815 through 1929 are very obscure. During that period, the value of Her art treasures continued to increase, but Her empire and influence evaporated."

"By 1929, the Vatican found itself in a very precarious cash bind. Going as far back as 1870, the Italian government had refused to reimburse the Papacy for the annexation of the Papal States. Then, in the early 1900's, Europe was devastated by World War I and the Bolshevik Revolution. The United States was in the throes of its great depression. Worldwide religious donations and charitable contributions were negligible."

Bishop Caesarinni drew a deep breath as if trying to suppress a great and troublesome secret. He refilled his coffee cup after taking several thoughtful sips, he leaned forward. With all the showmanship of an experienced actor, he spoke to Jamie in a conspiratorial tone.

"Now, Father," spoke the Bishop as he paused for effect.

Glancing at the banker, Nicholas Zapato, a sly grin spread across the Bishop's face, adding a slight crimson coloration to his cheeks.

"I'm going to tell you about one of the most bizarre and miraculous chapters in the history of the Holy Roman Catholic Church." Do you know who became the greatest secular hero of the Church during the 1930's?"

Jamie pleaded ignorance with a nod of his head and a helpless gesture of both hands while he edged forward in his chair.

"Benito Mussolini!" The words almost hissed from the Bishop's mouth.

"For the next fourteen years, IL Duce became the reluctant benefactor of Our Holy Mother Church. During that time, he flaunted his political relationship with that other despicable retarded individual!"

"You mean Adolph Hitler," asked Jamie expectantly.

"No, Father Bolin, not Hitler, D'Annunzio, Father, D'Annunzio!"

"I'm sorry, Bishop, I don't follow you. Who was D'Annunzio?"

"D'Annunzio was the Italian equivalent of the Marquis De Sade, a disgusting degenerate poet who played a necessary part in the political rise of Mussolini. In fact, at one time in the early 1920's, he almost became the king of Italy; but that's another story."

Jamie was stunned by the turn in the conversation. He leaned back hard against the chair, his left shoulder absorbing the impact. While the good Bishop continued to talk, Jamie sat transfixed. His left elbow rested on the dark mahogany arm of the chair. His hand, partially obscuring his gaping mouth, served as prop for his protruding jaw.

"Yes, Father Bolin, Benito Mussolini was an avowed atheist and also, as you mentioned, a bedfellow of Adolph Hitler. In fact, earlier in his career, IL Duce had published a pamphlet entitled 'God Does Not Exist.' But by 1929, he recognized the value of an alliance with the Vatican. Presto! Instantaneous enlightenment, the great man became a convert."

The Bishop continued his bizarre story.

"On February 11, 1929, he gained the everlasting gratitude of Holy Mother Church. On that day, Mussolini met with Cardinal Gasparri right here in Vatican City at the Lateran Palace and put his signature on the most important document in all of Christendom, the Lateran Treaty. By nightfall, millions of Italian Catholics were dancing in the streets. It became a national holiday. Then, at a later date, in recognition of that auspicious occasion, Pope Pius XI exclaimed, 'Mussolini was a man sent by Providence'. Overnight he became the Catholic hero of Italy. The populace toasted him in restaurants. His picture was placed in millions of homes. Young and old alike venerated him as a saint."

"I'm finding this all very difficult to believe, Bishop Caesarinni. How could the Italian people, let alone the Catholic Church, be so gullible?"

"On the contrary, Father Bolin, as you shall learn, it was the Duce, himself, who was used by the Vatican to meet the needs of the Church."

"Bishop, don't you believe the price for his services was very costly in the terms of humanity?"

"Come now, Father. It's Jamie. Isn't it?"

"Jamie, you Americans are hopeless. How do you account for the likes of John Kennedy and Lyndon Johnson? Give the Italians and the Church credit for being realists. When we discovered our mistake, the man was hung upside down like a side of beef!"

"Surely, Bishop, you don't equate the likes of Benito Mussolini with two of America's greatest democratic presidents?" shot back Jamie as he began to perceive he was going to be no match for Bishop Caesarinni on this matter.

"Frankly, the Church gained a lot of mileage from Kennedy, and we would just as soon leave well enough alone. We owe no such debt to Lyndon Johnson. I suggest if you're really interested, you can find a glimpse of the truth in a book by one of your own American authors, Norman Mailer. It's called, I believe, The Idol and the Octopus. His book reveals only the tip of the iceberg regarding war, sex and stupidity as an American way of life."

The Bishop smiled broadly.

"Then, of course, if you like, we can talk about Mr. Nixon. . ."

The Bishop's voice trailed off in an amusing fashion.

Jamie decided to back off.

"You're absolutely right. I suppose we Americans are political Pollyannas. Please continue with your story."

"We are all guilty of that human frailty," remarked the Bishop, not wanting to escalate the argument. "Now let me see, where was I? Oh yes! The Lateran Treaty. Even I find it difficult to believe. The Treaty was composed of three codicils: the Lateran Pact created the sovereign state of Vatican City; the Financial Convention awarded the Church compensation for the loss of the Vatican States; and the Concordat granted special powers and privileges to the Church."

"Would you care to enumerate the most important concessions to the Church, Bishop Caesarinni?"

Casearinni looked over at Nicholas Zapato, then back at Jamie. He held up his hands, using his fingers as an alphabetical checklist.

A. Exemption from all Italian taxation.
B. Sovereign rights, not only within the walls of Vatican City but To numerous properties in and around Rome.
C. Church canon law prevailed over Italian civilian authority. Church marriages did not require civil approval and divorce cannot be granted by the State.
D. Ninety million dollars was paid to the Church. Half in cash And half in interest-bearing government bonds.
E. The Church was given control of certain clerical and laymen organizations throughout Italy, including financial control. Clergy and citizens of the Vatican were exempt from personal taxation."

The Bishop hesitated.

"Have I forgotten any major considerations, Nicholas?"

"Possibly one," commented the banker.

"Oh, of course, such a trifle," laughed the Bishop.

"One little clause granted in the Financial Convention obligates the Italian government to pay a small wage annually to parish priests in Italy."

"Wait a minute!" exclaimed Jamie.

"You're telling me that in 1929, with the world engulfed in a massive economic depression, Italy paid the Vatican ninety-million dollars!"

"That's what I just told you, Father."

"But in terms of today's value, that would be equivalent to a billion dollars," uttered Jamie in complete disbelief as he shook his head. "With that enormous sum bestowed upon the Vatican, what is so significant about a paltry annual wage to a few parish priests?"

"Well, you see, Jamie, in 1959 the Vatican convinced the Italian government that the originally negotiated wage was too small, so the government amended the agreement with the approval of the Church and increased the annual wage to $1,500 American."

"So what?" asked a bewildered Jamie.

No longer able to contain himself, the banker interrupted.

"Father Bolin, there are 40,000 Catholic priests in Italy!"

"My God! That's sixty-million dollars a year," rejoined Jamie

"Surely you must be joking?"

Both men, grinning broadly, assuring Jamie that such was the relationship between Italy and the Catholic Church.

"But. . .but. . .that document, the Lateran Treaty, must represent the biggest political payoff in the history of ecclesiastical affairs."

"Most likely," said the Bishop.

"Except no one is quite sure about Queen Elizabeth, Henry VIII's daughter, and the Church of England. After all, look at what happened to Mary Queen of Scots."

Jamie recovered from the shock of Caesarinni's disclosures and asked, "I take it the Vatican wisely invested the ninety million dollars in 1929?"

Caesarinni acknowledged the money had been wisely invested.

"Mr. Zapato will fill you in on the details. Why don't you and he discuss it over lunch? Sorry I can't join you-perhaps some other time?"

"Before you leave, Bishop, could you take a minute to give me an opinion on the value of the Vatican art treasures and land holdings? I'm fascinated by the Church's treasures."

Bishop Caesarinni answered Jamie with several vague comments. "Da Vinci's one painting of the Mona Lisa in the Louvre if auctioned today would command a price of ten-million dollars. By comparison, the Sistine Chapel alone consists of entire walls and a ceiling painted by Michelangelo. In addition, there are hundreds of paintings here in the Vatican by old masters such as Giotto, Fra Angelico, Bellini, Lippi, Caravaggio, Da Vinci and Titian to name a few."

Raphael is not only represented by his paintings, but there are rooms here that were completely designed and hand-painted by him. The Vatican library houses seven thousand incunabula, precious illuminated manuscripts, by the greatest authors in history."

"As for real estate, the Church owns more property in the United States than anyone else, save the Federal government. Then of course, Mother Church has parishes throughout the entire world. Come, gentlemen, I really must be on my way. Why not walk with me before we part company?"

V. A PENNY SAVED IS A PENNY EARNED

Bishop Caesarinni waved as he separated from Jamie and Nicholas Zapato on the ground floor of the Teutonic College. Jamie turned to the Greek banker and suggested they have lunch in his suite at the villa of Pius IV.

Nodding in agreement, the banker led Jamie down a narrow corridor leading to the back of the building, then across an open courtyard. Vatican City lay beyond the guard gate. After displaying the proper identification, Jamie and Zapato continued on their way, passing through the lovely garden grotto between St. Peter's Basilica and its adjoining Sacristy.

Jamie called Nick's attention to a nearby minibïke station. Ten minutes later they parked outside the villa. During the short ride, Jamie thought about the great versatility of the Church. No longer a temporal power, consort to kings and queens as She had been during the Middle Ages; now She is disguised as a banker and multi-national business manager. Her spiritual presence is currently overshadowed by Her riches and struggle for power.

Upon entering the suite, Jamie wasted no time in ordering lunch.

"Two large fresh garden salads, blue cheese dressing on both and a bottle of American Rhine wine, Taylor of California preferred."

"Ten minutes, fine, thank you very much."

He then turned his attention to Nicholas Zapato.

"I'm looking forward to learning all I can from you about Vatican investments. I acknowledge the Bishop's disclosures this morning are well known to historians and Italian politicians. But I dare say it would come as jolting news to the majority of Americans."

The gregarious Greek laughed placing his hand on Jamie's shoulder.

"May I call you Jamie?"

"Of course."

"And by all means, please call me Nick. Jamie, I'm quite certain you will be equally astounded this afternoon by the wealth of the Church!"

At lunch, in between bites of his salad, Zapato took up the modern-day story of the Church where Bishop Caesarinni had stopped.

"Does the name Nogara mean anything to you?"

Jamie responded with a negative shake of his head and urged the banker to continue his story. Pausing to savor a taste of the California Rhine, the banker began to unfold the story of every investor's dream.

"The Lateran Treaty was signed on February 11, 1929 and ratified by the Italian parliament on June 7th. On that very day, Pope Pius XI appointed one Bernardino Nogara director of a new Vatican office called the Special Administration of the Holy See. Nogara, a close relative of the Archbishop of Udine, was scrupulously honest, a devout Catholic and above all else, an absolute financial wizard. Nogara would invest Church funds in a company and appoint one or more trusted Catholic laymen to the company's board of directors."

“A typical example of his financial acumen was demonstrated by numerous small investments in Italian natural gas companies. Eventually the companies became known as the Panzarosa group. During the 1930 depression, the Italian government refused to bail the companies out of trouble. The Church stepped in and purchased a majority of the stock for two million dollars. Nogara placed Senator Alfredo Trossati and the Marquis Pacelli on the board of directors. Pacelli's brother later became Pope Pius XII!"

"Today the Panzarosa group is better known as Italigas; the sole supplier of home fuel to approximately forty cities in Italy. In 1978, the company sold more than one billion cubic meters of natural gas. Over the years, Nogara continued investing in Italian companies concentrating in petroleum products, electrical power, communications equipment, banking, railroads, farm equipment, textiles and cement companies."

"While the Italian intellectuals inveighed to anyone who would listen the evils of the concessions made to the Church concerning Canon law under the Lateran Treaty, Nogara shrewdly took advantage of little-known or cared-about clauses 29, 30 and 31 of that document. Those three clauses excluded ecclesiastical corporations and the Vatican bank from Italian taxation!"

"Am I to assume from your remarks, Mr. Zapato, that Benito Mussolini was the financial dupe of Holy Mother Church?"

"Harsh words, Jamie. True perhaps, but such a condemnation of the Church should be tempered by an understanding of the world at that time. Cooperation between the Church and IL Duce reached its zenith in 1935. By then, Vatican-owned munitions factories were supplying Mussolini with weapons used to invade Ethiopia. In 1939, Pope Pius XI died. The new Pope, Pius XII, never got along with Mussolini."

"When the war ended in 1945, IL Duce had already been dead several years and the Church emerged in complete financial control of Italy's post-war destiny. In all fairness to the Church, Jamie, it was She with the help of Her business partners, who spearheaded the reconstruction of Italy's devastated economy."

Having brilliantly justified the Church's use of Her wealth, the banker raised his wineglass in a toast to the late financial genius of the Vatican.

"To a loyal Catholic layman, Salute Nogara, temporal savior of Holy Mother Church! God rest his soul."

The gregarious banker was obviously a great admirer of Bernardino Nogara. His toast to the financier ended his soliloquy on Vatican investments. Jamie, however, was determined to dig deeper. All three Vatican financial people had been very clever. The information divulged to Jamie dealt mainly with past history. Although shocking in detail, in no way had anyone revealed information regarding the Church's current wealth or political intrigues.

Jamie was prepared to deal with such evasiveness cloaked in the guise of complete disclosure. Intentionally, he had stretched out the morning meeting, hoping to contrive a one on one interview over lunch. Jamie also believed the morning meeting had been quite revealing, in an unexpected way.

Monsignor Anton had 'spilled the beans' about the Vatican third world strategy. *For that little slip up, Joe might kill him,* Jamie mused. Jamie intentionally had given the appearance of a priestly bumpkin when he had refused the bait to delve more deeply into Church politics. His ploy had worked; no one but Joe had seen any harm in letting the banker lunch alone with him. Now, thought Jamie, I need to ask just the right questions at just the right times.

Zapato, having made his carefully prepared speech, began to relax and finish off his salad when Jamie interposed the first of his queries.

"Nick, I've always been fascinated by international finance. Could you give me an estimate regarding the size of the Vatican bank's capital account, its customer profile and the magnitude in round figures of its demand deposits in foreign banks?"

The banker almost choked as he gagged on a mouthful of salad.

"Are you all right, Nick?" solicited Jamie, barely able to suppress an emerging smile.

Clearing his throat, Nick fatuously pressed a linen napkin to his lips, attempting to regain his composure. He knew that only a trained certified public accountant specializing in finance or an international economist would be astute enough to ask such a troika question. Who is this son-of-a-bitch anyway, thought Zapato. *Answering his question will completely disclose the Vatican's pre-eminent standing in the international financial community.*

The banker was nobody's fool but realized, as the Americans would say, 'I've been had'. Zapato decided to answer Jamie as succinctly and briefly as he could. He realized the moment Jamie sprung his trap that evasiveness would only prolong Jamie's interrogation until he got exactly what he wanted. Monsignor Anton and Bishop Caesarinni would not be pleased with Nick's report of this afternoon's revelations.

Putting aside his wineglass and dropping his napkin in his lap, the banker drank from his coffee cup. Slowly and very deliberately, he began to address himself to Jamie's question.

"For an American priest teaching history at a small Jesuit school in northern California, you certainly have one hellava grasp of economics, Father Bolin."

"Just curious by nature," replied Jamie as he accepted the veiled sarcasm.

Trying not to gloat, Jamie continued, "I'm just looking forward, Nick, to learning all I can--it's my job you know."

We'll see about that, thought Nick.

"I'll do my best," answered the banker.

He forced an affable smile across his clenched teeth. Beads of perspiration danced on his forehead.

Jamie pressed on.

"Sorry I interrupted; what were you about to say regarding the bank's capital account?" reminding the banker that the question remained unanswered.

Reluctantly, Nick divulged the information.

"The Vatican bank has on deposit approximately two billion dollars."

"I beg your pardon, you mean two million dollars, don't you, Nick?"

"No, Jamie, I mean two billion dollars; and what's more, I think you damn well know exactly what I mean!"

The banker was becoming a bit testy.

"Your depositor profile then," asked Jamie, "it must be very impressive."

"We have seven thousand depositors. Many of them are Italy's most influential businessmen and politicians, several high officials in the communist party, I might add. Those bastards are the biggest capitalists I know," replied Zapato, determined to keep his answers brief.

"Demand deposits?" urged Jamie.

The banker let out a sigh. "We maintain about one hundred and fifty-million dollars on account with a number of correspondent banks."

Nick saw Jamie's eyes light up as registers on a pocket calculator.

Nick was very nearly correct. Jamie began computing the value of the demand deposits in terms of international business transactions. Demand deposits accrue no interest to the depositor, in this case the Vatican bank. The deposits placed in another bank serve as a legal method used by an investor to pay foreign banks a commission on business transactions.

The foreign bank can invest or lend the demand deposits and earn interest at the rate of seven percent to fifteen percent. Jamie quickly calculated the Vatican bank's overseas business transactions by estimating the commission percentages represented by the size of the demand deposits. It's billions of dollars in international transactions.

"Are you telling me, Nick, that the Vatican transacts billions of dollars of international business every year?"

Jamie looked incredulously at the banker. His rhetorical question required no reply. *What then*, thought Jamie, *must be the enormous size of the Church's stock portfolio*? Bishop Caesarinni had mentioned a ninety million dollar payment to the Church in 1929! Jamie's mind wrestled with the magnitude of compound dividend rates. Hadn't Zapato just drunk a toast to a mysterious Mr. Nogara, the man who had guided Vatican investments during the world-wide depression of the 1930's, through the Second World War in the '40's and on into the post-recovery period of the 1950's. What a spectacular era for investment.

The post-war economic boom could have multiplied the original investment a hundredfold by now. Jamie wanted to find out exactly how much. Could the canny Greek banker be enticed to tell Jamie what he wanted to know?

Nick was just getting up from the table as Jamie's mind came back to the present. The banker was about to excuse himself when Jamie offered him a fine Havana cigar.

"I really do appreciate your frankness, Nick; it was information I really needed. Hope you didn't mind."

"Not at all," lied the banker as Jamie arose to light Nick's cigar.

"Care for another glass of wine?" suggested Jamie.

"Why don't we relax and move to the divan, it's already been a long day."

"Alright, Jamie, but I can't stay much longer--a bank meeting--you understand," said Nick.

The banker began to relax, sip the wine and slump down into the divan. Despite himself, Nick couldn't help liking Jamie. He liked the way the priest called him Nick. His friends all called him that. It fit the son of an itinerant steelworker who had immigrated to Italy after the war and rose from object poverty to his present lofty position.

"Tell me, Nick, how large are the Vatican stockholdings in Italy?"

"What value would you place on them?"

Caught off guard, the banker exploded

"They're not worth a rat's ass"

"Beg your pardon?" Jamie innocently responded.

"Excuse me, Jamie, it's not you. It's just that the subject is a very sensitive one with me."

Having regretted his display of anger, Nick began over-compensating by talking too much.

"One of my responsibilities is being a member of the Vatican investment advisory board. Italy, as you know, is in a state of grave civil unrest. The Church`s ownership of Italian industry is immense. It is only a matter of time before the communists with the assistance of the idiot socialist party take control of the central government. When that day comes, either the Vatican reaches an accommodation with the communists, or She can kiss Her Italian investments goodbye."

"How large a loss are you speaking of, Nick?"

"Conservatively, the Church directly holds fifteen percent of all stocks listed on the Italian national exchange. Actually, through its many corporate entities, She controls at least fifty percent of all the listed companies. The ninety million dollars originally invested by Nogara grew to half a billion dollars by 1950. In the twenty-some years since that time, their value on the Italian stack exchange was last estimated at six billion dollars!"

Jamie thrust his raised hand towards Nick, palm face up.

"Hold it, Nick, are you pulling my leg?"

"No, Jamie, oftentimes I myself wish it weren't true. The Vatican Italian investments consume a major portion of everyone's time here in Vatican City. Although the Church attempts to keep a very low profile, when difficulties arise, bishops and even cardinals, as the case may be, are constantly drawn into the decision-making process; persuading businessmen what course of action to take on this or that matter. Crises now arise on a daily basis."

Intending to test the validity of the banker's revelation, Jamie asked, "Nick, could you give me some specific examples of Vatican ownership?"

"Where are you staying in Rome, Jamie?"

"The Hilton atop Monte Morio, why?"

"Because," replied Nick, "the hotel with its lush gardens, restaurant-nightclub, 400 rooms, pool, tennis courts and seven-acre park is operated by Hilton International. But the hotel is actually owned by another corporation, which in turn is seventy-five percent owned by Americana Nicovi Alberghi, better known as IANA. IANA is a wholly owned subsidiary of Societa Generale Immobilaire. The Vatican owns seventy-five percent of all the stock in SGI. And that story is the same in all phases of industry throughout Italy."

"How so?" interjected Jamie.

"Take Finisider, Italy's steel group, for example," Zapato continued, "Its two largest stockholders are the Italian central government and the Vatican. Finisider itself employs over 80,000 workers. More importantly, it owns more than fifty percent of a holding company known as Italiader."

"Italiader owns or controls thirty to forty other corporations. The list of companies is endless--automobile manufacturers, utilities, ship lines, banks, insurance, machine tools, electronics, etc."

"Is it possible, Nick, that the Church is similarly heavily invested in the rest of Europe and America?"

"I really don't know the full extent of Vatican foreign interests, Jamie."

"But surely, Nick, as an officer of the bank, you have some idea."

"It isn't that simple. You see, Jamie, the Church's other interests are either controlled through foreign corporations or the Church's Swiss bank!"

"The Church's what?" As he spoke the words, Jamie leaned forward.

His eyes bored a hole right through the banker. *My God*, thought Jamie, *is there no end to all this? What have I gotten myself into on this assignment*?

"Jamie, Jamie, you Americans are so naive. I'm sorry you seem so upset. It's like your Mr. Nixon and Watergate. His real crime was being a Republican President with an extremely hostile Democratic Congress. Mr. Nixon projected no heroic image on your TV screens. After all, Roosevelt, Kennedy and Johnson perpetrated far more impeachable offenses. Most Europeans would even say treasonable ones. But those men projected images larger than life, and theirs was always the party in power."

"Look, Nick, I don't know how we got on this subject, but President Nixon was wrong and got what he deserved."

"No, Jamie! You're wrong. That's where we Europeans differ politically with you Americans. Just as the French abhor violence in films, Americans are obsessed with sex. President's Nixon's problem was one of appearance and public relations. Many of your Presidents could kiss babies and make women weep in the streets. This then gave them the privilege of sending thousands of boys off to needless wars, and then you Americans make these idiot Presidents national heroes."

"Nick, please, I'm not here to discuss European attitudes with regard to American politicians. Now what about this Swiss bank business?"

"The Vatican has its own Swiss bank, Banque de Rome Swisse. It's wholly owned by the Vatican and functions as a foreign holding company. It won't do you any good to attempt investigating the Church's foreign holdings. Under Swiss law, such information is beyond disclosure! To wet your obviously curious mental appetite, I can tell you in a general nature about the Vatican's success in American investments."

"During the 1960's, after the death of Nogara, one of the Vatican's most astute financial advisors was your own Cardinal Spellman of New York. Incidentally, he was a very close personal friend of old Joe Kennedy. For twenty years the Vatican did extremely well multiplying its investments in New York stock exchange listed companies. The dividend payments alone have been enormous."

Concluding his conversation, Nick Zapato, the Greek banker, said to Jamie, "The Church does have an unusual investment in Canada through SGI, the Vatican-owned construction corporation. It seems that the construction company owns ninety-five percent of Immobilaire Canada Limited. ICL is a Canadian holding company that among other things owns a 600-foot-high steel-reinforced concrete building in downtown Montreal. It's the tallest structure of its kind in the world."

"A very unusual investment, Nick, but I don't see how it sheds any light on the magnitude of Vatican investments in North America."

"Would it interest you to know, Jamie, that the building cost forty-seven million dollars to build in the 1960's and that its name is the Montreal Stock Exchange Tower! It houses all the Canadian stock exchanges operating in the Province of Quebec."

Zapato added, "Need I remind you, Jamie, that although Americans consider Canada of minor economic and political importance, in reality, Canada is the eighth ranking power in the world and that the Province of Quebec is almost entirely Catholic. In the Province of Ontario, in the city of Toronto alone, there are over three-hundred thousand Italians."

Zapato glanced at his watch. He was late for his next appointment.

"Sorry, Jamie, but I really must run. Besides, you have gotten more information from me than I should have given you. I'm not sure just who you are, but don't be too critical of Holy Mother Church. She is fighting for her life right now. You're a tough one, Father Bolin, but I would like you to call on me if you have any more questions. Good day, Father."

The banker stood up, shook Jamie's hand and seemed rather at peace with himself. It was as though part of the burden he always carried with him had been lifted, transferred somehow to this enigmatic Irish-American.

Without waiting for Jamie to escort him to the door, the banker turned and left. Jamie was certain that their entire conversation would be reported to Father Joe, Monsignor Anton and Bishop Caesarinni. Was he, Jamie Bolin, really up three to one on the Jesuits, or was the game, as the Brooklyn bookies would say, "A boat ride"?

It was getting late. Jamie was anxious to get to the Vatican library. But something the banker had said troubled him. Jamie stopped long enough to puzzle over the situation and make several notes. Then his anxiety surfaced from the depths of his subconscious. Jamie recalled that Cardinal Villot was a Frenchman and that France had very close ties with Quebec.

"Good grief," puzzled Jamie aloud, "I'm sitting in the middle of a multi-national financial empire, so artfully contrived that even a thorough audit of their books would disclose very little of the Church's enormous wealth. And what's more, the chairman of the board is responsible to no one, at least not on this earth. The Pope reigns supreme as corporate president, sovereign king and absolute spiritual head of seven-hundred million dues contributing members and doesn't even pay taxes!"

Gathering up his notes, Jamie left the suite. He rode his mini-bike through the Belvedere courtyard. A very real sense of uneasiness pervaded his thoughts. With the information acquired today, an entire new set of parameters had been added to the possible causes for the death of John Paul I.

VI. TOMBS ARE FOUND IN MANY PLACES

Jamie entered the portals of the massive Apostolic Library. Fleetingly, his mind recalled the many hours he had spent researching the grandeur of the Catholic Church of the Middle Ages. Glancing about, he recognized his old scholarly retreat, a small brown oak table in a dusty alcove, just down the aisle from the front entrance. The alcove was far enough removed from the central reading areas so that Jamie would not be disturbed by the constant noise of shuffling feet and restlessly moving chairs that so characterized most of the vast, main library chambers.

Twenty years ago in this same library, Jamie had researched very scholarly works, including many private papers of monarchs and cardinals. The Vatican meticulously preserves such documents. Today, his only interest was in the latest secular periodicals. It was simply more convenient to use the Apostolic Library than to visit the library in downtown Rome.

Jamie placed his attaché case on the table and laid claim to a nearby chair. He noted by his Seiko that it was almost two o'clock. Abandoning his daydreaming, he headed for the main library information center, rather flamboyantly identified as such by a large sign stating:

"INFORMATION", printed in seven different languages.

"Father, could you tell me the location of the periodical stacks?"

Without a sound, the young, dour-looking librarian priest whipped a sheet of paper off a pile, circled a location on what appeared to be a map of the library and thrust the piece of paper towards Jamie.

"Grazie prete!" taunted Jamie.

Silently, the young man glared back and ever so slightly wiped two fingers across the underside of his chin. Turning away, Jamie smiled broadly and thought, *certainly an uptight, unpleasant fellow; either trying to give up smoking or masturbation, perhaps both.*

Despite the unpleasantness, Jamie was thankful for the information. The Apostolic library contains 800,000 volumes. Directions to a specific location are an absolute necessity. Scouring the racks, it took Jamie forty-five minutes to gather up the magazines and newspapers he needed and return to the little table in the alcove.

Jamie glanced around at the several hundred people, mostly priests doing scholarly research. He marveled at the loveliness of this centuries' old building housing so many treasures of ancient and contemporary knowledge. He stacked the periodicals on the table, bent down and took out pad and pencil from his attaché case. Inconspicuously, he plunged into his laborious task.

A shadow fell across the table while Jamie continued to make notes. He felt the weight of a powerful hand upon his shoulder.

Father Joe leaned over and whispered, "Hello, Jamie. I can only stay a few minutes. Father John 0'Brien will accompany you to the Pope's funeral tomorrow. Is that all right?"

Unfolding a small scrap of paper, Joe laid it on the table. "It's Father 0'Brien's phone number. Call him and arrange a time and place for him to meet with you in the morning."

"Speaking of time, Joe, you're early, aren't you? I thought you said you couldn't get here until 4:30."

Joe laughed. "I'm running late, Jamie. it's already 4:45. Call me tomorrow evening, and let me know how you make out."

Turning abruptly, he left. Jamie was once again alone in the alcove.

Jamie placed his hands behind his head, leaned back and watched the priest move cat-like down the corridor. The silence was deafening. A slight shiver permeated Jamie's body. Now very tired, he yawned and realized how easily he lost track of time when he became absorbed in his own research. Another hour and a half passed before Jamie left the library. Riding a bike to St. Anne's gate, he caught a taxi to the Hilton. Traffic was unusually heavy at 7:30at night.

After a long, tough day, he unlocked the door to his rooms. Enough of Papal intrigue and Vatican finances, thought Jamie. Upon entering his bedroom, he removed his sport coat and tugged at his tie; dropping coat and tie over the valet stand. He tossed his attaché case onto the nearest chair. Bulging with notes, dates and names, the leather case nestled into the heavy brocade Italian Provincial material of the chair, as a little brown dog might cuddle up on a chilly evening.

Picking up the white, ornate phone, resting in its imitation golden cradle, Jamie plopped down upon the bed. Only to sit up with a groan, as his head accidentally struck the headboard. He had forgotten to prop up any pillows. "Serves me right," he muttered, rubbing a very tender spot.

"Every thought of that girl fogs my senses."

Rearranging the pillows, he heard a voice say repeatedly, "Number please, what number do you wish?"

"The Minerva Hotel please, operator. Thank you."

"Hello, the Minerva Hotel,"

"Miss Livingston's room, please."

Ring! Ring!

Reaching down, Jamie removed his English loafers and stretched his calf muscles.

"Hello?" came a tentative inquiry from the other end of the line.

"Carol?"

"Is that you, Jamie?"

"Of course, Love, and you could be a little more excited at the sound of my voice."

"Why you silly Irishman, I thought you were never going to ring me up. Besides, for the last two evenings my phone has jangled, but no one answers when I pick it up."

"Probably an operator error. By the way, Love, I have missed you."

"Well, you certainly have an odd way of showing it."

"I'll make it up to you Saturday."

"Sorry about the last two evenings. I've simply been very busy. I'll tell you all about it Saturday."

Jamie wanted to know if she could chat for awhile. In her most seductive manner, Carol intimated she had nothing else to do but wait for him on Saturday. Already, she was tired of killing time in Rome. Half teasing, she told him of her plans for the next three days, which included very explicit details of how she intended to sun at poolside in a pair of bright green, short shorts and a braless halter top.

"That is, Jamie, if you'll leave a key for me at the desk so I can change in your room. The Minerva doesn't have a pool-but I understand the Hilton does. I do so want to show off these shorts. I bought them in London, at an American shop. I believe they're called 'Dittoes'. Have you seen them on any American girls?"

Marvelous images of Carol cavorted through his mind. She continued teasing him. Frivolously, they bantered back and forth for the next half-hour.

"I really miss you Jamie. Be careful, I've had the funniest feeling."

"Don't worry love. If it weren't for this damn assignment, I'd be with you now. I'll wrap it up as quickly as possible."

"Damn you Irish," she answered. "How can you make being apart seem so romantic?"

Then Carol asked, "What time Saturday?"

"I'll be knocking' on your door at one o'clock sharp. I'll not leave your side for the rest of the day."

"Till then," mused Carol.

"I guess it will have to do. Good night, Jamie."

"Good night my lovely English girl."

Replacing the receiver on its cradle, Jamie dozed off with images of Ditto shorts and long legs dancing in his head. Several hours later, he awakened, remembering to call Father O'Brien. Still half asleep, Jamie stood up, turned on the bedside lamp and groped his way towards the valet stand. His fingers grudgingly probed the inside pocket of his sport coat for the scrap of paper containing the priest's phone number.

Standing beside the bedroom wall, he heard noises emitting from the suite next door. Angry muffled voices were coming from the adjoining room. Jamie was sure he heard a slight scuffle taking place.

A raised voice shouted, " . . . your instructions and mine:" Followed by a horrendous slamming of a door.

Once more Jamie's bedroom was cloaked in silence, as if nothing had disturbed its tranquility. Jamie was not adverse to a small diversion of eavesdropping on a domestic quarrel, but when the silence continued unabated, he returned to the bedside table and placed a call to Father O'Brien.

"Hello? Father O'Brien here."

Jamie hesitated momentarily, intending to return the friendly greeting of the priest. A look of consternation crept across the features of his face as he was distracted by a small buzzing sound coming from the suite next door.

"Oh: Hello father," said Jamie. "Sorry to call you at this hour. I just wanted to check on our arrangements for attending the Pope's funeral tomorrow."

"No problem, Jamie. You didn't disturb me. It's only ten o'clock. I usually stay up past midnight. Why don't you meet me in the grotto next to the Basilica about fifteen minutes before the scheduled service?"

Only half-listening, Jamie's attention again focused on the bedroom wall as he realized the noise was becoming more attenuated. Incredulously, as the priest's voice drifted off Jamie watched the plaster, next to a hanging print by Van Gogh, begin cracking up. Spindly pieces of white-gray plaster wafted their way through the air and fell to the floor.

Jamie murmured a quick good night to Father O'Brien after affirming their morning meeting place.

Replacing the telephone instrument on its cradle, he dumbfoundedly sat on the edge of his bed, staring at the crumbling plaster.

The spill of plaster chips was quickly followed by the protuberance of a solid, two-inch auger bit pushing through the vacated space. As quickly as it had appeared, the curled steel mass vanished. Jamie sat transfixed, staring at what he perceived to be a tiny black hole in space.

"What the Hell?"

Jamie instinctively hurled himself over the top of the bed. He hit the floor on the opposite side. Simultaneously, he reached up under the contour sheet, grasped the handles on the side of the mattress and yanked with all the energy that can be adrenalized by a single moment of mortal fear.

“Jesus H. Christ:" Jamie blurted out.

He half rose from the ambulance cot, holding his forehead with both hands. The pain was intense.

"W hat happened? Where am I?"

Seated directly across from him was a police officer from the city of Rome. Next to the policeman was an ambulance attendant, who, with a not too reassuring smile, leaned over and nudged Jamie back into a prone position on the cot.

"Perhaps, Mr. Bolin, you can tell us."

"Bolin? That is your name, is it not?" inquired a rather short, portly, no-nonsense policeman.

Before Jamie could reply, the attendant handed him a disposable plastic cup and three pills. Staring at the multicolored pain capsule and the two antiseptically pure white aspirin tablets, Jamie gratefully tossed them into his mouth, emptying the plastic cup of its watery contents in one gulp. Briskly rubbing his upper arms with his hands to ward off the night chill, Jamie let his head drop back on the canvas cot.

He winced as the sore spot on his head settled into the coarse fabric. He moved his fingers across his forehead in forbearance of the unrelenting headache, while he told the policeman about making a phone call and watching a hole being bored into the wall of his bedroom.

"Oh yes, and the last thing I remember was seeing a rather large projectile traveling through space. It was propelled through the hole in the wall. Funny it reminded me of a train engine, headlight ablaze, exiting a long, dark tunnel. Finding no track on the other side, it appeared to fall endlessly through space, its headlight still glowing brightly in the distance."

The policeman filled in where Jamie left off. Seems they found him on the floor. One entire side of the room had been demolished. Part of the mattress was ripped to shreds, with him underneath. "It was a miracle, Mr. Bolin, that you survived such a dynamite blast."

"Dynamite blast?"

"What the hell are you talking about?" shouted Jamie as he tried to get up and was restrained by two pairs of determined hands.

"Oh! My head," agonized Jamie as the ambulance pulled up to the emergency entrance.

Refusing to be detained any longer, he broke the grips of his restrainers and alongside the policeman, climbed out the back of the now-parked ambulance.

Jamie, the attendant and the policeman began an intense argument as only Italians can do, in good humor. Suddenly all three were spotlighted in the glare of headlights from a black Alfa Romeo sedan. From the innards of the black machine; a detective leaped to the pavement. The car screeched to a halt, almost pinning the three men between the ambulance and the automobile. Whereupon, the attendant made a very nasty, articulate gesture towards the car.

The policeman let go of Jamie's arm and began a verbal assault on the driver of the car, another policeman. Jamie moved in the direction of the detective, who motioned him towards a building doorway. The police, it seems, wanted Jamie to come with them to headquarters and make out a report. Jamie assured the detective he was quite all right and had no useful information concerning the bombing. What he wanted was to return to the hotel, get his personal belongings, another room and a good night's rest.

A compromise was finally reached; Jamie would be driven back to the Hilton, on the way he would be questioned and the conversation recorded. A policeman would be posted outside his new rooms for the remainder of the night.

By the time Jamie had been returned to the hotel, he, the police and the hotel management were all in agreement concerning the dynamiting incident.

"Obviously," summed up the Chief of Police, who had been called to the hotel, "It's just one more murderous attempt by the 'Red Brigade' to demonstrate their ability to roam practically at will. They are discouraging foreigners from vacationing in Italy so long as Christian Democrats remain in power. Undoubtedly, they know that Mr. Bolin is a freelance correspondent. They could achieve enormous news coverage by blowing up his suite. It would also serve as a warning to the press that they are not immune to danger and should treat the 'Brigade' with respect. After the death of Moro, the news media heaped scorn on the ultra-leftist terrorist organization. Perhaps this was their way of telling the press to ease up."

"Do you believe Mr. Bolin is still in danger?" asked the Hotel manager.

"No! No! No! I do not believe so. But to ease your mind, we will leave an officer on duty at the door of his suite all night. There are weekly shootings and explosions throughout the city as you well know. “It's most likely the terrorists didn't care whether or not Mr. Bolin was in his suite at the time. They simply wanted publicity. We have an unfortunate situation on our hands since the murder of Moro. You see, we have either rounded up or have under surveillance many of the suspected leaders of the 'Red Brigade'."

"This has left a motley assortment of lower-level malcontents, who without close supervision by their leaders, just carry out random, self-initiated terrorist activities. In fact, Mr. Bolin is probably very safe. I have been informed that shortly after the explosion, a young man was shot by one of my policemen. The man was seen running through the piazza. The officer called out for him to stop and shot him when he continued his escape."

"Today, in Italy, refusing such an order is tantamount to being guilty. I'm sorry to say, we have developed a 'them or us' mentality that leaves little room for regard to individual rights of a suspected felon. When you have innocent people having their kneecaps blown off, you're rather inclined to shoot first and question the remains later."

"Had anyone else been seen leaving the hotel just prior to the explosion?" inquired Jamie of the men standing outside his new suite.

The detective who had escorted Jamie back to the hotel shook his head in a negative reply. Jamie bid the police officers and the hotel management good night and asked the bellhop for the key to the suite. On impulse, he asked the boy if he had seen anything unusual in the lobby just prior to the incident.

"Not really, Mr. Bolin. There were a number of people milling around the foyer near the elevators. A young priest coming out of an elevator inadvertently bumped into an old dowager, setting her rump down pretty hard on the terrazzo floor. Several people rushed to her aid, but she wasn't hurt. The priest apologized. He left the lobby with her shrill voice hurling rather colorful insults in his direction. It was really very amusing and gave us all a good laugh."

Jamie took the key from the bellhop. He asked the policeman on duty to accompany him back to his old rooms so he could retrieve his belongings. He experienced a queasy feeling in the pit of his stomach when he entered what used to be his bedroom. The door was blown off its hinges. The room was a shambles. There were bits and pieces of his tie and sport coat scattered throughout the room. Jamie walked over to the far corner of the room, stooped down while clearing chunks of a crumbled wall away from an overturned chair and picked up a seat cushion. Safely tucked behind the cushion was his attaché case.

Recalling the life-saving qualities of his mattress, Jamie promised himself someday to do a free TV commercial for plastic foam manufacturers. Luckily, before leaving the library earlier that day, he had put his notebook and wallet inside the attaché case.

Patting the case, Jamie muttered how he was "still in business".

Moving to the bathroom, he picked up his toiletries; stuffing them inside the case. One of his traveling idiosyncrasies had also paid off.

He walked to the closet in the sitting room, reached in and took out his garment bag. Except for a sport coat and tie and what he had on, all of his clothes remained in the unpacked bag. Before leaving the suite, Jamie gave a puzzled look at the Black English loafers on his feet. He distinctly remembered kicking them off when he had telephoned Carol earlier that evening. This minor unsolved riddle would always remind him of his bizarre flirtation with death.

It was two in the morning before he fitfully fell off to sleep. For the remainder of the night, strange faces, in all manners of dress and expressions, raced through his dreams. Fortunately, the Pope's funeral wasn't until mid-day, and Jamie had left a wake-up call accordingly.

The phone went off with the painful reality that it was 10:00 a.m. Jamie woke up with a throbbing headache. His body felt like it had been kicked by an army of Missouri mules. His bedsheet was soaked through with sweat. Sometime during the night, his adrenaline had subsided and his body passed through shock. Very carefully, he slowly attempted a few modified yoga positions as he sat up in bed. After several audible groans, he gave up and urged his body to soak in a tub of hot water.

Leaving his rooms an hour later, Jamie thanked the policeman on duty, "No need to stay. I'll be gone all day and won't need anyone this evening."

Jamie knew he was being foolhardy. He could not abide being watched over by anyone. And yet, ever since he had taken this assignment, he had moments of uneasiness; a feeling that someone was constantly watching him.

Only a few more days and I can leave Rome, the Vatican and the Red Brigade far behind. Maybe I can spend some time in London with Carol or take her to the south of France, thought Jamie before his mind became preoccupied with the pain in his body, as he sat in the taxi on his way to Vatican City.

"How are you, John?" shouted Jamie.

He approached Father 0'Brien, waiting at the entrance to the grotto. "Fine, fine, Jamie. Although very sad at the prospects of never seeing the Pope's beaming face again after today. It'll be good to have you with me this afternoon. I feel a real downer coming on. Let's hurry along lad. The service is about to begin."

Jamie and Father O'Brien hurried toward the Basilica. Father O'Brien tossed off several anecdotes about the late Pope. Suddenly, he stopped. Taking Jamie's shoulders in both his hands, he turned Jamie half-way round.

"I just realized you look like hell!"

"What happened to you?"

"Oh, father, I wish you hadn't grabbed me like that. I hurt all over. This is no time to explain. I just hope it never happens to me again."

"I'm sorry Jamie. I didn't intend to cause you any discomfort. It just dawned on me how bad you look."

In silence the two men continued on into the side door of St. Peter's Basilica. Jamie immediately felt the immense psychological impact of the grandeur of the Holy Roman Catholic Church. All about him was a sea of red-robed Cardinals, one hundred and twelve strong. Behind them lay pew after pew of dignitaries, priests, bishops, monsignors, heads of states, several kings, prominent theologians, scholars and businessmen from all points of the globe.

Jamie spotted a small American contingent consisting of Lillian Carter (the President's mother), Senator Tom Eagleton of Missouri, Ella Grasso, the Governor of Connecticut and Ed Koch, major of New York. Jamie couldn't tell if the lady seated on the mayor's right was Bess Myerson or not.

Father O'ßrien tugged at Jamie's elbow and directed him to squeeze into the next pew that had been reserved for them. Several bishops muttered at the inconvenience of being crushed together.

Then a whispered voice said, "That's the late Pope's secretary!"

Suddenly, two large vacant areas miraculously opened in the pew. Jamie was awed by the testimonial of power which these Churchmen recognized in Father O'Brien's name. This must have been the way Moses felt when he parted the Dead Sea, laughed Jamie to himself.

Once seated, Father John explained that the actual mass would be held outside at the base of the Basilica, facing St. Peter's Square. The Mass would be broadcast inside the Church for the convenience of the dignitaries while outside the populace gathered in the square. Jamie tossed his head back and began to recall the impressive characteristics and history of St. Peter's Basilica. It was truly a magnificent edifice.

Originally constructed in 319 AD, the walls began to disintegrate during the fifteenth centuryAD. Reconstruction took almost two hundred years and encompassed the lifetimes of five great Italian artists, each of whom contributed to the majestic splendor; ßramante, Raphael, Peruzzi, Bangallo the Younger, and then Michelangelo, who at seventy-two became the last to take charge of the reconstruction. Even he died before its completion.

Somewhere hundreds of feet behind Jamie stood the five massive doors that led to the portico of the Basilica. Beyond those doors lay five more massive doors opening onto St. Peter's Square. Hundreds of steps led down and onto St. Peter's Square.

Inside the Basilica, everything was constructed on an almost unbelievable, perfectly proportioned, grand scale. Upon turning his head, Jamie's eyes beheld one of the tiny cherubs carved into the base of a pillar standing in the distance. Such a tiny delicate figure belied the true nature of it and its surroundings, thought Jamie. When one begins to walk directly toward the little sculptures in relief, they will grow in size at an alarming rate. Until finally, you stand adjacent to the carvings on the pillar. Then you realize that the once seemingly tiny cherubs have carved feet equal to the distance from the tip of your fingers to your elbow.

Ah yes, thought Jamie, *the Church's appearance and its reality are entirely two different th*ings! Again his mind focused on the Basilica. Embedded in the marble floor of St. Peter's are bronzed plates commemorating great Christian churches around the world. The distance between each bronzed plate is approximately equal to one of the ground floor dimensions of each church it represents.

St. Peter's Basilica encompasses 9,752 square yards of floor space. The church is 212 yards in length, 138 feet wide and 435 feet high. At one end is a very high altar reserved for only the Pope to say mass; while on a second tier above ground level, supported by four high arches, are niches holding statues of great churchmen. Inside the Basilica is St. Peter' crypt, surrounded by great works of art. Among them are Bernini's bronze throne (1656 AD) and Michelangelo's Pieta; considered one of his greatest works, created when he was only twenty-two years of age. Other artifacts of the crypt are a huge platinum chalice from an early king of Spain and the cloak worn by Charlemagne at his coronation.

The dome of St. Peter's, thought Jamie, was the envy of the Christian world, where everything of splendor was translated into terms of man's worthiness in the sight of God. Jamie's head rolled back until his neck ached. His eyes looked directly overhead, 435 feet above the floor to the dome's top. It can be approached by taking an elevator to the second level of the Basilica. Then you walk up one flight of stairs until you are 160 feet in the air. If you're inclined to be adventurous, you can ascend a second staircase reaching 235 feet above the Church floor.

You could, mused Jamie, *if you were downright reckless, do as he, himself, had once done. Climb another flight of stairs, at the top of which is suspended a small platform which can accommodate fewer than twenty people. From that small perch, one is treated to a magnificent view of the city of Rome.*

Jamie grimaced as he felt the aches and pains running through his still bruised body. He recalled how once he had stood on that very same platform. The return trip to the ground had been a very spooky experience. It had been late in the afternoon. He had traversed a narrow walkway across the wide expanse of the unlit dome.

The shadows cast by the glow of the setting sun played tricks on his perception, and there had been no railing. A memorable climb and descent thought Jamie. A journey you only made out of ignorance of the dangers involved. One slip and hundreds of feet below lay a cold, unforgiving, all-embracing marble slab.

"Come on, Jamie," whispered Father John O'Brien.

"They're transporting Pope John's body to the Mass site outside"

"Why are you staring at the ceiling, like some long-lost child?"

Without responding, Jamie leveled his gaze in time to watch the passing procession. The Pope's body rested in a simple yellow cypress coffin, suspended in midair by twelve pallbearers, who were preceded down the aisle by Cardinal Villot and Cardinal Carlo Confalonieri, Dean of the College of Cardinals. Villot would say the High Mass and Confalonieri would deliver the homily.

As the procession continued on, Jamie observed that the coffin was carried at a pronounced angle so that everyone could see the burial attire and facial features of the late Pope. Adorning the Pope's head was the traditional bishop's mitre.

The Pope was clothed in a red over-vestment. Underneath was a white silk cassock, trimmed at the sleeves with four delicate rows of lace embroidery. On his feet was a pair of soft, red satin slippers. His hands were gently crossed and wrapped with rosary beads. The Pope's thin black hair, streaked with gray, contrasted with his wide face. Thin rimmed, plain glasses rested on his prominent nose. Appropriately, a gentle smile countenanced his face. His wide chin and jawline were firmly set; giving credence in appearance to what Jamie had already begun to suspect was the character of the man.

Pope John Paul I loved the poor with all his heart. He had been determined to improve their lot in life . Too bad, thought Jamie, *the Pope hadn't lived long enough to do for the poor in the world what he had done for the poor in Venice.* Throughout Italy, Cardinal Albino Luccianì had been known as the "Bicycling Patriarch of Venice".

He ignored the aristocrats and tourists, who frequent St. Mark's famous church. He had spent his time across the lagoon in the industrial belt of the community. Here he visited factories, union halls, canal boats, churches and hospitals, clothed in the simple garb of a parish priest, not as a prince of the mighty Holy Roman Catholic Church. The Pontiff had never forgotten his origins as the son of a bricklayer.

"The Church," he had once so elegantly proclaimed, "is for the impoverished."

Standing up after vacating the pew, Jamie and Father John watched the cardinals file out in pairs to take their places on the dais. The cardinals faced the crowd waiting below in St. Peter's Square for the Mass to begin. Jamie and Father John followed the cardinals out of the Basilica. Father 0'Brien motioned Jamie to an obscure corner outside the portico. From this vantagepoint they waited for the ceremony of the Mass to be completed.

Before beginning the service, Cardinal Villot sprinkled the casket with holy water and reached out with a small silver hammer tapping lightly on the head of the deceased Pontiff.

In so doing he exclaiming, "Albino, Albino, Albino, you are dead!"

Great cries of anguish rose from the crowd below in the Square. Women mourned and swooned as if their own son had died. Everyone's attention was caught by the anguish of the crowd, everyone's that is but Jamie's. He continued to follow the movements of Cardinal Villot. The Prelate moved to the side of the casket. Villot lowered his arm to pick up the Pope's hand while raising the little silver hammer above his head to strike a symbolic blow.

Jamie was captivated for a moment by the sight of the old Cardinal standing aloof from the 50,000 mourners below, holding the hand of a lifeless, undoubtedly sainted Pope. The sun's glittering rays reflected bright bursts of light from the raised little, silver hammer. Then, just as quickly, with a surprised look on his face, Cardinal Villot let the Pope's hand drop. His arm, questioningly holding aloft the silver hammer, returned to the Cardinal's side.

How very odd, thought Jamie. *Perhaps Father 0'Brien will comment on the Cardinal's absentmind*edness.

Without further ceremony, Villot motioned the pallbearers to seal the lid of the coffin. The Cardinal moved towards the altar to begin the Mass. The lid of the coffin was secured. A single, tall, white candle was lit and placed alongside an open bible atop the coffin. Shortly thereafter, Cardinal Villot motioned to Cardinal Confalonieri to begin the homily.

"We have scarcely had time to see the new Pope, yet in one month it was enough time for him to have conquered our hearts. It was for us a month in which to intensely love him. Remember, my good brethren, it is not the length that characterizes the life of a Pontiff, but rather the spirit that fills his life, however short."

An hour passed as Jamie stood on the steps. A light rain fell. Cardinal Villot completed the communion of the Mass. The crowd of 50,000 stayed to the very end. The pallbearers carried the casket to a small cemetery inside the Vatican walls for a very private burial ceremony. Pope John Paul I was laid to rest in a tiny grotto surrounded by 146 of his predecessors. Present at the burial were his immediate family, thirty close relatives and five cardinals who were his lifelong friends.

The Pope's plain cypress casket was placed inside another made of oak. In turn the Oak casket was sealed in a lead outer coffin. The coffin was lowered into a stone sarcophagus, on whose uppermost surface bore the single Latin inscription:

"Icannes Paulus PPI"

There would now be nine days of official mourning. On the tenth day, the new conclave would begin, October 14, 1978. Its purpose is to elect a new pope.

Jamie waited until the pallbearers disappeared into the grotto with the Pope's body. He turned to Father 0'Brien as the two of them sat on the steps outside the Basilica.

"Why did Cardinal Villot raise the little silver hammer and hold the hand of the Pope, just prior to the casket being closed?"

"Jamie, before a Pope is buried, the seal of His office, which is cast on the surface of his golden papal ring, must be marred by a blow from the little hammer. It signifies papal authority rests in the living, not the dead."

"Why didn't Villot strike the blow? He seemed rather perturbed at the time."

"It's all my fault, Jamie. I should have notified the Cardinal days ago, and I'm certain I'll hear about it tomorrow. Villot doesn't like any surprises, least of all in the presence of 50,000 people. You see, the Pope never received his final fitting for the ring. There wasn't any ring on his finger:"

"Are you absolutely certain about that, John?"

"Absolutely. Pope John Paul had just recently, in fact, the day prior to his death, received a second fitting. The Pope mentioned in chambers that it fit too tightly. He told one of his aides to pick it up later and return the ring to the Vatican jeweler. Come on Jamie; let's join the reception for the visiting dignitaries back at the Apostolic Palace. It's the nearest thing to an Irish wake you'll find in Italy, and I badly need a drink."

"Death, Farther 0'Brien, is certainly the great equalizer. Most of the conversation here seems to center on speculation as to whom the next Pope will be. I think I'll wander around a bit by myself. Do you mind?"

"Not at all, Jamie. You know where to find me."

Strolling through the menagerie gathered at the Palace, Jamie wondered how poor people lived. The Apostolic Palace was the largest of its kind in the world. The Palace had a central core structure and a number of attached buildings. Try to imagine, if you can, a majestic building some 700 years old containing more than 1,400 rooms and surrounded by twenty courtyards. By comparison, the Palace of the Wizard of Oz looked like a pauper's place.

On the top floor of the Palace, the Pope occupies a suite of nineteen rooms. He can look out over St. Peter's Square. His office on the floor below is a commodious forty by sixty feet in width and length. At his disposal is a fleet of not less than ten papal automobiles. *What a sense of humor the Church has*, Jamie chuckled to himself, as he recalled the two mottoes stamped on Vatican coins.

On one side of a coin is printed, "This is the root of all evil" and on the opposite face, "It is better to give than to receive"

Most likely the shock alone of living every day amidst such garish splendor would kill a man who had all of his life loved the poor: That last thought almost made Jamie sick to his stomach as he stood on a balcony and watched the reception in one of the main ballrooms.

Meandering through the crowd for the better part of an hour and a half, he heard the name of the Pope spoken in only the most loving terms. One remark often repeated, allegedly had originated from James V. Casey, Archbishop of Denver, Colorado, on the morning of the Pope's death. It clearly summed up the frustration of Catholics everywhere:

"When we awoke this morning, we were a little disappointed and annoyed with God."

A number of people at the reception recalled the Pope's love of children. Jamie overheard a cardinal repeating for the ears of several foreign dignitaries the last public audience Pope John Paul I held in the presence of 10,000 people on the Wednesday prior to his death. The Pope initiated a brief interview with a youngster, Daniele Bravo, whom he had coaxed to the microphone:

"Do you always want to be in the fifth grade?" inquired The Pope after the boy had told his age and grade.

"Yes," replied Daniele, "So that I don't have to change teachers."

Whereupon the Pope laughed, recalling to mind his own school days.

"Well, you are certainly different from the Pope. When I was in the fourth grade, I started worrying if I would ever make it to the fifth:"

Two other quotations attributed to the late Pope piqued Jamie's morbid curiosity. One related to a highly publicized give and-take discussion between the Pope and the press at his investiture ceremony.

"If I hadn't become a bishop of the Church, I would have wanted to be a journalist."

The other quotation had sent shudders through much of the Church's hierarchy:

"The real treasures of the Church are the poor."

Walking through the crowd, Jamie searched for Father 0'Brien. Coming toward him from across the room, he saw Father Gault.

"Jamie, I heard about the attempt on your 1ife last night. What happened?"

Damn it, thought Jamie. *Does the Vatican know everything?*

Eerie scenes of an engulfing spiderweb passed through his mind's eye. The web changed into a vast spy network. Jamie found himself trying to remember something from the past. Of course, that's it! The Vatican is the best-informed organization in the world. Their scholars were masters of all the known languages, and then there's the Vatican news. Six times a week it reaches 75,000 subscribers. A yearly subscription is $25 for Italians and $55 for foreign readers. Written mostly in Italian, it nevertheless carries articles in Latin, German, English, French, Spanish and Portuguese. The title of the paper is very bland, L'Asservatore Romano.

What had truly been imprinted on Jamie's mind years ago came back in a flash. He now understood the magnitude of what he had discovered when he was an honor student at Oxford. It wasn't so much the Vatican newspaper, but rather his interest had been in a particular religious order that operated the newspaper and printing plant. At the time, only their workmanship and scholastic endeavors had interested him, but now . . "Jamie, are you feeling okay?"

"Why are you still shaking my hand and staring off in space?"

"Perhaps you have a mild concussion from last night?"

"What? Oh, beg your pardon, Joe. My mind did wander off, but I assure you I'm feeling fine, just preoccupied with this assignment."

"About last night, Jamie?"

Quickly, Jamie rattled off an explanation of his horrible misadventure with the Red Brigade. He shrugged the whole thing off as a statistical possibility of random coincidence.

"What's your opinion, Joe?"

"Nothing that band of cutthroats does is left to chance, Jamie. Forget about the pep talk by the Police. Those people are professionally trained terrorists. If I were you, I'd be less flippant about such a close shave with death. Stay in the Vatican until your assignment is completed."

"Oh, I don't think there's much to worry about, Joe. I think the Italian police are keeping a pretty good eye on me."

Just then Father 0'Brien joined the twosome. He suggested they accompany him to his rooms, where he kept a very special whiskey on hand. The liquor served as an inducement to attract affable and conversant acquaintances to long hours of conversation; an Irishman's favorite pastime. well, second or maybe third favorite, third at least for secular Irishmen.

"Argumentative dialogue gentlemen, argumentative dialogue!"

It was apparent to Joe and Jamie that father 0'Brien was very much "in his cups".

"Later in the evening, I'll break out the Irish whiskey," lamented the priest.

"Afraid not, John," said Father Gault, "too many things to do."

"And you, Jamie?"

Jamie laughed and laid his hand on 0'Brien's shoulder.

"A rain check, John? Please, until Friday night. I promise, I'll come, okay?"

"Be seeing you gentlemen," muttered the good father as he ambled off into the crowd like a lost soul in search of the Holy Grail

Pope John Paul I had meant a great deal to him, and he had come to love the Pontiff in only a few short weeks. Spotting an old, Irish politician across the room, he turned to shout back at Jamie

"I'll expect you at 7:30 Friday evening, top floor of the Palace, room IVCXXIII," laughing at his own inside joke.

The priest threw out his hands and embraced his old friend.

Jamie turned his attention to Father Gault.

"Joe, tomorrow I'm going to sequester myself in my hotel in order to review a great dealof information I have accumulated. Saturday, I have some personal business in Rome, I'd like to give you a call late Thursday evening or early Friday morning, okay?"

"Certainly, Jamie, but is there anything I can do for you now? I have some time to kill."

"Yes there is, Joe," as the idea suddenly struck Jamie.

"Could I tour the Vatican broadcasting facilities?"

"You mean right now?"

"Yes, is it inconvenient?"

"A bit unusual, Jamie, but yes, I believe it can be arranged. Are you ready to go?"

"Fine, father, lead the way?" said Jamie, as if the priest needed his approval.

Joe was already elbowing his way out of the ballroom. Behind him, Jamie lumbered through the crowd, trying to catch up while singing a little tune under his breath

"We're off to see the Wizard, . . ."

Father Joe led the way into the courtyard of St. Damascus, which is enclosed by the Palace. The two men walked a considerable distance. After crossing a long open portico, they arrived at a three-pronged fork in the road, adjacent to the Papal Gardens.

Father Gault flagged dawn a Vatican limousine, which somehow miraculously appeared out of nowhere. The priest instructed the chauffeur to head for the broadcasting facilities.

Jamie noticed the car was heading for the highest ground at the western end of the Papal Gardens. The car came to a small rise in the road. The radio station popped into view, just over the horizon in a rather foreboding and isolated location.

Pointing toward the station, Father Gault explained, "Jamie, that building houses our main transmitters and there are more ancillary equipment, taping studios, conference facilities and recording equipment located in Rome."

"Joe, do you mean that the Vatican Studios in Rome are larger than the one we are about to tour?"

"The facilities in Rome, Jamie, cover a two-square mile area to the north of the city. It is completely walled-in. Thanks to the Lateran Treaty you heard so much about the other day, it is located on Vatican soil, not Italian. The Italian government has no legal authority on that piece of property in Rome."

"Excuse me, Jamie," said Joe as he reached for the mobile phone in the limousine.

"I'll have to get security clearance to enter the radio station."

While Joe was busy on the phone, Jamie's thoughts flashed back to his earlier revelation concerning the Vatican newspaper. *Of course, that's it*, he thought. *That obscure religious order is the greatest group of cryptographic experts in the world. The KGß and CIA pale by comparison. Jamie tried to recall the name of the order?*

The Sons of St. John Bosco, that's the order! These were brothers charged with also printing all secret and confidential Vatican documents as well as translating and issuing publications in a variety of Languages. As I recall, they are knowledgeable in 120 different alphabetical systems. Besides printing and translating all the commonly spoken Languages in the world, they routinely publish and analyze documents in hieroglyphics, Chinese ideographs, Coptic, Hebrew, Arabic, Braille and Glagolitic.

"Good God!"

Father Gault completed his call. Jamie's head ached, not only from last night's explosion but also from the exertion of putting his memory to work. Jamie began to realize that he was in deeper than he ever dreamed possible. Last night's attempt on his life was no random coincidence. The limo pulled up to the radio station. A Swiss Guard met Father Gault and Jamie at the entrance.

"Father Bolin and Father Gault?" came the searching inquiry.

“Yes"

"Yes."

"Does one of you have the code clearance? We just received word about your visit," said the guard.

"621GH," replied Father Gault.

"Do either one of you have a camera, weapon or recording equipment on your person?"

"No. "

"No."

"Would you please step through the security checkpoint?"

“It’s simply a series of X-ray and electronic detection equipment. Please check back with me before you leave the premises."

"Joe, why all these top security measures?"

"Because the Vatican doesn't want unsanctioned information about these facilities getting into the newspapers. As you should know from last night, the Red Brigade might get it in their heads to occupy these premises and use its worldwide broadcast facilities. The Vatican has enough problems right now without a mini-revolution on the premises."

"Its no wonder, Joe, the Church has survived for 2,000 years."

"They don’t leave much to chance, do they?"

But somehow Jamie was not convinced the priest was telling him the whole story, and that's precisely why Jamie had asked for the tour.

Father Joe hurried Jamie along, giving him a quick, barely minimum look-see at the facility. That was to be expected. Jamie had formulated other plans for finding out much more about the Vatican's vast communications network. He remembered that day in Father Rene's office; where he had first gotten a small taste of the Vatican's sophisticated electronic capabilities. Jamie suspected that more than religious broadcasts were emanating from inside these walls.

If his suspicions were true, he needed hard evidence. Throughout the tour, Jamie watched for "Authorized Personnel Only" signs and made mental notes of their exact locations. Near the end of the tour, it was time to put the first part of his plan into operation. Father Joe led the way up a narrow flight of gray metal steps to a catwalk that passed in front of a large glass enclosure. From here Jamie could look out over the installation of main broadcast transmitters.

Jamie reached inside his coat and withdrew a small notebook and pencil. With one hand, he pointed the pencil in the direction of the nearest transmitter.

"How much did the main frame equipment cost?"

Father Joe's eyes followed Jamie's hand pointing the pencil. Jamie use two fingers of his other hand to slip a small piece of fiberglass reinforced tape from between two sheets of cellophane paper tucked inside the small notebook.

Joe responded to Jamie's question, "Both transmitters in this building cost at least five million dollars."

Before Joe's head turned round again towards Jamie, the small piece of tape had been palmed, and the notebook was transferred to the hand holding the pencil. Jamie's youthful days as an amateur magician had not been misspent. Joe and Jamie met each other's solid gaze. Each realized he had just unnecessarily revealed information to the other, thus suspicions were aroused in both men.

Jamie had spoken the words "main frame cost", inadvertently using electronic manufacturing terminology. Joe would know that Jamie was most likely an expert in the field and had more than a passing interest in the Vatican's communication systems. On the other hand, Father Gault had mentioned "both transmitters in this building". Jamie realized from the inflection on the word "this", that there were other transmitters, possibly a great many more; not just in Rome but around the world.

Father Gault broke the embarrassing silence. "Have you seen enough Jamie?"

"Yes, thank you, Joe."

Retracing their steps to the building entrance, Jamie moved toward a side exit door he had passed earlier in the tour. It was unmarked and had a rather large door handle mechanism. Jamie gambled it was an emergency exit leading directly outside. Stopping near the door, Jamie started to say some thing to Joe and let his notebook fall to the floor. Gault stooped to pick it up.

“Jamie blurted out, "What's in here?"

He pushed down on the lever with his right hand and shoved. The door popped open. Jamie stood staring at the outside of the building at grounds behind the broadcasting station. Father Joe stood up. Jamie opened the palm of his left hand and pressed the tape across the cam locking mechanism on the side of the door. Backing up, with an embarrassed look of stupidity on his face, Jamie quickly drew the door tightly shut.

"I'm sorry Joe; stupid of me, wasn't it?" apologized Jamie, taking the notebook from the outstretched hand of the priest.

"Clumsy too, thanks Joe."

Father Joe smiled broadly, supposedly at Jamie's faux pas.

The two men wasted no more time and hurried to the front entrance, checked out with the Swiss Guard and stepped into the waiting limousine.

"Take us to the Gate of St. Anne, please," said Father Gault."

"Jamie, why not let the driver take you back to the Hilton? If you're not going to heed my advice about staying on Vatican grounds, at least I'll sleep better knowing you got safely back to the hotel."

"Thanks very much, Joe. I accept your offer. Where shall we drop you?"

"I'11 get out at thc Gate. I need a bit of fresh air."

At the Gate, Joe said good bye and again cautioned Jamie to be very careful.

"Goodnight, Joe; don't worry."

The ride to the hotel in the plush upholstered limousine was uneventful except for a brief conversation between Jamie and the driver. "This is a very fine automobile. What make is it?" inquired Jamie in all sincerity.

"Excellent ride, too."

"It better be, Father."

"Why so?" Jamie asked.

"I thought you'd know, Father. Alfo Romeo provides the Church with its very best cars. After all, the Vatican owns the company outright. ""You're kidding?"

"No, Father, I thought everyone in Italy knew that."

"I'll be damned," sighed Jamie.

When the limousine pulled up to the hotel, Jamie tipped the driver 1,800 lira and strolled into the lobby of the hotel. He was worn out from the day's activities. He was sore all over. The pain didn't seem to matter that much as a glow of satisfaction warmed his insides. He thought about the taped exit door, hoping no one would bother to examine it too closely.

VII. THE EVIDENCE MOUNTS

"Hello?   Room service? This is Mr. Bolin, Suite 812."

"Let me have two eggs over easy, four strips of bacon, toast and breakfast tea. Send up a morning newspaper as well."

"Yes, that's all, thank you. About how long will it be?"

Within thirty minutes Jamie had completed a light session of yoga, showered and shaved. He heard a knock on the outer door just as he was about to don an old sweatshirt and pull on a pair of faded jeans.

"Come in. The door is unlatched."

Quickly slipping on the jeans, Jamie walked part way into the sitting room as the waiter entered from the hallway through the unlatched door.

"Would you put the tray on the table by the window?"

"Margari, Mr. Bolin."

"Il conto, pere favore."

Following the waiter, Jamie accepted the bill, added the gratuity and returned to the bedroom to finish dressing.

"Molte Grazie, Signore!" sang out the waiter as he left.

It was still early morning when Jamie sat down to breakfast. Sleepy-eyed Rome yawned and stretched out beneath his window. One by one, its heartbeats multiplied. Crowds of shuffling pedestrians and honking cars poured into the city's arteries. Pushcarts of flowers rolled onto the piazza.

More than once Jamie's eyes caught and pursued a long pair of shapely legs striding boldly along, while a gentle breeze, heaven sent, pressed already clinging skirts and blouses amorously tighter to the curvaceous, full bodied, young Italian women moving about in the streets below.

"Whewee" exclaimed Jamie.

"Enough of this, I'll never get started on today's work."

Laughing with regret, he reluctantly arose from the breakfast table, tea mug in hand, and moved to a black leather upholstered wingback chair. Edging himself forward, Jamie reached out and switched on the bulb of a tall, beige, glazed marble lamp gracing the center of a tooled, inlaid leather desktop.

The steaming mug of tea sat on one edge of' the desk like the puffing smokestack of an idle freighter on a calm sea. "Pop! Pop!" snapped the latches of his attaché case as Jamie carefully removed various documents and notes relating to several interviews and his visit to the Vatican library.

Pulling his chair snugly against the desk, his elbows resting on its surface, Jamie pushed up the sleeves of his old sweatshirt. Picking up a long orange-colored #2 pencil, he slid a lined, yellow, legal-size pad of writing paper in front of him as he began digesting the accumulated information laid out on the desk.

Five hours later, he leaned back, stretched, tossing the pencil stub onto the desktop. Jamie's body groaned as he got up to order something for lunch. Stripping down, he headed for the shower and turned on the ice cold water.

Although a shock to his nervous system, he had found that over the years it was the quickest way to revitalize his brain cells and his body awareness. He toweled down and slipped on his robe. Then Jamie retrieved the morning newspaper that the waiter had placed on the coffee table. In his haste to begin working, he had forgotten about it. His body sank comfortably into the deep pile cushions of the couch. His eyes scanned the front page of the news.

Jamie sat bolt upright. Italians had a flair for the dramatic. Incredulously, he read the entire front page without stirring from his upright posture, line by line, sentence by sentence. The top half of the news was ablaze with an editorial and full color photo of Pope John Paul's funeral. The bottom half was split into two equal parts.

In the lower left-hand section was a photo of Jamie's bedroom as it looked after the dynamite explosion. The midpage left-hand headline read, "Red Brigade terrorizes Hilton Hotel!" The written account made no mention of Jamie and dwelt on the mindless attacks upon foreign visitors. The article then summarized the Brigade's atrocities to date.

It was the mid-page headline in the right-hand section of the paper that had first startled Jamie. It read, "Who Killed the Pope?"

The article included a sketch depicting the Pope serenely reading in his bedchambers, while a sinister shadowy figure lurked in the background, an evil sneer spreading across his villainous face as he poured a vial of poison into the Prelate's coffee cup. The editorial quoted directly from a news release issued by none other than the Civilita Christiana, the ultra-conservative Catholic organization that was even now employing Jamie to investigate that very possibility.

"We have concrete evidence to back our demands for an investigation but we cannot release it at this time."

The editorial went on to explain that the evidence would be given to the "Vatican prosecutor" and not to Italian civil authorities in an effort "to avoid scandal" and because only the Vatican had jurisdiction over crimes, even murder, within its own sovereign territory.

Jamie realized that the news release was a ploy to keep others from investigating the death of the Pope. It was meant to give Jamie time to complete his investigation. Apparently, rumors of an assassination had sprung up all over Italy. Too many people were beginning to ask questions.

Now everyone would wait to learn what evidence would be turned over to the Vatican. Very few Italians would be shocked at the news. After all, through the long history of Mother Church there had been many attempts on the lives of various popes, some of which had been successful.

Jamie got up and went to the desk. He rummaged through his notes and found what he wanted, a page full of information extracted from last week's issue of "Time" magazine about the sordid history of murdered popes. There have been two hundred and sixty-four popes. At least six were known to have been murdered.

One pope had died from wounds inflicted during a civil war. Then again, there was Pope John XXI who was killed in the year 1277 when a ceiling fell on his head. Prior to the death of Pope John Paul I, there had been thirteen popes who had held office for less than a month. For example, there was Pope Stephen, who died in the year 752, three days after his election to office.

During one unsettling period in church history, the years 895 and 896, there were four popes in a little over twenty months. But, thought Jamie, now is the first time in church history that three popes will have held office within three months. He presumed the forthcoming conclave would not last but a few days.

Jamie continued to review his notes on the "Time" article. He was struck by some of the more gruesome periods in the history of the Church. Pope Stephen VII had the body of his predecessor, Pope Formosus I disinterred. Stephen had hated the dead pope and had his decomposing body dumped on the Vatican throne in St. Peter's Basilica. Then He promptly invoked a synod and posthumously denounced the dead pope and declared the previous election invalid. Whereupon Stephen ordered the dead pope's ring cut off and had the decaying body tossed into the Tiber River.

In the year 974, Pope Benedict VI was forcibly removed from office by an anti-pope, Boniface VII. The anti-pope then had Pope Benedict strangled in his jail cell.

During some of the Church's turbulent times, cardinals did not fair too well either. In the year 1241, a powerful prince locked up the cardinals. While in confinement the cardinals held a conclave and elected a new pope. Meanwhile, three of the cardinals died of inhuman treatment. The newly elected pope excommunicated the prince but died sixteen days, later, presumably murdered.

A t one point in history, the Borgia family controlled the destiny of the Holy Roman Catholic Church. Somehow against their wishes, a very old cardinal was elected pope and became Pius III. Numerous Vatican bureaucrats pillaged his old lodgings. This followed an old church tradition. Once a man became pope, supposedly everything he needed would be given to him. But Pius III didn't have any place to sleep and had to buy back his own bed. Twenty-five days later, he died of the gout, or was it Borgia poisoning?

Jamie felt certain that within a week he would know whether or not Pope John Paul I would be added to the list of murdered popes. The evidence in hand was not conclusive but pointed in the direction of a possible conspiracy by an unknown group. A group that wanted absolute control of the Holy Roman Catholic Church.

There were certain pieces of key information that Jamie felt were crucial to his investigation. One of those pieces was an approximation of the wealth of the Church. So, having hastily eaten the salad and ice cream delivered by room service, Jamie immersed himself in his notes. By late afternoon, thanks to information obtained from the U.S. Catholic Almanac in the Vatican library, Jamie had constructed a summary of the approximate real estate wealth of the Church, at least in the United States.

Jamie meticulously had listed the kind of holdings by "Category" and the quantity of each type by number of units as listed in the Almanac. Then he estimated an average replacement value of each type. He reduced the assigned value by estimating a reasonable encumbrance of debt. Jamie purposefully underestimated each unit's replacement value to allow a considerable margin of safety, thus preventing an over-estimation of the worth of the real estate holdings. The figures were enormous.

ROMAN CATHOLIC REAL ESTATE HOLDINGS IN U.S.A.

Category Total	No. of units	Estimated per Unit Replacement Value	Total Estimated Value
Catholic Hospitals	671	$ 20 Million	$13,420,000,000
Special Hospitals	90	$ 4 Million	360,000,000
Nursing Schools		$ 5 Million	705,000,000
Missions	3,760	$ 1 Million	3,760,000,000
Universities 8c Colleges	251	$ 100 Million	25, 100,000,000
High Schools	1,676	$ 8 Million	13, 408,000,000
Seminaries	269	$ 3 Million	807,000,000
Elementary Schools	8,539	$ 2 Million	17,078,000,000
Parishes	18,500	$ 1 Million	18,500,000,000
		Grand total	**$93.138 Billion**

The information obtained from the U.S. Catholic Almanac indicated a 20% decline in the number of parochial schools in the last eight years. Such a decline reduced the Church's biggest single cause of negative cash flow. Schools would continue to close or become self-supporting.

The Almanac further disclosed that there were 48 million Catholics in the United States, including 18 thousand seminarians, 59 thousand priests, 9 thousand brothers and 135 thousand nuns.

What a superb intelligence network, thought Jamie. Somewhere in his notes, Jamie remembered that an unidentified source had indicated that besides its vast real estate holdings in America, it was rumored that the Catholic Church owned 33% of all the land in Mexico!

Jamie recognized that the numbers were becoming unreal. Such estimates were necessary from his point of view to perceive the Holy Roman Catholic Church for what it really was, not as everyone thought it might be. Jamie could then better analyze every nuance of intrigue with which the Pope had to contend. In turn, such thinking might assist him in uncovering an international assault on the Vatican.

Jamie was absolutely certain that Christian as She may be, the Vatican was also the headquarters of a colossal financial empire. The Church had achieved this dubious distinction by single-mindedly following the eight rules of ultimate financial success. Bernardino Nogara established those rules some fifty years ago. The very day the Church began its negotiations with Benito Mussolini, which culminated in the Lateran Treaty of 1929. Of those eight rules, it was apparent that four of them always remained uppermost in the minds of Vatican administrators.

Rule 5 - By increasing the size of your organization, its personnel can be organized more efficiently and therefore can be better utilized in a more rational manner.

Rule 6 - By increasing the size of your organization, it makes it more difficult for governments to fiscally restrain it.

Rule 7 - By increasing the size of your organization, you can offer the best technical products.

Rule 8 - By increasing the size of your organization, it will in itself generate additional increases.

How very clever of the Church, mused Jamie. *By the introduction of ideas expressed in Vatican II, the Church had outflanked all its competition by technically upgrading the world's best-selling product, Religion!*

Given time to ride out the turmoil created by Vatican II, the Church had the financial ability to offer a shiny new product which would appeal to the world's religious consumers who could not be reached by the old doctrinaire methods.

It reminded Jamie of the great financial gamble taken by IBM's historic move in the 1960's when the company risked its entire corporate future on the development and introduction of their Series "360" giant computers and won!

The difference being that the Vatican's risk was much less pronounced because the Church employed the proven management techniques used by major US corporations in their successful development of new products.

The "Church" would likewise change her product to fit her needs, and her customers would always believe it was done for them and because it was morally right.

It was getting late in the day and Jamie had philosophized enough. It was very important that he review the itinerary he had prepared the other night. Just this morning he had further condensed the information to its bare essentials. He must get a hold of Father Gault to arrange a series of last-minute interviews.

Perhaps Joe could arrange appointments for Friday of this week, as well as Monday and Tuesday next. If the parties to be interviewed were no longer in Rome, Jamie might try to reach them by phone. Jamie left a message for Father Gault, and the call was returned by early evening.

"Hello Jamie, Father Joe here. What can I do for you?"

"Joe, I'd like you to set up a series of interviews for me as quickly as you can."

“Who did you have in mind, Jamie?"

"I have a rather extensive list, Joe."

"Read me the lot."

Jamie read off the long list slowly, allowing the priest time to jot down names. When he had finished, Jamie detected a disgruntled sigh on the other end of the line.

."I'll do what I can Jamie, but quite frankly, it is most unlikely you'll interview any of the cardinals directly. You might be lucky enough to get one of their administrative assistants to cooperate."

"Joe, it is extremely important that I speak directly to those involved. I was under the impression that I would have ready access to whatever information I needed? Should I call father Rene?"

"No, Jamie, I'll do the best I can, but the climate has changed since the editorial today about the possible assassination of the Pope. No politically astute cardinal is going to give out any information on the subject. And quite frankly I have never known of any such cardinals. Let me do what I can, and then we'll go on from there. Father Petri, for instance, is currently a guest at the Vatican, and I'm certain he can give you a concise review of John Paul's speech to the College of Cardinals. "

"When Joe?"

"If I don't call back, I will meet you with Petri at your suite on the Vatican grounds at ten o'clock tomorrow morning, okay?"

"That's great, Joe. Thank you."

"Oh, by the way, Jamie, you can eliminate from your list the possibility of interviewing Nickodem, the Metropolitan of Leningrad."

"Why?"

"He's dead, Jamie."

"Dead! Under what circumstances?"

"I'm surprised Father 0'Brien didn't tell you. It happened during his audience with the Pope on September 7. Niekodem had a massive coronary. Before help could be summoned; he died on the spot."

"Joe, you mean to tell me a Russian cardinal died suddenly in the presence of Pope John Paul I, and no one has investigated the circumstances of that death?"

"He had a history of poor health, Jamie, that's all. I can save you some time regarding Father Giovanni Cereti's discussion with the late Pope as well."

"How so?" responded Jamie, disappointed and suspicious that Father Gault was not being very cooperative.

"'Everyone in the Vatican is aware of Father Cereti's views, and those views are also well published. In his recent audience with the Pope, Cereti reiterated his warning and concern about the Church's dependency on income from multi-national corporate investments. Hold on a minute Jamie, I'll read you something."

A few moments later the priest returned to the phone.

"This is a recent article written by Cereti. It was published in the International Theology Review. I'm quoting verbatim. 'It {the Church) depends on the benefits of the big multinationals, who take out everything, even from developing countries. It finds itself on the side of capitalists in certain social conflicts.'"

Then Joe continued to tell Jamie that the facts should be self-evident from Jamie's own meeting Tuesday with the finance group.

"Father Cereti is a much respected Italian priest and theologian. I, myself, have heard him say, 'the Vatican depends upon the capitalist system.'"

"Personally, Jamie, I don't see any harm in it."

"That's helpful, Joe."

"I can see how a man like John Paul would be torn between assisting the poor and amassing a fortune for the purpose of expanding the Church`s international influence."

"Tell me Jamie, why would you want to speak with Eduardo Luciani, the Pope's younger brother?"

"Frankly, Joe, I want a member of the immediate family to give me his impression of the Pope's physical and mental health. I'm not convinced the Pope was the type of person who neglected his health."

"Look Jamie, Eduardo has been called to Australia, just today on Church business. And also I suspect, to keep him away from the Italian press."

"He has made some embarrassing, counterproductive statements about the late Pope's prior physical fitness."

"I'm sure you read today's papers about the possible assassination of the Pope. Eduardo's statements were lending support to that theory."

“How so, Joe?”

"After the pope's death, the general consensus was that the papal responsibilities simply overwhelmed him."

"In the past few years, the Pontiff had four operations of which two were for gallstones, one for a broken nose suffered in a bicycle fall, and the fourth to correct an eye affliction."

"It was also well known that he had contracted TB as a youngster and might be functioning on only one lung."

"Wouldn't an autopsy be in order now, Joe?"

"It would solve a lot of problems Jamie, but it can't be done."

"What do you mean, can’t be done?"

"Pope Paul VI declared in the papal edict of 1975 that autopsies were not to be performed on the bodies of popes."

“What!”

"Don't ask me any more about that point. The entire Curia is very upset over its implications.”

"Well, what about Eduardo, Joe?"

"It seems the Vatican physician diagnosed the Pope's death as havring been caused by a massive coronary due to his excessive work load. As you know, his face was rather gruesomely distorted. The heart attack was so severe that the Pope didn't have time to reach his bedside buzzer. Eduardo wasn't satisfied. He complained that the Pope, his brother, was in excellent physical condition. All his operations had been minor and were strictly routine surgical procedures. He claimed the Pope had completely recovered from TB and that he had two very good lungs. After all, Eduardo insisted, he was a prodigious walker and rode his bicycle all over Venice before becoming the Pope."

"Why didn't you tell me all this earlier, Joe?"

"You never asked, Jamie. Hell, if I took seriously every conflicting rumor concerning the Pope's death I'd spend all my time investigating a fait accompli. There's no evidence of foul play, and without an autopsy, there's not likely to be any."

"Then you have done some investigating, haven't you?"

"Look, Jamie, everyone loved the Pope. Let`s consider the matter closed, shall we? Goodnight Jamie, see you tomorrow morning."

Sitting by the phone, receiver in hand giving out an eerie squeal, Jamie was getting a very uneasy feeling. Either the Vatican knew more about the Pope's death than he was led to believe or he was being used as a decoy so someone could find out what really happened. Secretly, a vast internal struggle, more like a war, seemed to be taking place inside the Vatican. Was it possible that the Church could split wide open? Very unlikely, thought Jamie, realizing that history tended to repeat itself.

No matter how horrible the situation, somehow the Church always came out on top. After all, as a group, She commanded the world's best educated men and had developed an espionage system vastly superior to the combined networks of all the world's governments.

Jamie recalled a Napoleonic quotation.

"One well-planted spy is worth 20,000 troops on the field of battle!"

Returning the phone to its cradle, Jamie moved to his desk for several more tedious hours of reviewing his notes and condensing his interview list based on his conversation with Father Joe. He summarized and he studiedthe supplementary background material. By nine o'clock that night, he had neatly assembled the following information:

I.Interviews of relevant audiences
Pertinent to the Reign of John Paul I

A. September Schedule of Daily Appointments

Date	Person \Group	Subject Matter
4th	College of Cardinals	General Assembly Address
5th	Cardinal Vagnazzl	Vatican Finance
5th	Father Carl Petri	Review of Response to Gen. Assy.
7th	Metropolitan Nickodem	Private Audienco
8th	Eduardo Luciani	Breakfast
11th	Father Giovanni Cereti	Capitalism
14th	RAbbi Rosenbaum	Israeli Diplomat
19th	Pironia, Eduardo	Latin American Bishops' Conf.
27th	Patriarch Narimos Hakim	Antioch - Arab Christians

B. Evening Conferences

8th	Cardinal Bernadin Gantin of Benin	African Affairs
15th	Cardinal Johannes Willebrands	Western Europe
25th	Pik Roelof - Foreign	South Africa
27th	Cardinals Villot and Baggio	Urgent Business

C. Staff Meetings

9th	Review of the realities of Salt II
16th	Latin American Conf. of Bìshops
23rd	African Catholicism

II. Miscellaneous Random Events and Information

Item

World Council of Churches, represented by 293 Protestant and Orthodox member denominations, disperses 2.6 million dollars in charity. Approximately one-half of this amount goes to black African guerrilla organizations. A singularly large amount went to the Rhodesian patriotic front movement and to Joshia Nkomo, co-leader of the Patriotic Front that is located in Zambia. They are fighting the whites of South Africa.When the W.C.C. again this year decided to fund such charitable causes, the Salvation Army withdrew from the council and many other members were considering similar action.

Item

Quotation attributed to his Holiness on the Wednesday before his death at a papal audience of 10,000 people. "Private property does not constitute for anyone the absolute unconditional right to hold to himself more than what he needs, especially when others have less and suffer."

Item

The Pope's investiture High Mass was stripped of its usual pomp. The Pope did not participate in the one thousand year old coronation ceremony, and the jeweled tiara crown was relegated to the trash heap. The new Pope also did away with the enthronement tradition, choosing to walk instead, after which he drew laughter and cheers and blessed 200,000 people.

Item

His selection was the shortest conclave in modern times, the first ever to pick two names and the first in over one thousand years to pick an original name.

Item

France's rebel Archbishop Marcel Lefebre was concerned.about the new Pontiff's ability to carry on the work of his predecessors.

Item

Close Vatican associates claim the Pope was a very effective pastoral bishop; able and used to handling extremely difficult situations.

Item

He was constantly in touch with Holland and West Germany, at least the liberal element, but was shunned by the conservative element there.

Item

In a prior quote on Communism, the Pope was heard to say; "We make no distinction as to race or ideology, but seek to secure for the world the dawn of a more serene and joyful day."

Item

President Jomo Kenyatta died in early September 1978; his successor is Arap Daniel Moi, age 54. Kenyatta was eighty some years old and ruled 14 million people. Although he had been educated in a Scottish mission, years later he was quoted to have said:

"The African had the land and the missionaries had the bible; they taught us to pray with closed eyes; when we opened them, they had the land and we had the bible."

Kenyatta resided in England for sixteen years. He had shared a London flat with Paul Robeson, the American Entertainer who later immigrated to Russia. Kenyatta, made two trips to Moscow studying at the Lenin School, a famous training ground for Marxists revolutionaries. He married a white woman and in 1946, returned to Kenya.

The British claim he was the infamous "Burning Spear", leader of the Mau Maus. Kenyatta became head of state when Kenya gained its independence from Great Britain. Previously it had been known as Nairobi. His methods of revolution are grotesquely described in Robert Ruark's book, "Something of Value". The successful campaign followed a standard Marxist pattern; terrorize the innocents. The Mau Maus killed only two hundred British, but they killed thirteen thousand natives. He was beloved by his people, and during his reign Kenya was one of the most progressive countries in Africa.

Representative Charles C. Diggs, Jr., long-time member of the United States House of Representatives, was indicted on eleven counts of mail fraud, eighteen counts of making false statements to the United States government. He was convicted by a predominantly black jury. There was a stream of nationally known Negro leaders who served as character witnesses at the trial. Among them were Coleman Young, mayor of Detroit; Coretta Scott King, wife of the deceased Nobel prize winner, Martin Luther King; Jesse Jackson, a Chicago preacher; and the Reverend Andrew Young, U.S. Ambassador to the United Nations.

Item

White House staff rumors persist that Secretary of State Cyrus Vance is miffed that Andrew Young has for some time been in complete charge of U.S. African affairs. Young has outstanding rapport with African black leaders and other third world United Nations diplomats.

Item

The press reported that the body of an ex-CIA official was pulled from the Potomac River last night. Although the government believes his death to be suicide, the circumstances are rather unusual. His prior position was in the office of CIA Strategic Research from which he had retired in 1974. He was an expert scuba diver and sailor. Cause of death was a 38 caliber slug behind his ear, and there was a 40 lb., diver's weight tied to his feet. He was wearing dungarees, a T-shirt, and gloves on his hands; coroner reports death occurred on Sept. 24.

Returning to the phone just long enough to order a burger with onions and relish and a glass of milk, Jamie then began the laborious final phase of his research. Comparing information he had gathered at the Vatican library, he correlated it with the discussions he had already held at the Vatican. Jamie prepared himself for the remaining interviews. He would make certain that no one would lead him astray.

He committed as much as he felt necessary to memory and made cryptic notes for ready reference regarding his next Meeting, tomorrow morning. Hopefully Father Joe would give him the dates and times for each subsequent interview.

By 11:30 that night, Jamie was mentally exhausted. His body still ached from the explosion. Wearily he snapped off the desk light and in semi-darkness moved to the bedroom, where he flopped on the mattress and slept fitfully through the night.

Jamie awoke the next morning. It was already 9:00 AM. He had forgotten to leave a wakeup call. He was due at the Vatican at 10 AM. Jumping out of bed, he experienced a slight case of dizziness. No time for a shower, thought Jamie. He headed for the bathroom. In eight minutes he sponged off, shaved, brushed his teeth and dressed. He hurried to the desk. scooped up his notes, yellow pad and pencils and stuffed them into his attaché case.

It was quite a sight watching him hustle down the steps of the Hilton and commandeer a taxi. The taxi deposited him at the Gate of St. Anne in record time. After entering the Gate, he swiped a mini-bike, which undoubtedly belonged to some poor priest or nun who would wonder where it had gone.

"Hope it belongs to a Jebbie!" laughed Jamie as he barreled the bike over the Vatican grounds, arriving at his suite in the Villa at 9:50.

He arrived with just enough time to order coffee, tea and roll. *Can't very well order breakfast*, thought Jamie. *Must play the good host, but I'd rather have some eggs and bacon. I'm starving.*

"Ah," sighed Jamie.

"The sacrifices one makes for journalistic integrity."

If only the hacks at P.J. Clark's in New York, nursing their hangovers from last night with Bloody Marys this morning, could see him now.

What the hell, thought Jamie, *is any self-respecting Irishman doing in Italy investigating the death of a saintly old man, while almost being blown to smithereens. I could be off to London with the likes of Carol. Why not leave the Vatican intrigues to the Italians? Who love them so. The answer, he knew, was simple, as he waved a hand in the air and said out loud, "I know Jamie, me boy, it's the money: And my own damnable curiosity. Umm, why not take the money and run?"*

Then Jamie sat fantasizing about his rendezvous with Carol tomorrow. He heard footsteps in the hallway.

"Trick or Treat?" mumbled Jamie.

Swinging wide the door to his suite,, his day was about to begin. Jamie offered a friendly greeting to Father Joe and his companion.

"Come in," as he glanced down the hallway.

"Expecting someone else, Jamie?" asked Joe.

"I ordered some coffee and rolls, Father, expected them before now."

"Father Bolin, I'd like you to meet Father Petri."

“My pleasure," said Jamie.

"I'm looking forward to our talk."

No sooner had he closed the door when room service arrived.

"Umm”, mused Jamie, "Trick? Or Treat!"

"What did you say, Jamie”"

"Say? Oh nothing Joe, just mumbling to myself."

"Here, why don’t you and Father Petri help yourselves?"

"Sorry, Jamie, I have to run. Here is a written schedule of your appointments. It's the best I could do. Call me Sunday evening after six, will you?" I'm leaving you in Father Petri's good but clever hands,."

"Thanks Joe, any cardinals?"

"Only one, Jamie, His Eminence Catin of Benin; a black prince of the Church,a member of the Curia. A super guy, tell me what you think, Sunday."

“I’m certain Carl that you and Father Bolin will hit it off. Just level with him, he can be very persistent."

"I know, Father Joe.”

"How so Carl?"

"The word from the Vatican finance office is they are going to request he be transferred from Santa Clara University to their offices here at the Vatican, as an auditor."

"You're kidding," snidely laughed Joe.

"Grapevine has it that Nick Zapato was very impressed."

"Stanford," said Joe, "is really getting its money's worth from the grant for this assignment."

"Right Jamie?"

"Anyone would think you were working for big bucks."

Joe slapped Jamie on the shoulder as he left the suite. Carl thought it was an affectionate gesture. Jamie believed it was more like a controlled shove. With the physical contact, Joe seemed to be saying, *Alright smart ass, how much more trouble are you going to give us?*

Jamie no longer felt paranoid. He was certain he was being followed and observed by more than one person, not including the Italian police. Got to get this business over with quickly, thought Jamie. The more distance I put between myself and the Vatican, the better.

"Why don’t we sit over here, Father Petri?"

"Carl, if you please, Jamie.”

VIII. THE BODY POLITIC

Jamie sat down and focused all his attention on Father Petri.

"Father Joe tells me, Jamie, that you are interested in the substance of the late Pope's address to the College of Cardìnals."

"It was my understanding, Father Petri, that you were an astute observer of those proceedings. As Dean of the Catholic University of America, I was hoping you would be an impartial judge of the reactions the cardinals had to Pope John's speech."

"Perhaps," said the priest, "I might start by giving you a thumbnail impression of Pope John Paul I. You see, Jamie, the Pope came from northern Italy. His father had been a bricklayer all his life and also an activist in the Socialist party. Because of his simple origins, Albino Luciani considered himself a very fortunate individual. Throughout his rise in the ranks of Holy Mother Church, he remained a very humble human being. The Pope had an abiding deep concern for the poor, the ignorant and the oppressed. His chief concern throughout his ministry was shepherding of his flock."

"Was he himself a simple man?" asked Jamie.

"Contrary to popular opinion, he was anything but that. Pope John Paul was very well educated and extremely intelligent. He was a doctrinal conservative regarding the Holy Scriptures. Yet in matters concerning social responsibilities, he was far more outspoken and aggressive than most so-called liberals or left-wingers."

"It was common knowledge throughout the upper echelons of the Italian Church that the Pontiff was culturally very impressive. His reputation for digesting classical works of literature was well known. His tastes ran from Goethe to Mark Twain. He also spoke and read several languages fluently."

"I understand Father Petri," interrupted Jamie, "that he was a lively and entertaining speaker as well as an accomplished writer."

"Yes, Jamie, the Pope was very much at home in the arts and letters. Even more importantly, to the dismay of the Curia, he was a very inquisitive man, with a great depth of knowledge. He was mentally very tough. He was by all accounts a very flexible and kindly man. Behind his bright smile, there was ostensibly a significant verbal bite awaiting anyone who underestimated him. In his coronation speech, he came out very loud and clear concerning matters that were uppermost in his mind. I paraphrased some of his remarks and wrote them down for you."

Jamie reached out and took the notes from Father Petri, digesting the information as he scanned the notes

"The Church's efforts on universal Christian ecumenism have been sadly lacking. Our efforts must be accelerated, particularly in regard to reaching an accord with both the Anglican and Lutheran Churches."

"The Church's first duty is evangelism. We must seek union without diluting the true meaning of divine doctrine, but we must go forward rapidly, without hesitancy. Regardless of economic costs, my abiding concern is for the people of Africa, Asia and Latin America. Let us not forget that the Church is for the impoverished . . . We must initiate a dialogue, unknown in previous times, to anyone who will listen. We are bound by the precepts of Vatican II."

Jamie put the typewritten notes aside and expressed an anguished sigh.

"Quite a man, I guess. Wouldn't you agree, Carl?"

Father Petri acknowledged with an affirmative nod of his head.

"What was your personal opinion of those remarks? What was the general tone of his acceptance address?" inquired Jamie.

"As Americans, Jamie, we should both be concerned over the long-range implications of his speech. The Pope showed no interest for the more sophisticated moral and emotional needs of Western Catholics, a trait uncommon in Italian prelates. They have all taken Machiavellian delight in watching elite Western nation Catholics hoisted, time and again on their own petards. Little by little the Church always gives them some more room on the road to salvation before abruptly shipping them off to hell!"

"Oh! Ha, ha! Carl," laughed Jamie painfully, "That really hurts. How true, how very true."

"Oh! That really hurts," as the wisdom of Father Carl Petri's last remark nearly brought tears of laughter to Jamie's eyes and internal regret as well.

"Seriously, Jamie, it's surprising to all the clergy that the new Pope's cry for Christian unity was so pronounced. It was as though he could feel communism nipping at his heels. What troubled everyone was that as a doctrinal conservative, what inducement could he offer the Protestant clergy? Sooner or later the Church would have to abandon its most cherished eccentricities."

"And what might those be, Carl?" spoke Jamie with concern in his voice and fully recovered from his laughter.

"What else but papal infallibility, divorce and birth control. Rather three large impediments to his plans, wouldn't you say, Jamie? Yet his appeal to the poor was inspiring and at the same time vexing to the Curia. The Church was seeing a grass roots shift in the attitude of their priests in third world countries. These countries represented the bulk of future populations most susceptible to conversion and control."

"I see what you mean, Carl," interrupted Jamie.

"I had heard that in countries where people's armies are toppling governments. The young priests are very socialistic. They equate Marxist Communism with the Christianity of Jesus even if the vehicle, itself, is dripping with blood. Which path do you believe Pope John Paul was advocating?" Co-existence with Communism? Unheard of twenty years ago, it was given some consideration by Pope Paul VI as the Vatican found itself about to be surrounded by an Italian Communist government one of these days."

"Hell, Jamie, the latest Italian laws permit divorce and abortion."

"Meanwhile, some politicians are demanding taxation of the Church. My impression is that the Church is on the verge of reaching a monumental decision. It could change the course of world history. The cardinals are divided into three camps. The conservatives remain dogmatic and intransigent, fight Communism to the bitter end and believe in nurturing the vast wealth of the Church."

The liberal Western Europe and American groups would prefer an American pope and would relocate the Vatican in North America where the Curia would be safe from Communist intimidation. Then there are the third world cardinals, mostly of Negroid, Spanish and Portuguese extraction."

"They truly represent the wave of the future. They see national Marxist governments as most representative of their people. For these cardinals, Western civilization is rapidly declining and well on its way to becoming the next historical Holy Roman Empire"

"What a mess," Jamie blurted out.

"Unfortunately, Jamie," said Father Petri, "if you unemotionally step back and evaluate the knee-jerking symptoms of senility apparent in Western civilization, one might tend to agree with the latter group."

"Surely you're joking, Carl?"

"Not if you consider, Jamie, that Western civilization spent many centuries cradled in the bosom of Mother Church and with no apparent interest in displaying the primary ingredient of adulthood, as characterized by a compassionate display of productive and creative intelligence. The West wasted the last one hundred years in Christian puberty, of late engaging in born-again Christianity! A sure sign of premature senility and second childhood foolishness!"

"Oh, good Lord, Father," shouted out Jamie as he again burst into laughter. "Are you by any chance Irish?"

Both men laughed vigorously. But behind their sardonic humor, as bright scholarly men, they feared the truth might be just as Father Petri, acting as the devil's advocate, had so eloquently stated.

"You know of course, Carl, that the Church Herself is greatly to blame. At various times in history, She has been dragged kicking and screaming into several 'renaissance' periods. I speak not of that period when art flourished and was so mystically endowed throughout the pages of history in terms of great cathedrals, paintings and all manner of art forms."

"What then are you suggesting, Father Bolin?" asked Father Petri in a quizzical tone.

"I'm talking about intermittent periods of enlightenment which were touched off by the creative ideas of such diverse people as Galileo, Da Vince, Voltaire, Franklin, Thoreau, Curie (Madame), Gurdieff, Ouspensky and Einstein."

"Jamie, your insight amazes me," answered the astonished priest.

Jamie remembered how his own mental processes had been altered by dedication, discipline and creative thinking, triggered by ideas he had gathered from the histories of such extraordinary people. Voltaire's "Candide" had a singularly profound effect on his life and altered forever his attitude on certainty and morality. Plato's "Allegory of the Cave" was also never far from his thoughts.

It seemed to Jamie ironic that whenever the Church was faced with a moral, political and, or financial decision, She, Herself, displayed many of the same characteristics as Voltaire's wanderer whom the Church considered immoral. The major difference being that Voltaire acknowledged subjective truth while the Church denies it, while practicing it with impunity and great self-righteousness.

As Father Petri apologized to Jamie for being so morbid about the present state of Vatican affairs, Jamie shook off his inattentiveness and forced his mind back to the present conversation.

"Don't apologize, Father. I find your candor and humor very refreshing. I very much appreciate your views on the late Pope."

"It's time I was leaving, Jamie," said Father Petri as he stood and shook hands.

"When you get back to the States, look me up if you get the chance."

"I'll do that, Carl. Thanks very much for your help."

"Don't bother seeing me out, Jamie . . . and good luck:"

As Father Petri left, Jamie's thoughts focused on the many implications of Father Petri's disclosures. If a decisive course of action had been agreed upon by Pope John Paul and his advisors, could such an agreement have led to his death? What party or parties stood to lose the most? If he, Jamie, continued to investigate the Pope's death, would he be exposing himself as a target for elimination by a radical zealot? Even worse, was he unknowingly stepping on the toes of an entire malevolent organization?

Jamie turned his attention to the appointment schedule provided him earlier by Father Joe. "Hmm," muttered Jamie. The mere thought of Joe was beginning to bristle the hairs on his body. How much longer would their mutual mistrust continue, until a real confrontation took place? It might help if I could really get him hopping mad. Jamie neglected to consider the possible consequences of such a ploy. Who really was this Father Joseph Gault?

Consulting his schedule,, Jamie saw that at 2:30 this afternoon he had a meeting with a Mr. Tom Johnson at the American Embassy.

"Best I could do," was scribbled next to Johnson's name; followed by, "I think you'll get what you want from him." signed Joe.

*Hel*l, thought Jamie, *what I need and what I have to do right now are two separate realities. Believe me,*

What I want has absolutely nothing to do with Holy Mother Church. Cloistering his libido, Jamie realized that this afternoon's meeting might shed some light on:

A. The Pope's audience with Rabbi Rosenbaum, an Israeli diplomat.

B. The Pope's audience with Patriarch Narimas Hakim, representing Arab Christians.

Jamie was grateful that the American Embassy was almost next door to his favorite Italian watering hole, the Giggi Fozzi. It was about one o'clock when Jamie reached the restaurant.

"Hey, Toni!" shouted Jamie.

"Got a table for an old friend?"

"Jamie, is it really you? Where the hell have you been? It's been almost two years."

"Three actually." Laughed Jamie as he bear-hugged the headwaiter.

Toni, unraveling himself from Jamie's grasp, leading him through a maze of crowded, noisy tables.

In his loudest voice entreated, "Jamie, my younger sister, Marie, you remember."

"Mama Mia! She is pregnant and still unwed."

"The bastard, a Frenchman, I will kill 'em, tear him limb-from-limb!"

"The filth, what shall I do?"

"Help me plan the perfect murder!"

"Here is your old table."

He then whispered in Jamie's ear, "Yes, I know I have no sister, but the patrons love it, and it's good for business."

"Honest to God, Toni, some things never change, you're marvelous!" shouted Jamie as the waiter rambled off, still venting his passion, as only an Italian can.

Such antics were part of the Giggi Fozzi scene. No one ever tired of them. Jamie was almost in tears watching his old friend's performance as the waiter danced away in a pretended rage, giving Jamie a wink of his eye.

The table waiter arrived, and Jamie ordered. "Birra Peroni over ice and lasagna, please."

"Very good!" saluted the waiter as he left to fill Jamie's order.

The beer was a local brew. The lasagna was the house specialty, three inches thick, smothered in onions and mushroom sauce. It could ward off hunger for days. Jamie decided to eat heartily now and forego dinner. Quaffing the beer, he ate the lasagna with obvious delight. The meal was topped off with spumoni for dessert. All the while, Jamie enjoyed watching the late lunch crowd and catching the eye, every now and then, of a flirtatious woman. On the way out, he chatted briefly with his old friend. Jamie then strolled across the street to the Embassy.

"Identification please," said the burly Marine Corporal as Jamie's way was barred at the top of the Embassy steps.

"Your passport will do. What is your reason for visiting the Embassy?"

"I have a two-thirty appointment with a Mr. Tom Johnson," said Jamie as he returned his passport to his inside coat pocket.

Scanning his clipboard, the Corporal checked off Jamie's name and let him pass. Jamie headed for the seated receptionist.

"Why the Marine guard?" Jamie inquired as he reached the front desk.

"I'm sorry sir; it's a necessary precaution these days because of the terrorist activities of the Red Brigade. The Ambassador is a firm-believer in preventive medicine, as you can see." Her hand swept the room. She pointed out three more Marines, armed and stationed at various strategic locations throughout the lobby.

"I have a two-thirty appointment with Tom Johnson."

"Oh yes, Father Bolin, isn't it?"

"We have been expecting you. Mr. Johnson called down earlier and said to bring you to his office as soon as you arrived."

"Follow me, please."

Jamie followed a lovely pair of long legs up the steep flight of marble stairs to the second-floor landing. He patted the pocket containing his passport. *Father indeed.* He hadn't realized the Vatican would officially identify him as such to the Embassy. Was it intentionally planned to cause him some future unforeseen difficulty?

The splendid legs in the high arched pumps suddenly disappeared through a nearby door. Jamie's eyes rose past the short skirt and slim hips just in time to see a very affable stranger stride across the room, arm extended.

"Ann, you know I'm expecting Father Bolin."

"What can I do for this gentleman?"

"This is Father Bolin," blurted out the receptionist.

"Oh! Excuse me, Father."

"As an old Notre Dame grad, I cannot get used to priests in layman attire. Old prejudices die hard."

"Thank you Ann, that's all for now," spoke the Charge d'affaires as he too watched the slow rhythmic exit of the tall, lithesome blond.

Both men's eyes met in mutual understanding.

"Welcome, Father," said Tom Johnson as he offered Jamie a chair next to his desk.

"The Vatican called and told us of your project. Since I work very closely with the Church, the Ambassador asked me to give you whatever information I can."

"That's very thoughtful of the Ambassador," sighed Jamie.

He feared the worst in rhetorical discussion of non-information which might follow such a pleasant and non-committal introduction. Jamie was summarily caught off guard by Tom Johnson's open and forthright detailed briefing.

"It just so happened the visits of Rabbi Rosenbaum and Narimos Hakim to the Vatican were immediately followed up by visits of both gentlemen to the Ambassador's office. I was present at both meetings."

"Please continue, Mr. Johnson."

"If I have any questions, I'll fit them in as we go along."

"Just call me Tom, Father Bolin."

"It's Jamie then, Tom," replied Bolin.

Slouching back in his large, dark leather upholstered chair, Tom Johnson swung around to more comfortably face in Jamie's direction. He cast one foot upward, letting it come to rest on an open drawer top.

"As you know, Jamie, President Carter is attempting to resolve this ongoing Middle East crisis. Both the Rabbi and Hakim were sent as goodwill ambassadors to ascertain the Vatican's attitude regarding a pending Egyptian-Israeli peace treaty. I'm positive that our discussion this afternoon will give you a concise view of the historical significance of a great Middle East paradox presented to the Catholic Church during the reign of Pope John Paul I."

"Paradox, Tom. What paradox?"

"Jamie, it's not very often one has the opportunity to have his remarks quoted for posterity in the archives of Holy Mother Church. I would like to strike a bargain with you before I continue."

"What did you have in mind?" responded Jamie with a rather quizzical expression.

"I would consider it a great favor if in exchange for this information you will be so kind as to mention my name and footnote my remarks as such. You may be sure that although some of my comments may be indiscreet, you will be given no information which violates United States security regulations or compromises confidential Embassy information."

"The least I can do, Tom. I appreciate your frankness. F ire away," said a relieved Jamie as he, too, relaxed into a more comfortable sitting arrangement

"You see, Jamie, the whole world is sitting on a time bomb. The outcome of such a minute-by-minute precarious situation may not depend on the armed might of the super powers. The resolution to the problem may well rest in the hands of one man and what he decides is the best long-run interest of the Holy Roman Catholic Church."

"Are you serious, Tom?"

"Very much so, Jamie, I assure you."

A grotesque picture flashed across Jamie's mind as his macabre Irish sense of humor grasped the urgency in Tom Johnson's voice and manner. A pope, standing upright, was holding a shining golden crucifix clasped in both hands, extended above his crowned head. Encircling the pope is a huge crowd of priests and nuns, huddled together in a large cavern in the foothills of Rome. Outside, the world is being devastated by neutron bombs.

"Fear not, my children," benevolently speaks the Pope "our financial well-being is secure. With great foresight, the Church invested in property, not people. In celebration of our good fortune, there will be a temporary dispensation of the vows of chastity and poverty. My brother priests may take as many wives as they choose from amongst our dear sisters."

"How long, Holy Father?" shouts a jubilant young priest already fondling a pretty nun.

"How long what, my son?" asks the pope.

"How long wills the temporary dispensation last?" sighed the now almost breathless priest as his excitement rose.

Putting down the crucifix, the Pope begins counting heads and then pulls from under his robes a tiny Texas Instrument's statistical business management calculator.

"I believe 5,000 years should do it!" laughs the Pope as he plunges headlong into a great group of nuns rushing toward him.

The priests begin performing their own instantaneous weddings, thereby initiating a massive orgy, which lasts for fourteen weeks. Then, after trying to subsist on the nuns' cooking, the priests annul the marriages. The Pope rescinds his dispensation, and the nuns praise God!

Although this vision only preoccupied Jamie's mind for an instant, he lost the thread of Tom Johnson's conversation.

"I'm sorry Tom, would you mind repeating that last comment?"

Jamie shook his head. He promised himself he would stop castrating the Church. It was childish and vindictive. The current problems of nations and religions are immense, and no amount of sarcasm would set things right.

"As I was saying, Jamie," spoke Tom Johnson as he stood up and moved next to the wall behind his mahogany desk. He pulled down a large map with one hand and reached for a long hollow aluminum pointer with the other.

"Yes, by all means, Tom, go ahead with your explanation," responded Jamie.

"The Russians, Father, are fifty years behind the United States in technology. They are about a century behind in logistics. But they are a thousand years ahead of us in practicing the art of duplicity. Temporarily, the mismatches appear to cancel each other out. But slowly, Jamie, the world is being cut to pieces by a grand Russian strategy."

Tom Johnson's pointer lingered on the country of Iran. He continued speaking, "The situation developing in Iran is the real reason behind the Camp David accords between Israel and Egypt. Turkey, although part of NATO, has moved closer to Soviet influence. The Americans have refused them arms shipments because of their spat with the Greeks."

"In fact, Bulent Ecevit has told the West that Russia is no threat to world peace. He then proceeded to sign a friendship pact with the Soviet Union. For all practical purposes, the Russians have neutralized Turkey, the strong southeastern arm of NATO. You can see Turkey is the next door neighbor to Iran."

"Wait a minute Tom; I thought this Iranian uprising was a popular democratic movement supported by the Shiite sect, very conservative

Muslims. They hate the Marxists as much as they hate Mohammed Reza Pahlavi, the Shah of Iran."

"You are very well informed Jamie, but things are not always what they seem.

"The spiritual leader of the impending revolution is the aging Ayatollah Khomeini. Originally exiled by the Shah in 1964, he took up residence in France where he has become spiritual leader of Iran's thirty-four million Muslims. Their stronghold inside Iran is the city of Quam, the center of their religion."

"This anti-Shah movement contains all elements of the society, a very loose knit hodgepodge, just the way Marxists love it. At the appropriate moment, the leaders of the revolution, including the old one, will be victimized. If the Shah falls, you can bet the country will go communistic, although it might take a few years. Maps don't lie, Jamie."

“Look here!” as Tom tapped Afghanistan.

"Its people's revolution was a cover for a Marxist government. Someday the Russians will physically occupy the country. Here in Afghanistan, as well as Iran, the Russians are simply playing cat and mouse with the West. The big prize is not Iran but Saudi Arabia."

God, he's right, thought Jamie. *It's all so simple if you just look at a map and pay no attention to theories.*

"I see Tom, the Saudi's are being trapped between the communists' movement in Africa and the Russian involvement in Afghanistan and Iran."

"All the oil in the Middle East will fall to Russia. Syria is already pro-Russian, so who does that leave?"

"Of course," Jamie continued, "the only two powers remaining in the Middle East are Egypt and Israel. Egypt has the manpower and Israel has the guts and the technology. The Saudi royal family will need the help of both countries to stave off a Marxist takeover after Iran falls."

"Yes Jamie, and the Jews are very well aware of their painful situation. By nature they are very tough negotiators. Therefore, every day they delay an Egyptian-Israeli peace treaty brings the entire Middle East closer to collapse. The Egyptians are in an appalling situation. Communism is sweeping across Africa. The Egyptians see themselves as first cousins of the Jews, not brothers of the Negroes. The Egyptians are in a bind because of American stupidity. The Russians made idiots out of us in Africa. The English knew what was happening but are absolutely powerless to help."

"What was the essence of the Ambassador's discussions with the Israeli and Arab diplomats then?" asked Jamie.

"It was agreed that somehow between the Christian Arabs and the Israelis they had to:"

"1. Convince the United States that Iran is the endangered queen guarding the king of Saudi Arabia from being checkmated by the Russian bear"

"2.They needed someone to rally the black Catholics of Africa to protect their flanks. After all, Africa was once the cradle of Mother Church. Even now, Africa numbers sixty million of the faithful. So you see Jamie, the Pope is really the key to peace in the Middle East."

Jamie was just beginning to realize how very small and very hot the world had become.

Tom Johnson continued, "Rabbi Rosenbaum received his audience with the Pope through Rabbi Marc Tanenbaum of the United States, whom the Pope held in warm regard. Tanenbaum was head of inter-religious affairs for the American-Jewish Committee. Previously, Pope Paul VI had attempted to make friendly overtures towards Israel. The Arabs gave him such a bad time that the Vatican did not follow through. Rosenbaum had hoped that Pope John Paul I would send a papal delegate to Israel and rally African Catholics in opposition to the Marxists."

"Both Rosenbaum and Narimos were very disappointed, not by what this Pope said, but by how noncommittal he was. That's when they came here, to the American Embassy and voiced their deepest fears. It appears that the Holy Roman Catholic Church is in a great dilemma."

"We must remember, however kindly Pope John Paul was, he was above all else, Protector of the Faith. Thus, we come to the crux of' the Vatican paradox regarding the Middle East."

Tom Johnson summed up by saying, "The Church is still based on one irrefutable doctrine as is the entire Christian community. Should that doctrine fail, there would no longer be one way to God, which in the eyes of Christianity is only through Jesus Christ. Therefore, in the long run, beliefs of the Jewish faith and those of the Muslims might as well be lumped in with the atheists, and particularly Marxist atheists, except that the people in Soviet Russia and Eastern Europe have their ancestry deeply rooted in Christianity. Poland, so far as the Church is concerned, is a Catholic country."

"After all, render unto Caesar . . .and unto God . . . could work in Russia as it had in old Rome. Look who came away a winner in the long run. Save the Middle East and you harden the Communists against Catholicism. The Church aids and abets her sworn theological enemies, the Jews and the Muslims, who most certainly are not open to evangelization. No one knows which way the Church will play her cards. And now, Father Bolin, you know as much as I do about the two audiences the Pope had concerning the Middle East."

Jamie responded for argument's sake, to see if he could gain more insight into the direction that the Church would take on this particular issuc.

"But Tom, the Jews and Muslims believe in God the Father, and the Marxist atheists don't. Surely that makes all the difference, doesn't it?"

"No, Father, I'm afraid not. You see, the government of Russia is made up of card-carrying Communists. Almost assuredly also atheists, but only five percent of the Russian population are permitted to be Party members. The Church knows this, and the Church is very patient. After all, the Church co-existed very nicely with the Nazis during World War II. They don't abandon their people because of the type of government. Remember, up until now it has been the Communists who have rebuffed the Church, and not the other way around."

"Soon the Italian Curia has to learn to live with Communist Italy or physically abandon the continent of Europe. If the Church believes the United States can no longer be trusted, She might attempt the impossible, a reconciliation with world Marxists. I must say, the last forty-year history of American foreign policy makes me believe no one has any faith in America. Our nation lacks the ability to carry out any long-range foreign policy program. Incidentally, that last remark is off the record, okay?"

"Agreed," responded Jamie."

"Well, that should about wrap up this interview."

"Tom, would you like to join me for a drink?"

"Sorry, Jamie, I'm leaving for a weekend in Nice and will be catching the train as soon as our meeting is finished."

The two men parted cordially, and Jamie said he would be certain to include Tom Johnson as one of his sources, if not in the body of the work, at least as a footnote. It was 4:30 when Jamie caught a taxi. No sooner had he opened the door to his suite at the Hilton than the phone rang; it was Carol calling.

"I'm glad I caught you in and just want to tell you I have been thinking about you all day."

Jamie responded, "If the decision were mine, I would just as soon start our weekend right now. Unfortunately, I have a meeting at the Vatican between 7:30 and 8:00 this evening. I have just enough time for a nap and a quick shower. But I am very glad you called, Love, and yes, I do miss you."

Slipping out of his clothes even as he hung up the phone, Jamie rang the hotel desk and left a wake-up call for 6:30 that evening. He quickly fell sound asleep sprawled out on the bed. At 7:45 he knocked on the door of Father 0'Brien's room.

"Room IVCXXIII?" he inquired, as the priest opened the door.

"Oh Ho!" sang out Father John, "You caught my little joke the other day. And how would the good Father Jamie Bolin be himself this fine evening?"

"Look, Father, I might as well level with you. I'm not a priest. I'm an investigative reporter on special assignment here at the Vatican. Knowing that, would you like me to leave? It's just that I've been almost run down by a car, blown to hell and back and have just learned that the Vatican might be turning Communistic. I'm just plain tired of all the bullshit."

"But, Jamie," said the priest, with a devilishly sweet smile, "we all know that. But, you must play the game by the Vatican rules."

"Now, what would you like to drink?""

Oh my God, thought Jamie, *what chance does the rest of the conniving world have with all these smiling innocent priests, always ten steps ahead of everybody else?*

Jamie asked for a double shot of Southern Comfort as he bent down and took off his shoes. Then, as if he was home with his 'ol mom', he stretched out in a large, overstuffed chair. His feet rested comfortably on an ottoman. Father 0'Brien returned with Southern Comfort and a side chaser of water for Jamie. In his other hand he held a tumblerful of whiskey for himself.

The priest sat down across from Jamie and told him what a wonderful man the Pope had been and how the office should be delegated to a tribunal of at least five men. As it was now, all the cardinals who reported to the Pope were as good as popes themselves. They treated each other as such in privacy. The only way the job could ever hope to be done. He told Jamie that eventually such a tribunal would replace the Pope. It would eliminate one stumbling block to amalgamation of all the Christian churches under the banner of the Vatican, thus doing away with the doctrine of papal infallibility

If only the Church could wiggle its way out from under Pope Paul's biggest mistake, his "Humanae Vitae" encyclical of 1968. Then, the Church would easily agree to let the clergy marry, and Protestants would agree to speak out against divorce. The Church could forever close the door on Martin Luther and all who came after him.

Protestant ministers would have what they have always secretly cherished the most, a shot at getting a red robe and all that it stood for. Jamie found Father John refreshingly honest and outspoken. He had already come to respect his thoroughness and his intelligence.

"Father, I must admit that the rumor about the Pope being murdered had some merit."

"Would you mind if I asked you some questions about that particular morning?"

"Not at all," responded Father John, "but other than what has already appeared in the newspapers and magazines, I can't recall much else."

"I really have three important questions on my mind," said Jamie.

"The first one concerns the documents the Pope had been reading. Have you found out any more about them?"

"No, Jamie, I couldn't even find the last page which I had originally discovered under the bed."

"John, who was the bishop that was to say mass for the Pope that morning?"

"What bishop?" asked Father 0'Brien.

"The one you mentioned to the newspapers when you told them about entering the Pope's chambers and finding him dead. Just before you entered his room, it was reported that you saw a bishop standing by the chapel entrance."

"Wait a minute, Jamie; let me think?"

"Why? Yes that's correct. I had forgotten all about it. Strange, I didn't remember telling the reporters about it."

"How did you know it was a bishop, Father?"

"I only guessed, because although the man had on simple white vestments, he was toying with a large ring. I'm not really certain he was a bishop. In fact, everything happened so fast, possibly I only imagined someone was standing by the chapel door. Perhaps, in my mounting panic to arouse the Pope, my subconscious wanted to see someone near the chapel. That someone could.have been the Pope. You see, Jamie, no one ever said mass for the Pope. Hie held his own mass every morning by himself."

"Obviously it was an aberration; otherwise, why would I have seen a bishop's ring at that distance? I wanted to see the golden papal ring and the comfort and authority it stood for. Remember at the funeral I told you one of the last things the Pope did on Thursday afternoon was to request that the jeweler pick up the newly-minted ring? It was too tight on his finger. I believe it pained him somewhat."

"I had hoped, Father John that you would have been able to verify a theory I have been tossing around in my head. Is it possible an unknown assailant had entered the Pope's quarters, snuffing out his life with a pillow? He could have been after the report the Pope was analyzing. Maybe as he propped the Pope into a sitting position, he noticed the gold ring nearby. Because of its value, the assassin picked it up, about which time Sister Vincenza started knocking at the door."

"The killer could have panicked. Run out through the sitting room. The killer started to pass behind the nun, who was in the alcove knocking on the Pope's bedroom door, when she abruptly turned and headed for your rooms. He could have flattened himself against the wall as the nun came out of the alcove and turned in the opposite direction."

"When she disappeared from sight, the killer started to follow her out and realized he had forgotten the papers clutched in the Pope's hand. Before he could return and get them, he heard you and the nun coming down the hallway. That's when he would have ducked into the entrance to the chapel. He then waited for an opportunity to sneak back and recover the papers Becoming interested once again in the ring, he inadvertently leaned out into the lighted hall, and you caught a glimpse of him. After you and the nun found the Pope and went for help, the murderer could have returned to the bedchambers and removed the papers from the Pope's hand."

"One of the papers could have fallen under the bed either in the original struggle or when the Pope's body had been rearranged in a sitting position. But now, your answer to my question throws cold water on the whole theory. Particularly since the one thing in my concocted theory which even I couldn't find, was a valid motive."

"Killing for the documents the Pope had been reading just doesn't add up"

"No." said Jamie.

"Those papers were removed after the Pope's death for some other reason. Someone could have simply re-filed and forgotten about them because of their insignificance. So much for a quick and easy solution to the death of Pope John Pau1 I."

"Does seem rather far-fetched, Jamie," said John.

"Now, what was your third question?"

Jamie decided to ask the priest straight out his impression of the Church's interest in reconciliation with the Communists around the world.

"Tell me, John, is the Catholic Church turning towards the acceptance of Marxist political doctrines?"

The priest's drink almost spilled out all over the floor. His wrist gave an involuntary jerk, and liquor ran over his hand and down onto his black, slightly rumpled trousers.

"May the saints preserve us, Jamie. Damn, if you don't think like a Jesuit even if you aren't really one."

Father O'Brien went on to explain that the answer to Jamie's question was the most complex issue facing the Vatican. His response confirmed to Jamie what Tom Johnson had told him earlier today.

"You see, Jamie, the members of the Curia, most of them, are diametrically opposed to conciliatory gestures of any kind towards Marxists. The Jesuit order is in vehement opposition to co-existence in any form. However, when financial and political realities are in conflict with Church dogma, somehow the Church always managed to slip out of Her virginal robes and prostituted herself politically in the short run. She hopes in the long run to be born again a virgin. Jamie, is my metaphor too obtuse? If you wish to pursue this line of inquiry further, you should consult none other than Father Joseph Gault."

Then, raising his now almost empty tumbler of whiskey, John proposed a toast.

"To Holy Mother Church, be She harlot or saint. She has never failed to do what had to be done. It bothers Her not, a little red paint!"

For the next three or four hours, the two Irishmen swapped stories and argued over Church policy, altruism vs Christianity. The bottle of Southern Comfort noticeably emptied. They talked about their roots and lamented over the lack of real compassion and understanding in a world wherein the Irish penchant for lyrical solutions to world harmony were considered madness.

Upon leaving the rooms of Father 0'Brien around midnight, Jamie seemed further from the truth about Pope John Paul I than he had ever been. His spirits, however, had been rekindled by the intellectual and emotional stimulus of the past few hours. Reaching the Gate of St. Anne and feeling no pain, Jamie had a slight altercation with a young Swiss guardsman. It appears no one was permitted to enter or leave the Vatican after 11:30 PM. without a special pass. One quick call to Father 0'Brien settled the dispute, and the young guardsman diplomatically convinced Jamie to wait while a taxi could be called to take him to his hotel.

IX. WEEKEND RESPITE

Saturday morning came and almost expired before Jamie groggily responded to the bedside alarm. Incessantly its aggravating tone amplified the throbbing pain that laced his forehead. His Irish common sense mentally extolled the many virtues of a frontal lobotomy. Such not being immediately available, vengeance is mine sayeth the Lord! With, one great sweep of the right hand Jamie simply yanked the clock, cord intact, from the wall socket. Sweet silence momentarily soothed his aching cerebral cortex.

Pleading an emergency, room service rushed to his aid. His gut reaction, until its arrival, was to hunker down beneath the covers, bury his head in the pillows, and curse, which is exactly what he did. By 11:40 AM, having downed a "Virgin Mary" heavily dosed with black pepper, a hottle of herbal tea with a bit of lemon and a lightly buttered English muffin, civility permeated his gray matter. The bawdy, off-key strains of "Mary Murphy" rose above the decibel level of the steamy shower spray; his taut, muscular frame outlined in the silhouetted, frosted glass doorway.

A short interval elapsed, after having shaved and otherwise refreshed, Jamie lounged serenely in a russet color, terry cloth robe on the living room couch, mulling over his next move. *Tomorrow I'll phone Gault and insist he meet with Father Rene and me first thing Monday morning.* Jamie was opting for a direct confrontation that should create a showdown when he divulged the probable cause of the Pope's death. Having no other leads, what was there to lose? Little did Bolin realize his naivete with regard to Vatican intrigue.

His thoughts were purged of Catholic-Marxist machinations. He wondered about more pleasurable contemplations. What should he wear? How would he look? Where should they dine? One quick glance at the cherub facade, gilded gold clock on the mantle brought him to the abrupt realization he would be late for their rendezvous. Observing the bright, sun-filled clouds above and the bustling gaily dressed crowds in the piazza below, Jamie determined the air was chilly, but radiantly warm.

Strolling the streets of Rome with her on his arm would indeed be a delightful way to spend the afternoon. Jamie put on beltless gray slacks, black wool, turtleneck sweater, wool socks and Johnson-Murphy matching shoe boots. From the adjacent closet he selected a dark herringbone sports coat, casually tossing the coat over his shoulder by crooking a forefinger in the elastic band inside the collar. A fluorescent hued blue and gray floral handkerchief festooned the breast pocket. Before exiting the lobby of the Hilton, Jamie retrieved $200 from the manila envelope in the hotel safe and converted it into a like amount of lira at the cashier's counter.

Carol unlatched the door to her apartment at twenty past one in the afternoon, having answered Jamie's knock in anticipation of spending a lovely day with him. He immediately saw how pleased she was to see him again. She responded to the touch of his fingers as he reached out and ran his hands lightly over her sleeveless arms. His caress deliciously and instantaneously sensitized her entire body.

The stroking tenderness of his palm raised goose bumps wherever it roamed. The radiant warmth ran to the small of her back, wrapped around her waist and raced for a haven within her upper thighs. Fluid muscles just beneath the epidermis of her smooth buttocks pinched together. His head and shoulders bent as he moved toward her, he felt the rays of wanton warmth emanating from her body.

His eyes basked in the soft, billowy fluid flow of her blonde hair. Carol had taken care to please him. She wore little makeup. A diminutive amount of blue and silver eyeliner gave a bright, haunting appearance to her light, full eyebrows, long lashes, and emerald green eyes. Jamie loved the perfect angle of her Grecian nose and the sensuous invitation of her slightly open mouth, framed by full, pastel pink lips, ever so inviting, especially when slightly wetted.

Her head nuzzled his shoulder, hands pressingly spread across his back. His fingers, spread wide, traversed the nakedness of her exposed bare back. Her arms slid downwardly and encircled his waist. For several moments the couple stood locked in a mutually shared affectionate embrace, as if they had been lifelong lovers.

Carol whispered softly into his nearest lobe, "Give me a minute to get my wrap and we can leave."

Reluctantly disengaging, Carol moved to the divan and Jamie stood watching, his eyes taking in every delicious movement of her limbs. She had, for his enjoyment, chosen to wear slender, high-heel, azure blue, open-toed shoes. The high heels gave her legs the line and appearance of being a mile long and extraordinarily curvaceous. How could she possibly, in those heels, stroll all afternoon in Rome? Then he noticed that sitting by a large shoulder bag at one end of the divan was a very attractive and comfortable pair of walking shoes.

His eyes caught the flow of her skirt upon her hips and he wondered where she had been able to find the flesh tight pale blue sleeveless sweater. The sweater demurely covered her bodice, complete with a soft, furry turtleneck collar, before seductively plunging, exposing her bare back. Velvety smooth in texture, her creamy skin created a tiny cave at the base of her spine. Her petite waist accentuated the exotic curve of her hips.

Jamie had been so intent on touching her, he hadn't noticed her outfit. He now understood why she seemed so soft and warm when he had held her. Her pleated skirt was the color of a light blue sky and made of the finest wool. Her skin hugging, Lycra sweater held her braless breasts in almost obscene distention. Her nipples were still erect from his earlier caresses.

As Carol put on her matching light blue suit coat, Jamie realized that she had dressed entirely to please him and no one else. With her suit coat in place, what little amount of the sweater remained uncovered gave the upper part of her body an almost serene, sedate appearance, although no one could deny she was beautifully endowed.

Jamie had, in fact, sighed with relief when Carol slipped into her suit coat. Moments before, he had visions of literally beating off hordes of Italian men and boys alike. Carole took hold of Jamie's arm. She lightly kissed him as they moved from the hotel room toward the elevators.

As they descended in the lift, Jamie whispered, "You are a devil, and I love it."

"Thought you might. Shall I take off the coat?" she teased.

"God no! Are you going to behave like this all afternoon?

"Lovely thought. I think I will. Would you like that?"

"Need I reply?" responded Jamie, helplessly, as the lift reached the first floor.

Hand in hand, he and Carol headed for the Piazza di Spagna.

"Shall we walk?" she asked.

"Marvelous idea," said Jamie.

"Are we going to the Piazza?"

"Yes, the restaurant is not too far from there."

"Good: I'm famished."

The Piazza di Spagna had the aura of New York's Greenwich Village, the old village, circa late 1940's. It also had a touch of atmosphere similar to the artist colony near Sacre Coeur in Paris. Jamie knew it would be a delightful afternoon, watching the artists paint and hawk their creations.

"Jamie," Carol spoke hesitatingly as they walked along the Via del Corso.

"Someone broke into my room last night. No! Don't be too upset. I wasn't there at the time. My dresser drawers and suitcase were a mess, but fortunately nothing of value was taken. Whoever it was didn't even bother to take my traveler's checks or my plane ticket to London. I imagine I was very lucky. I understand such things happen all the time here."

"Frightfully inhospitable of the Italians, don't you think, Love? I thought those early evening phone calls all week long were a bit strange."

Then she gave Jamie a good-natured shove.

"What was that for?" asked Jamie as he caught the faint smile in her eyes.

"Well, damn it! You weren't up to calling all week. So why should I mind if every time I answer the phone, the person on the other end hangs up; just wanting to know if I was in the room. Maybe he was dangerous and good looking; at least he called."

"Good heavens, Carol, I adore your sense of humor, but now I'm worried. Do you have any reason to think they might come back?"

Further discussion exhausted the subject. Both Carol and Jamie agreed she was a poor robbery choice. After all, the hotel clerk told her that thirty percent of female tourists are robbery victims in Rome. Most of the crimes were either purse snatching or room break-ins similar to her experience.

"Speaking of purse snatching, I hope you have a firm grip on your shoulder bag," cautioned Jamie.

"One hand for my belongings and one for you," Carol smiled, as she spoke, and tightly squeezed his hand.

"Hold up a minute, while I change into my walking shoes; but first sir, just for you."

Carol lightly spun around, giving Jamie one more look at her lovely legs. Then, propping herself up with one hand on his shoulder, she lazily reached down and changed shoes.

If an afternoon drunk had chanced by just at that moment, he might have gotten a touch of seasickness. There stood Carol on one leg in a five-inch heel; while listing to starboard as her other leg in the walking shoe touched the pavement. Carol completed the exchange of shoes. Jamie jokingly turned around as if looking for something he had lost. The sweet scent of her hair just below his nostrils told him she was very close by, but a head shorter.

"Carol, look over there. An artist seems to be doing excellent charcoal sketches."

"Come on, I'd like one of you."

Several hours passed in what seemed like a matter of minutes. Jamie and Carol enjoyed the carnival atmosphere of the Piazza. They wandered in and out of the small shops amongst the adjoining side streets. Coming upon a small postal station, Jamie mailed the charcoal sketch, now protectively placed in a mailing tube provided by the artist, to his home in the United States.

"Let's grab a snack; it will tide us over until dinner," said Jamie.

"If you don't mind, Love, it's already four in the afternoon. I've had too much of Rome and not enough of you."

"Let's have an early dinner, and then go back to the Minerva. You know, Jamie, I leave for London tomorrow," she reminded him.

"Why the hell didn't I think of that?"

" Taxi, taxi!" shouted Jamie."

He stepped from the curb, after momentarily wrapping both arms around her in a bear-like hug, to grab a cab.

"Stop here, driver, please, by the Piazza Norona," said Jamie. Carol alighted, and Jamie rummaged through his pockets for payment.

Oh: How enchanting," sighed Carol.

"What a lovely cascade of water."

"It's the 'Fountain of the Rivers,' designed by Bernini. It really is something. Hollywood made a movie about it in the States some years ago. Come on, let's get closer. The spray from the splashing water is marvelous," shouted Jamie.

"I hope," he then gently whispered in her ear "that you can recall the cool, gentle freshness of this mist, later this evening."

"Oh, Jamie, do we have to have dinner?"

"Let's go back now."

"Just a bit longer, love."

"There, just across the way, is a great little restaurant, the La Macella. A quick bite and we'll be off."

"Enough of this fountain now, or we'll be soaked to the skin."

“Jamie tossed several coins into the fountain and shouted, "Make a wish as we leave!"

"Shame on you!" as he playfully nudged her a minute later.

"You're a dirty old man, and a mind-reader, I might add," laughed Carol as he guided her across the street into the restaurant's interior.

The rush hour was over. Only a few patrons were in the front lounge. Jamie asked to be seated in the back room.

"Look out:" called Carol just as she was about to sit down.

"No, Carol, it's not real. It's just a very large stuffed eagle hanging in the ceiling rafters overhead," laughed Jamie.

"God, what a fright," she halfheartedly laughed and caught her breath.

What interested Jamie more was the Roman Catholic Cardinal. Jamie spotted the prelate sitting at a small table in the corner of the room, directly under the eagle. Jamie summoned the waiter and inquired, "Who might His Eminence be?"

"He is one of the Polish Cardinals. His Worship comes here quite frequently when in Rome," replied the waiter.

"I'm familiar with both Cardinal Filipiak of Poznan and Stefan Wyszynski."

"What is this Cardinal's name?" Jamie asked the waiter.

"Cardinal Karol Wojtyla of Krakow."

"Haven't heard of him before," mused Jamie, "and what is your name?"

"Dante," replied the waiter, expecting the usual tourist crack to follow.

Later, Jamie would recall how prophetic this brief-encounter would seem to him.

"What is the good Cardinal having this afternoon?" inquired Jamie.

"Freshly caught fish of the day, smothered in mushrooms, with a carafe of house wine, a white Grottaferrata, and a side order of Caciotta Romana," answered the waiter.

"Sweet sheep's milk cheese," interpreted Jamie as Carol looked on quizzically.

"Shall we dine as the Cardinal, Love?"

Carol nodded enthusiastically, and Jamie said, "Two of the same, please."

"Excellente!" was the waiter's response.

A few minutes later, Jamie poured the wine while Carol sliced the cheese and arranged the platter between the two of them.

"Until London, then," toasted Jamie.

"And a long, quiet, lovely evening," proposed Carol.

"Salute", they both whispered as the glasses tingled upon touching.

Carol let her hand fall casually on Jamie's thigh. Leaning over, she kissed him tenderly on the neck while playfully squeezing his thigh.

She teasingly whispered in his ear, "Is the Cardinal watching?"

"I assure you, Love, Cardinals are immune to street demonstrations of any kind. Oomph!"

Jamie groaned playfully, recovering his balance as Carol almost knocked him out of his seat with a not too gentle shove.

"Wench," he laughed, "You have a wry sense of irreverent humor; I love you for it."

His remark caught them both by surprise. Was it possible, thought Jamie that at last he had found someone who could fill the emptiness he so often felt? It's almost too good to be true, but one can always hope.

"Your entree," said the waiter.

With the help of two large silver spoons he deftly transferred the baked fish from a steaming serving platter to their plates.

"Tea please. English Gray if you have it, for the both of us," said Jamie.

"Dante, we won't be having desert, so you can prepare the bill. Thank you."

Reaching over, Carol pressed his hand in hers and said, "It's a lovely meal, Jamie, but can't we eat quickly?"

"Honestly, I have never felt like this before. Nor have I ever said what I'm saying now. My legs are very, very warm, Love."

Without another word, Jamie filled the wineglasses once more as they hurriedly ate dinner and ignored the tea.

"Dante, the bill, if you please."

Jamie left a large tip and he and Carol rose to leave. Jamie thought he caught the eye of the Cardinal in such a manner as to convince Jamie that both men knew who was the luckier in life.

"Crazy tourists," shouted Dante, as Jamie and Carol exited the restaurant.

The waiter was not the least impressed by the large tip.

"That's no way to treat the Cardinal's favorite dish."

"Taxi!" shouted Jamie

He turned to Carol and said, "At heart, the Italians are really Epicureans, not lovers.

"The thought of women simply whets their appetites. In mathematical terms, you might say it this way. Ardent practitioners of the Karma Sutra have a propensity for material ingestion inversely and geometrically proportional to their erotic endeavors."

"Is that why the waiter yelled at us?" laughingly responded Carol as she nestled into Jamie's arms while the taxi sped towards the Minerva. Carol didn't see the wry smile on Jamie's face as he recalled making a similar remark years ago to a very attractive but overly endowed American housewife.

The woman equated bonbons with amore. Unfortunately for Jamie, she was also the wife of the company president at the time. Jamie later learned she had graduated with honors in mathematics from a prestigious

Midwestern university. The day he left the company, she had sent him a cryptic "good wishes" card on which she had scribbled "Bon Appetite."

Snuggled together in the back of the taxi, Jamie and Carol were happily engaged in conversation as the cab reached its destination. The afternoon walk and the wine, coupled with a slight chill in the air, had taken their toll. The pair slowly unbundled and headed for Carol's room. Carol entered first. She switched on the light and headed for the "telly." It sat just opposite the divan.

“Mind if we watch the tennis matches? The semis of the Italian Open are on today," she tossed the remark over her shoulder as she bent down to adjust the set.

"Splendid idea, Love," yawned Jamie.

He again marveled at her long, curvaceous legs. Carol slipped out of her shoes and joined him on the divan. Removing her jacket, she threw it over a nearby chair. She moved close to Jamie, drawing her feet up under her as she lay back against his chest.

"You forgot to turn on the sound."

"No, I didn't; I like it better this way, you'll see."

Jamie liked it just fine. The two of them pressed closely together. He caressed her arms and shoulders. Carol felt the surface of her skin respond to Jamie's stroking as he alternately played with her legs in the same manner.

"More, more," murmured Carol.

She gathered her skirt high above her hips, deliciously revealing her panties and thighs. Jamie tousled her hair and massaged her scalp while listening to her little sighs and moans. Carol arched her back and rose up to brush his cheek with her own. Jamie caught her silent ache and ran both his hands, spread wide, over the voluptuous mounds of her distended breasts. Her nipples became rock hard. Playing with her tits through the tightly stretched, soft fabric of her jersey, Jamie could sense her tiny bodily tremors, followed by soft cries of pleasure.

After prolonged caressing, Carol murmured, "Please, Love, take me to bed before I melt."

Very slowly, they stood up so as not to disturb their reverie. Carol slid the coffee table out of the way and converted the divan into a queen-size bed. Jamie undressed with the exception of his tightly fitting European briefs of muted, mixed earth tone colors. Carol handed him two large pillows from a nearby dresser. Jamie fluffed them up and stretched out on the bed. Carol stood to the left of the bed. The sun began to set in the western sky. Its light, passing through the window, played delicate shadows across her body as she very slowly undressed for him.

Catching her long blonde hair at the nape of her neck with both hands, Carol walked around the foot of the bed. She stopped just short of

Jamie's reach. Still holding her hair, she thrust upward with her elbows, giving a goddess-like lift to her breasts. Her nipples, now on fire, were diamond hard and bright red. Pivoting to a sitting position on the side of the bed, Jamie caught her small waist in both hands. His fingers lightly manipulated the tiny hollow at the base of her spine. Carol's back arched ever so slightly, as Jamie drew her close to him. With delicate care, his lips brushed back and forth on her upper thighs.

Gently, Jamie eased Carol down on the bed beside him. From her earlier remarks at dinner, he knew she would come very quickly if she hadn't started already. Then he felt the dampness on her legs. He remembered her mind had been playing with his image all week long, and by now her fantasies had reached their limit. Sliding off his briefs, Jamie teased her deliciously all over.

Carol came in rockets and rainbows. Jamie withdrew. He held her languid and drowsy body close in his arms. Although physically spent, she was still emotionally aroused and excited about her new love. To Jamie's great pleasure and surprise, Carol began playing her hands lightly over his taut, muscular body. Her mouth moved with sweetly placed kisses down past his waist.

Later that evening, much later, Jamie called room service.

"Beer and sandwiches all right with you, honey?"

"Whatever," came back a sleepy reply from Carol lying cradled in his arms.

Then, for hours they talked about their feelings, their passions, and their work. "My lover in England, you know, Jamie, the Frenchman, was really a very kind and generous man. But until this evening, I hadn't experienced the real pleasure of total sensuousness. I expect most women never do, at least not the ones I know. We have orgasms, now and then and at certain times animal sexual gratification. You know, making love while holding the image of some rock music star in your head. Actually, I slept with one once. What a downer! He was strung out on drugs. We met at a party. I was alone and thought it was time to put one of my fantasies to the test."

"It was one of the most dreadful experiences of my life. Never, before tonight, have I experienced such incomprehensible joy of erotic loving."

"God! Love, you have marvelous hands. I suspect there's lots more to you than I even dare think about, isn't there, Jamie?"

Carol was still in love with her dream of him. It was a far better beginning and, in fact, a better ending than he had encountered with most women. Carol was first to fall into a deep sleep, still sensually bemused at his ability to utterly exhaust her. She hoped he was as contented as she was. Jamie kissed her neck and shoulders, while his mind dwelled on the trouble women create for themselves. If they could all let go of their anxieties as easily as this lovely creature, we'd all live long and happy lives. His mind still full of the pleasure of her, Jamie, too, fell off to sleep.

It was mid-morning when he awoke. Carol was already up and about. Half-dressed, she sat on the bed next to him and bent down and kissed him several times. Jamie teasingly moved his hands across her bare back, shoulders, and neck. He was about to undo her bra strap when there was a knock on the door.

"Oops," cried Carol as she slid from his grasp, checked her strap, and put on a frilly, softly textured, long-sleeve blouse.

"She announced, "Breakfast for two!"

Jamie protested slightly at the timing. The waiter entered and watched the two of them making funny gestures in pantomime to each other. "Hush, Irish," She said as she signed the breakfast tab, uncovered the food, and moved the large silver tray to the bedside. It was eleven o'clock by the time they finished breakfast.

"My plane leaves at one, Jamie. I have to go to the airport shortly."

"I'll dress and ride with you."

"No, I'm sad enough as it is already. You stay in bed a while longer. When will you come to London?"

"Katherine remember, my daughter is arriving Wednesday. If she agrees, we'll both come to London on Thursday, and she will be with me through Saturday, all right?"

"Whatever, Love, just be there as soon as you can"

"I'm getting lonely already," replied Carol.

"I'll call you Wednesday night to confirm our arrival time."

"Could you meet us at the airport?"

"Who could stop me, Jamie?"

"If you don't mind, Katherine will be going out with us in the evenings, until she leaves for the U.S.A. on Saturday."

"Jamie, I want to meet her very much, please encourage her to come."

"Carol, I'm going to get up and at least see you off in a taxi, okay?"

"Besides, lying here in bed, I'm beginning to feel like a kept man."

"And you love every minute of it, don't you?" said Carol as she lightly slapped his backside.

The taxi pulled out. Jamie waved to her until she was out of sight. *Funny*, thought Jamie, *already I miss her. I'll walk for a while to clear my thoughts*. Later that evening, Jamie placed a call to Father Gault.

"Joe, Jamie here. It's urgent that I see you and Father Rene first thing tomorrow morning, before my ten o'clock meeting with the members of the late Pope's administrative staff."

"Rather short notice, isn't it, Jamie? Let's try for later in the week, shall we?"

"No, Joe, I don't care about schedules or routines. I want to see you and Rene first thing in the morning."

Joe was about to get hard nosed. He thought better of it.

"As you wish. Meet me at Rene's office at 9:00 a.m. sharp. We'll only have a few minutes."

"Thanks, Joe, see you then," Jamie said curtly.

Jamie felt things were going to move along very quickly after tomorrow morning. He wondered if he could maintain control over the events that would follow. He plopped himself down on the bed to watch an old American movie on TV Twice he rang up Carol's number in London, but there was no reply. Probably visiting her father, thought Jamie. I'd better get some shuteye. It's going to be a long day, tomorrow.

He had made up his mind to break into the Vatican broadcasting station tomorrow evening. Although he needed his rest, Jamie tossed and turned all night long due to a constant cast of characters, all with villainous intent, meandering through his dreams.

X. THE SPY NETWORK

The phone rang incessantly. Jamie picked up the receiver. Still clutching his razor in one hand, shaving lather began to drip from his face.

"Hello!" spoke a disgruntled Jamie.

"Did I disturb you Jamie boy?" sang out Father 0'Brien.

"What is it, John? I was just shaving."

"Just friendly concern, Jamie; be very careful, will you? After our talk the other evening, I remembered something important that happened shortly before the death of Pope John Paul. I was reluctant to tell you because you may jump to conclusions which could lead you to some rash action."

"Come on John, you obviously called knowing I would insist you tell me. What is it?" asked Jamie.

"Well," explained Father 0'Brien, "It's true Pope Paul VI held his office for many years and apparently died of old age. Has it occurred to you, Jamie that in less than forty-five days, including the death of Paul, that Pope John and the Russian prelate of Leningrad, Nïckodem, have all died? Nickodem died in a private audience with Pope John Paul."

"Yes, of course John, I realize the implications of that short span of coincidences. Surely you didn't call to remind me of that."

"Can you hold just a minute, Father? I'11 be right back."

Jamie went to his bathroom and grabbed a towel before returning to the phone, leaving the razor on the countertop. "Please continue, John," Jamie again spoke into the phone as he wiped the lather from his partially unshaven face. He cradled the phone in his shoulder blade and toweled the wetness from his hand.

"Jamie," said Father 0'Brien, "there was a fourth death link to the other three. At no time throughout Church history have four such related deaths occurred in such a short time. It seems the fourth link was overlooked in al l the confusion."

"Good Lord, John, do you mean to tell me that another prince of the Church has died in the last month or two?"

"Who was it?" Jamie asked.

His brain had failed to recall such a vital piece of information. A frequent failure of the intellect, overlooking the obvious, is a fact of life for which every magician is forever grateful.

"Does the name Yu Pin mean anything to you, Jamie?"

"Yu Pin? Yu Pin? Cardinal Yu Pin of the People's Republic of Mainland China. Oh, how dumb! You're right, John, he did die just recently."

"Do you remember the circumstances?" groaned Jamie.

"He collapsed at the funeral of Pope Paul VI; died two days later. The medical examination cited cause of death as heart failure. More importantly, Jamie, the Cardinal came to Rome for a private audience with the Pope. Be careful, Jamie. May God go with you."

Jamie heard the click as Father 0'Brien put down the phone, but the line remained open. Then a second click and the familiar monotonous tone began.

"God damn it!" exploded Jamie.

"If I get my hands on those **** ing bastards."

Jamie quickly completed shaving, Put on a black sweater. Angrily snatched his attaché case and sport coat from their respective resting places and stormed out of the apartment.

He arrived at the Gate of St. Anne at 8:45. The Swiss Guard, who by now recognized him on sight, glanced at his pass and let him into the Vatican grounds. Jamie hurried down the Via del Pellegrino and came out of the street facing the north entrance to the Belvedere Palace. No one was in the outer office of Father Rene as Jamie entered.

He went directly to the inner office door. Realizing there was no knob, Jamie knocked to gain entrance. The door swung open. As he entered, Jamie noticed Rene's hand withdrawing from the remote control console. Father Joe stood off to one side.

"Where's your watchdog, Laurent?" inquired Jamie in a hostile tone.

"Called home, sickness in the family," shot back Father Gault.

"I'll bet," mumbled Jamie.

"But let's not waste time in idle sarcasm, Jamie. Why did you call this meeting?"

"Look Joe, if it kills me, I'm going to get to the bottom of this mess."

Under his breath, Joe murmured Jamie just might get his wish if he wasn't careful.

"What was that crack?" Jamie fired back.

For several moments, the two men glared at each other before Father Rene intervened. "Calm down, Father Bolin; after all, we're both here at your request."

"First of all," retorted Jamie, "cut out the Father crap."

"You know I'm not a priest. Gault knows it. As far as I'm concerned, the whole damn Vatican knows it!"

"Take it easy, Mr. Bolin. Sit down, sit down. Relax. Perhaps this assignment is just too difficult. Maybe we can wrap it up here and now, and you can be on your way."

"I'm sure you would both like that very much and if I don't? Perhaps you can help me disappear:"

Father Gault took a step toward Jamie. The husky priest stretched out his arm, extending a very large, menacing hand pointing his forefinger directly at Jamie's face.

"Look here, Bolin, I've had just about enough out of you and your investigation. We had orders to cooperate, against my better judgement. Now just how quickly can you finish up and get the hell out of here?"

Jamie stifled a small smile. He knew his plan was beginning to work. The cool exterior of the priests was beginning to crack. If he could survive the day, he might, with the help of the Italian police, set a trap for his quarry. Regaining his composure, Jamie threw some blarney in the direction of Father Rene to see his reaction.

"Originally I thought the assassination theory was ridiculous, but for ten grand American, who was I to complain? But now I know the real reason why the Pope was murdered."

Father Rene was visibly shaken. He appealed to Father Gault to explain away Jamie's accusation.

"What ridiculous notion gave you an idea that there was a conspiracy in the Vatican?" asked Father Joe.

"Conspiracy? Did I say conspiracy? I didn't say it, Joe. You did," responded Jamie.

"Look Joe, I need some information, and then I'll tell you what I know, deal?"

"Okay: what do you want to know?" asked Joe in an apologetic tone.

"What is the capacity of the Vatican's radio network, both in terms of long and short-wave channels and the nature of her broadcasts over a twenty-four-hour time span?" asked Jamie.

"Why didn't you ask me that on our tour last week?" inquired the priest.

"Because at the time, it didn't seem important. It does now," responded Jamie.

"The Vatican emits worldwide broadcasts every day in some thirty to forty languages as well as Latin and English. Many programs reach behind the Iron Curtain and have a greater impact on people in Russia and Eastern Europe than does Radio Free Europe. The programs vary in content from daily masses and religious music to priestly messages of hope and encouragement. The transmitters operate on twenty or more short-wave bands and five to ten medium wave bands."

"Of what possible interest could this information be to you?" asked Father Gault.

Both priests exploded out of their chairs when Jamie replied, "I believe that the Holy Roman Catholic Church operates the biggest clandestine intelligence network in the world. Furthermore, I believe the Pope was murdered by ultra-conservative elements of the Church because of secret accords being negotiated between the Vatican and Marxist communists in Africa, the Soviet Union, Latin and South America. I suspect that Pope Paul VI did not die of natural causes and that the two cardinals from China and Russia who were privy to these negotiations were assassinated as well."

"My God, Bolin, are you going public with these wild allegations?" shouted an incredulous Father Gault.

"Look, two attempts have already been made on my life, and I am under constant surveillance. My phone is monitored around the clock."

Stretching the truth, Jamie continued, oblivious to interruptions and stammering denials by both men.

"I have substantial, well documented proof, and should anything happen to me, the information will become public knowledge within twenty-four hours."

"What do you want from us?" replied Father Rene.

"I want you to call off the dogs for seventy-two hours, and let me complete my investigation. If I'm wrong, perhaps you can convince me. My untimely death would be absolute proof of my published evidence."

Without waiting for a reply, Jamie excused himself and left for his ten o'clock appointment at the Apostolic Palace.

The priests stood with clenched fists, mouths agape, as Jamie left the office. He wondered if his bluff would work. At the very least, it would buy him some time. Father Gault moved to Rene's desk and activated the switch on the console, securely sealing the office entrance.

Turning to Father Rene, he smiled and said, "I believe Jamie is beginning to grasp the situation, but of course he doesn't have any proof.

He could, however, do a lot of harm by pure speculation. No reputable news service would touch his story without substantial proof."

"He has a nice touch though," said Rene, "and runs a good bluff."

"He's your responsibility, Joe. What next?"

"I think it's time I arranged a little meeting of my own with our Mr. Bolin, and perhaps I can get him to see the light."

"I know just where to find him this evening."

"I believe we have just caught a common sneak thief."

"What in the world are you up to now, Joe? Just hurry up and clean up the mess, whatever it takes."

Unaware of the conversation taking place between Father Rene and Gault, Jamie rather smugly entered the Apostolic Palace. He felt very pleased with the turn of events. He had forgotten one very important legal technicality. Vatican City was a sovereign state with its own courts, prosecutor, judges and laws.

Jamie had picked the worst possible time and place to confront the conservative elements of the Curia. He was on Vatican property, and there was no Pope. If Jamie's suspicions were correct, it could mean his death. No one would ever know what happened to him. His grandstand play was dumber than bluffing in seven card poker with a three-card fandango in the hole.

Jamie walked up the stairs to the third floor and found the right conference room. Inside, he introduced himself to two older men.

"Pleased to meet you, Father Carey," replied Jamie.

"Just call me Francis, Father," said the priest.

"And this is Mr. Suti, correct?" inquired Jamie.

"Vincent or Vince, Father, please, whichever makes you more comfortable," spoke the gracious layperson.

Both men were genuinely friendly. Father Francis had been instructed to fully inform Father Bolin on what took place between Pope John Paul I and his staff when the Pope had asked for an update on the Salt II talks between Russia and the United States.

"We have a lot of ground to cover, Father Bolin. May we begin?"

"By all means, Francis and make that Jamie, will you."

Vincent Suti spoke up, describing how military and political data was presented to the pope, At the Pope's briefing one team of assistants represented the Russian interests and another team represented the United States. Each team would describe their military might and what military advantages their enemy possessed. The team representing the Russian interests was most concerned about the American thermonuclear weapons, transportation, storage and delivery systems.

Each team in turn would privately disclose to the Pope their strategies before entering into simulated negotiations with the other team.

The teams acted as if they were the military and political leaders of the two superpowers. Each team employed to the best of their ability the logic of each group they represented. From such a sophisticated briefing, the Pope could ascertain the relative strengths and weaknesses of each government.

Vince continued, "If you will join us it the conference table, Jamie, I'll represent the Americans and Father Francis will represent the Russians. You, of course, will be getting a very condensed version of the original briefing given Pope John Paul I. His briefing required in excess of five hours."

Jamie was diverted to the head of the table, and Father Francis and Vincent sat on opposite sides of the table. Each man had access to a set of electronic controls from which they could project motion pictures, slides, document enlargements, markers and pointers on to an 18-foot by 7-foot silver screen. If necessary, they could also project closed circuit television and videocassettes.

Jamie looked on as he watched half of the opposite wall slide behind a recess in the lower section, exposing the large projection screen. At the same time, Vincent Suti depressed a button on his console. The windows were shuttered and three small spotlights were activated, one light over each man's head, bathing them in a soft glow. The remainder of the room was pitch black. Jamie realized he was in the Vatican War Room or at least a facsimile of one that was probably buried deep underground.

Vincent began the presentation by displaying and commenting on the changes in American military might over a fifteen-year period.

"The United States presently has over 8,000 hydrogen bombs besides its already immense atomic arsenal. The United States still holds a decisive edge in most weapon systems, but the Russians now lead in the number of tanks, bombers, and submarines. To counter this loss in conventional weapon superiority, America is developing a neutron bomb and a very inexpensive cruise missile."

"Russia has a tremendous first strike capability in their SS-18 intercontinental ballistic missile system. A single missile can deliver multiple fifty megaton atomic warheads. Next in priority of concerns is the general state of Russian troop readiness along the borders of Western Europe, combined with overwhelming Russian tank superiority."

"Vince, what is the size of the U.S.A. military Budget?" asked Jamie.

"The United States spends over one-hundred billion dollars a year on its military budget. Would you like to comment, Francis?"

"Yes, thank you Vincent, if Jamie doesn't have any more questions."

"No, please go ahead Father," urged Jamie.

The priest projected onto the screen a comparison of Russian weapon capability for the years 1963 vs 1978:

Soviet Union	1963	1978
Troops (millions of men)	3.9	4.5
Combat Planes	Unknown	9,000
Transport and Short Take-Off	Unknown	3,000
Ocean freight Tonnage (millions)	4	16
Combat Naval Vessels	165	250
Submarines	430	234
Artillery Pieces	Unknown	9,000
Tanks	36,000	45,000
Intercontinental Ballistic Missiles	65	1,500

"It should be obvious from this chart that the Russians were gearing up for an all-out conventional offensive war supported by enormous atomic missile capability. Their dramatic increase in deadweight ocean freight would indicate developing a capacity to control key countries even further away than Eastern Europe, thereby widening Russia's sphere of influence beyond inland borders."

The priest paused to light a cigarette and then continued, "It is estimated the Russians could overrun Western Europe in a week. Only West Germany, if warned in time, could repulse a Russian invasion and only if the Germans resorted to atomic weapons. The key phrase warned in time left the statistical probability of that likelihood at near zero. Despite evidence to the contrary, we do not anticipate an attack on Western Europe because the implied Russian threat accomplishes their real objectives."

"1) It provides absolute control over Eastern Europe.

2) It brings terrible pressure on West European governments who in turn keep the United States guessing as to the reliability of NATO. Such confusion misdirects the Americans while the Russian bear continues its magic of deception and slight-of-hand tricks. The real tip-off to Russia's intent is hidden in the following figures."

Father Francis, with the aid of a slide projector, then threw onto the screen in large block print:

THE MILITARY HARDWARE SALES TO THIRD WORLD GOUNTRIES BY RUSSIA IS F IVE BILLION DOLLARS A YEAR.

THE CURRENT NUMBER OF RUSSTAN TECHNICIANS IN AFRICA ALONE IS 9,000!

Father Francis Carey continued, "Due to inflation, the United States military expenditures in real dollars had not changed significantly since 1965. Soviet Russia had increased her expenditures in real dollars from forty billion to one hundred fifty-eight billion dollars, a fourfold increase in thirteen years. The Russians are not really concerned at all about American cruise missiles now."

"Ten years ago NATO might have in fact considered attacking Russia if NATO had such a weapon, but today it only represented parity, and NATO is considered nothing but a paper tiger. Italy and France are as good as Communistic, already. Even Japan, America's Far East ally, saw the handwriting on the wall and is turning towards China."

"In possibly ten years or less, a very strange and perplexing world situation is likely to become a reality. America's greatest, and for all practical purposes, only potent military allies will be England, Germany and Israel. The series of events leading to such a scenario would be greatly accelerated if Iran becomes a Marxist country."

Father Carey activated another touch button that returned the screen to its hiding place behind the wall; un-shuttered the windows and bathed the room in soft light. The electronic consoles automatically lowered out of sight beneath the conference table.

Jamie asked, "What had the reaction of the late Pope John Paul been to this general review of the comparative military strengths of the Russians and the Americans? What would be the impact of a Salt II agreement on both countries?"

Vincent Suti responded, "Surprisingly, the Pope's first question had dealt with the destructive power of atomic and hydrogen weapons."

"And?" asked Jamie.

To which Vincent replied, "A short explanation had been given regarding modern weapons in the unlikely possibility of a third world war. It seems that each of the two atomic bombs dropped on Japan in 1945 were in the neighborhood of twenty kilotons, meaning each had the explosive power of twenty-thousand tons of TNT. Whereas currently, a Soviet SS-18 can deliver to a designated intercontinental target, multiple warheads of 50 megatons each."

"A fifty megaton bomb is equivalent in explosive power to fifty million tons of TNT. Therefore, the power contained in a single atomic warhead would be equivalent to, shall we say, in American terms, of covering the entire state of Michigan four feet deep in sticks of dynamite and then lighting a match to it! Americans, always believing that bigger is better, have perfected hydrogen weapons. As you saw on the screen, they now have at least 8,000 such bombs. A hydrogen weapon the same size as an atomic weapon can generate 100 times more explosive force."

"What then," asked Jamie, "with enough destructive power on both sides to destroy the entire world a thousand times over, was the real purpose behind the Salt II agreements?"

Father Carey said that too had been explained to the Pope.

"American politicians require paper victories to reassure naive voters that everything possible is being done to make the world safe and peaceful. Congress can then increase military expenditures so that such agreements can be reached, a true paradox."

"The Russians love the game of playing with the elected and appointed officials, who the American people, in their greed for an unreal world without discomfort, keep sending them. While the Americans worry over nuclear holocaust and the Russians play their role of poor dumb bureaucrats trapped in their own system. American politicians stroke the people while the Russian Bear, one paw behind its back, gobbles up the world bit by bit, piece by piece. The Americans are always kept busy watching his other paw pounding the table in front of them. A magician's magician; if you know what I mean."

Father Carey snuffed out his cigarette and said, "As a group, we told the Pope that the western multinational companies represented a real economic force in the world fed by western scientific technology. As a political force, the western world was, if you'll excuse the expression, like a bad Polish joke. Salt II was meaningless to the Russians except as a diversionary device. They simply went about their real business of subversion. The Pope thanked the staff for their thoroughness and adjourned the meeting. He had given no hint as to why he had requested such a briefing, and his comments during the meeting were short and of a technical nature."

Father Carey and Vincent Suti sat with Jamie a while longer and discussed various aspects of the overall Russian strategies for the advancement of world Marxist doctrine. The conclusion was that Russia didn't care about Marx or Lenin or anything else. Some old men had gained power fifty years ago, learned how to use it to stay in power, and now they, as well as everyone else in Russia, had a government and a system that no one knew how to dismantle or change. Politically, the Russians had to function much like the Church did economically, through expansion and growth.

By now it was one o'clock in the afternoon. Jamie thanked both men for their disclosures surrounding the Salt II briefing for the late Pope and left the Palace conference room. Some time later, Jamie sat in the living room of his suite at the Vatican, realizing that the world he knew was obsolete. Universal forces were once again at work. Despite the silly efforts of all the governments and all the religions of the World, once again the human race, grabbed by the scruff of its neck, would be shaken unmercifully one more time, in the hope of knocking some sense into its childish head. The Universe was growing very tired of its shoddy plaything.

Jamie, having finished his lunch, stretched out on the couch to take a nap. At first he didn't sleep very soundly. Images kept cascading through his head in a surrealistic ballet of popes, cardinals, dollar bills, planes and tanks, gigantic buildings and atomic explosions.

His subconscious mind sought her out. Smilingly, she beckoned to him, arms outstretched, and peacefully he fell away into a dreamless sleep. Jamie woke up at 3:40 PM. It was five minutes before his Seiko alarm was due to go off. He went into the bathroom to shower and shave. At 4:05 there was a knock on the door. Jamie went to open it, expecting to greet Cardinal Gantin of Benin, a member of the Curia under Pope John Paul I, and the only black prince of the Church residing in Vatican City.

Standing in the doorway was a tall, very handsome, young black priest in his middle thirties. He was immaculately dressed in his austere black garb and white Roman collar.

"Father Bolin?" he inquired.

"Yes," answered Jamie.

"I bring apologies from His Excellency, Cardinal Gantin. He was called out of the city on urgent business. I'm Monsignor Jack Richards. I was sent by the Cardinal's office to be of any service I can to you in the Cardinal's absence."

Momentarily, Jamie was disappointed. From a personal point of view, he had heard of the reputation of the Cardinal as a brilliant and incisive mind on African affairs and had been looking forward to probing that mind. From a purely reporter's viewpoint of gathering information, Jamie was much more likely to be able to dig deeper into the affairs of the Vatican by speaking with a member of the Cardinal's staff rather than with the Cardinal, himself.

"Won't you come in, Father Richards?" said Jamie.

"I'm sorry the Cardinal has been called away. I hope to eventually have the pleasure of seeing him."

As the two men talked, Jamie learned that by birth the priest was an African. At the age of fourteen, a white Protestant missionary couple ministering to his village had adopted him. The next year Jack and his parents had been sent back to America where they stayed for five years, and then the couple returned to Africa without him because having finished his high school education, they had enrolled him in Yale University theological studies. The year after he enrolled, his foster parents were murdered when a terrorist group swept through his native village.

At Yale, Jack Richards became acquainted with several older Catholic priests who befriended him. The priests were taking post-graduate studies there. They sat by the hour and discussed theology and race relations as practiced under the guise of Christianity. Through these discussions, Jack had been converted to Catholicism. He attended a seminary after graduation from Yale and was ordained ten years ago. Father Richards then spent the next eight years in Africa and the last two here in Vatican City.

Jamie, counting backwards in years as the priest talked, recognized that the man, through experience, had been privileged to watch his race emerge as a power in the United States during the early sixties and had been present in Africa at the time western colonialism had ended. Jamie was anxious to listen to the priest's views on the Church's attitude toward the emerging African nations.

Jamie asked, "Would you care for something to drink, Father, before you tell me about the purpose of the meeting between Cardinal Gantin and the Pope several weeks ago?"

"I'll have some tea, please."

Jamie called room service before returning to his location on the couch and urged the priest to begin.

"It seemed the Pope had wanted the Cardinal to simply give him a rundown on Africa, particularly as it pertained to the relationships between the Marxists, the priests and the tribal families," said Father Richards.

"I caution you, Father Bolin, that the information I'm now imparting to you will contain my own feelings and understandings of those relationships."

Jamie nodded his head, indicating he knew only too well the distortions that were created in the process of secondhand descriptions of an event.

Father Jack Richards spent several hours talking about his native land. As a brilliant and well-educated person who had great ideals and a consuming knowledge of his subject matter, this opportunity to speak openly acted as a catharsis for his own emotional insecurities. His narration of African history was so vivid; Jamie could almost see the elephants stampeding across the plains and the Zulus warring against other tribes.

For the past hour, Father Jack had elaborated on the current status of Africa.

"It is a pawn to be exploited either by multi-national companies or by Russian, European or American political interests. On the other hand, one cannot take a simplistic view of blacks against whites. In many cases, there was more hatred amongst blacks, themselves. And the

Egyptians, represent over ten percent of the population of Africa. Then the priest spoke about the Zulus, the long ago disenfranchised rulers of many African tribes.

"It wasn't until the end of the seventeenth century that the Boars settled in Southern Africa. Until that time, In their conquest of the region, the Zulus literally annihilated many other tribes. The Kaffirs, for instance, lost ninety percent of their population in less than thirty years warring with the Zulus."

"In other parts of Africa, educated black Africans have one or more languages in common with their former colonial rulers: French, Dutch, English, Portuguese or Spanish; whereas, in the lower portion of Africa, the Zulus controlled many tribes of Bantu Negroes who spoke over 250 different dialects. Most of the territorial control of Africa, until the middle of the eighteenth century, was gained by running battles between opposing tribes."

"By 1950, only one hundred years later, there were only three countries in Africa ruled by the people who inhabited them, Liberia, Ethiopia and Egypt. Today, only twenty-eight years later, whole new nations have appeared. Except for South Africa and Rhodesia, all of Africa is now a continent of recently formed independent nations. In many cases, their internal tribal differences are far greater than their previous differences with the colonial powers. Today there are only three great forces in Africa: Marxist communists trained in Russia. Catholic priests trained in Rome and multi-national company employees."

Father Richards paused for a sip of tea and then continued.

"The Marxists and the village priests have much in common in theory. In practice they are light-years apart. In many cases they cooperate with each other for mutual benefit. At the same time, neither group trusts the other."

"What about the future?" asked Jamie.

The priest answered, "If South Africa falls into the hands of the Communists, the Church has one of three choices: get out of Africa, cooperate fully with the Marxists, or attempt, with the help of the multi-national companies, to stalemate the Marxists for as long as possible. In the end, the Marxists would win."

"Why," asked Jamie, "is South Africa the key?"

"Because," explained the priest, "it would be economically advantageous for the Russians to move in and exploit the resources and to control the world's supply of gold. Such a move would create havoc with Western monetary policies. However, if South Africa could form a truly democratic government, the multi-nationals would be encouraged to up their investments in many African countries. The Church could go about its business without total domination by Marxist governments."

Jamie then asked, "What will most likely happen?"

Father Richards answered, "Believe it or not, the future of Africa might well hinge on the decisions of one man, the Pope, and one country, South Africa. It could go either way."

The priest then said a peculiar thing that saddened him greatly.

"The historical truth of the interrelationships of Africans, Europeans and Americans has been so distorted that all sides share the blame."

Jamie asked for a further explanation.

The priest, shaking his head, said, "If only the whites had been willing to teach and the Africans had been willing to learn. If both races had not consorted to buy and sell people, Africans would now be ready to enjoy the greatest prosperity in their history."

Jamie knew only too well how right the priest was, as Father Jack continued. "The white man hadn't invaded Africa and stolen slaves. Whites had brought their ships only to coastal cities. Tribe after tribe sold their enemies freely and willingly. Yesterday's seller might be today's slave, as each tribe won or lost in its hunt for human products. Then, after two hundred years in America, the blacks gained their freedom little by little. Not because Lincoln was a great emancipator, but because the system became uneconomical."

"Slowly and painfully the blacks tried to crawl back up the ladder of human dignity after being slaves for so long a period. By 1945, the whites began to respect their courage shown in World War II. Black athletic ability was already legend because of such people as Jesse Owen and Joe Louis, to be followed shortly by the baseball feats of Jackie Robinson. Their small and growing private educational institutions turned out articulate and brilliant individuals. One man had become a legend in his own time, Luther Burbank."

Father Jack began pacing the floor, shaking his head.

"Then came the Supreme Court decisions abolishing school segregation and job discrimination, and just as the three hundred year-old goal was in sight, they blew it. 'Get whitey' and 'cheat the system' became the battle cries encouraged by radical elements, perhaps Marxist oriented, but certainly socialistic in nature. Liberal white Wasps, Jews and Catholics joined with the radicals."

"Conservative middle-class Negroes, who knew better, sheepishly stood by and watched as an entire generation or perhaps two generations of Negro children were lost to society. Negro political leaders opted for economic gains and power. Now, twenty years later, they still complain about discrimination." "Had the right decisions been made, the American Negro movement could have been a positive force in African affairs before it was too late. Now the American Negro has to wake up and start all over again."

"America could have used their strength and Africa their example. But in trying to leapfrog economically, without discipline and basic educational skills, American Negroes have become their own worst enemy and now those whites opposed to integration can sit back and say, 'I told you so.' If Africa, whose majority is black, not white, follows the lead of its American cousins, then only the fear instilled by Marxist political-type processes can keep their nations functioning. The Church would be forbidden to develop an educational system in competition with the state."

Father Richards finished by stating what both he and Jamie knew to be true.

"Unless African nations attract industrialization and encourage the whites to provide black children with the best possible education, then the road ahead will be long and bloody. Likewise, the Negroes in America are sitting on a powder keg. America for better or worse is the most sophisticated technologically oriented society the world has ever known. It is likely to maintain, if not expand, its leadership in the future."

"The American Negro community cannot afford to be well fed, well housed, well dressed and not well educated. In times of deep recession or depression, they will become an enormous welfare drag on a faltering economy. When any majority's economic interests are seriously threatened, an uneducated minority is the usual victim. In times of inflation, black purchasing power disproportionately decreases."

"African and American Negroes' number one priority should be to staff their schools with the finest white teaching talent in the world. The Negro community should back them one hundred percent on discipline; demanding absolute proficiency in reading, writing and arithmetic.

These teachers should have great community respect and thereby create an elite educational system. Only teachers black and white who have expert teaching skills in mathematics, phonics, science and literature would be eligible for the country's highest-paid teaching positions. And then, get rid of all the layers of administration and social service functions."

Here it was eight o'clock in the evening, and Jamie had been distracted from his original purpose while Father Richards spoke of the needs and priorities of his race. From the tone of his voice, Jamie could tell the priest knew it would never happen, and he was almost certain Africa would remain in turmoil for many years to come.

Marxist terrorists or military strongmen would form one government after another. Only by warring on their neighbors could they distract their people from their poverty. If the multi-national companies pulled out, Africa's only customer would be Russia, and Cuba knew what that meant. Would Africa soon follow the same road?

As the black priest took his leave with an apology to Jamie for becoming so adamant in his convictions and for staying so long, Jamie's mind drifted off when he said goodbye. Putting himself in the Pope's place without knowing any more than he did, surely the pontiff would steer the course of the Church toward accommodation with Marxist nationals and in particular Soviet Russia, for what other choice did he really have?

By now it was very dark outside, and Jamie had to complete one more assignment yet this evening. He gave himself two hours to be certain that not many residents of the Papal City would be out and around. Picking up the phone, Jamie ordered a hot roast beef sandwich with mashed potatoes and gravy and a large glass of milk. No, he cancelled the milk and asked for water instead. If he ran into any trouble tonight, he didn't want to be sleepy. He wanted to be very alert when he broke into the Vatican radio station. If what he suspected were true, then perhaps he would have enough proof to take his story to a publisher.

This morning he had dressed in dark blue trousers, black turtleneck sweater and black walking shoes with rubber soles and heels. If he hadn't donned his herringbone sport coat, any mystery buff would have immediately taken him for a second-story man. In his attaché case he had stuffed a dark blue windbreaker. Having eaten dinner and relaxed, Jamie tossed his sport coat aside and donned the windbreaker. On Vatican grounds, he would look like any other priest out for a late night constitutional.

Checking to be certain he had the key to his suite and his mini-bike metallic card, Jamie reached inside his attaché case once more and drew out a penlight, a small crowbar and his compact black, electronics tool kit. The kit held such unlikely tools as a miniature metric screwdriver, wire splicers, socket wrenches and various circuit padder devices and test probes.

The case itself could be held in the palm of one hand but was rather thick. Built into the bottom, top and sides of the case were special meter-reading devices and frequency monitors. Jamie was not necessarily a paragon of virtue when it came to obtaining information. He never traveled without his little tool case

One set of items was really extraordinary; tiny thermite explosives disguised as resistors for blowing off locks or hinges and the like. He had purchased several hundred of them one night years ago in an Irish pub from a disgruntled IRA man who needed some drinking money and showed his box of wares to everyone in the pub. The man had been on his way to Ulster in Northern Ireland and was none too happy about it.

Once outside the villa, Jamie headed due west toward Vatican City high ground where Father Gault had previously driven him. After jogging for about ten minutes, he came over a small crest of the hill and not fifty yards away, outlined in the night sky, stood the radio station. The grounds around the station were not well lighted. A haze had begun to settle due to the night dampness.

The eerie appearance of the station took on the form of a crippled praying mantis that glowed erratically in the dark. There were banks of fluorescent lights over the main entrance, and off to the side of the building, Jamie saw a bright, single floodlight over the emergency exit door he had tampered with on his previous visit. Looking upward through the haze, he saw warning beacons for low-flying aircraft.

Adjacent to the tower, reflected moonlight penetrated the haze. Jamie scrutinized the large parabolic dish, telltale evidence of a microwave relay station, a direct line-of-sight alternate means of communication with the other Vatican broadcast facilities located in the city of Rome.

The complexity of the exterior structural nature of the broadcast and relay facilities plus the five million dollars worth of radio transmitters inside the building attested to the sophistication of the Vatican's communications network. Jamie was very anxious to get inside and verify his hunch that Father Joe had not fully informed him of the complete network capabilities.

He cautiously approached the emergency exit. He could feel the perspiration rising to the surface of his palms and forearms. Jamie could not afford to hesitate for a moment once he placed himself directly under the exit door floodlight. Its heavy gauge Lucite type enclosure made it impractical to think of breaking the light. The noise, God knows, would carry how far out here?

Reaching into his poplin jacket, he withdrew a three-inch diameter rubber disc, on the back of which was a strap secured at both ends to the disc. Jamie placed the four fingers of his left hand through the strap. His thumb was positioned over the top of a small protuberance on the side of the disc. The undersurface of the object served as a large suction cup. He quickly moved past the door. His left hand pressed the suction device onto its outer surface.

Now he would know if the tape over the locking cam had been discovered. Pulling on the suction cup, the door failed to yield. In desperation, Jamie rotated his shoulders as a street fighter might; trying to land a haymaker. The door swung open. As it did, his thumb released itself from the air valve maintaining the vacuum. The suction device came free from the door. Jamie spun inside. With his right hand, he caught the inside door leverbar, pulling the door shut behind him.

It had seemed like an eternity, but he had only been exposed outside the entrance for less than four seconds.

Jamie retraced the route of his previous tour. He came to the catwalk leading to the large wire-mesh glass, viewing window. Down below were the broadcast transmitters that he had seen the other day. Jamie spotted a door in the transmitter room marked "Absolutely No Admittance, Authorized Personnel Only". What made it stand out in his mind was the language in large red stencil. It was in Latin. Now Jamie had to get inside the transmitter room and then down the steps to the floor level.

There was no one in sight as he turned the knob on the outside of the steel door next to the viewing window. The door was locked tight. Jamie ran a slender steel ruler up and down the door edge and found the door was secured by a deadbolt on the inside. Opening his tool kit, he removed several items. He fastened the suction device to the viewing window immediately adjacent to the deadbolt location on the inside of the door.

Jamie sealed the air valve with a small plug and placed a circumferential glasscutter in a blind hole located in the center of the suction cup device. Pressing on the outside of the glasscutter, he cut a one-eighth inch circular slot part way through the plate glass until he reached the depth of the wire mesh.

He removed the cutting tool and lit a miniature oxy-acetylene torch. He moved the torch slowly around the circumference of the slot cut in the glass until the wires melted. Reinserting the glasscutter, he cut through all but the last eighth-inch of the remaining glass circle. Holding onto the strap of the suction device, he pushed slightly forward, snapping the glass free. He withdrew the suction cup holding a five-inch circle of glass.

Two minutes after unfastening the deadbolt, Jamie glued the cut glass back in place, scampered down the several flights of stairs and was zigzagging across the floor of the transmitter room toward his objective. He heard an abrupt noise to his left. He flattened himself against one of the transmitter housings and held his breath. Several minutes passed, and he heard no further sound.

Peering cautiously around the transmitter, he saw no one and chastened his overactive nerves. Ten steps later, Jamie found himself alongside the room he wanted so much to inspect. On the outside of the door was an electronic combination locking mechanism. He was in luck, because the lock itself was a conventional cam action, the only difference being that the lock was solenoid controlled by an electronic system.

Using one of the thermite explosives, Jamie blew open the lock. If anybody was inside the room, Jamie would be caught. It was too late to go back now. One turn of the knob and he stood at the entrance to the room. Inside were several dozen devices that Jamie had suspected he would find. Two other devices surprised him. Most of the devices were code transmitting and receiving scramblers tied into continuous printout devices.

The units functioned automatically; remote terminals for input or output transmission were also on line. The two devices that surprised him indicated the high level of technology being employed. The devices were a photo transmitting device coupled with a scrambler and its companion receiver device. This last item was a very complex, high-priority system. To be certain of its purpose, Jamie had to measure its input and output voltage and current levels as well as its signal generation frequencies. He had to activate a keyboard to generate those frequencies.

It took him about twenty minutes to examine the unit. It was a scrambler comprised of a digital to analogue resolution. The analogue computer portion had a changeable set of parameters keyed by on line computer signals to translate in any one of a number of languages. The computers were triggered by the initial noise generator signal. No noise generator signal, no activation. Once activated by a given noise generator, the operator had to speak in the correct language or no message was transmitted through the scrambler device.

Tearing off several of the data transmission sheets, Jamie had hard evidence of at least one kind. The Vatican could and did operate a worldwide network of short-wave radio transmitters requiring a high degree of secrecy. Their scrambler devices and coding techniques would make the KGB and the CIA blush.

Jamie thought he heard someone trying to enter the outside room and decided he had better get out before he was discovered. His luck so far had been almost too good. Crossing the room as quickly as he could, he raced up the stairs, retracing his original route. Once outside the transmitting room and back on the platform overlooking it, Jamie slowed down. He folded the data sheets neatly and tucked them in the pocket of his jacket.

Walking down the hall, his adrenaline pumping for all it was worth, Jamie kept telling himself to calm down.He reached the exit door and began to relax; believing the worst was over. He opened the exit door, and a terrible blow to the stomach doubled him up in excruciating pain. Before he could gasp for breath, a knee slammed into his mouth. In agony, he crumbled on the grass outside. His hands covered his belly as if to pray away the pain.

Turning his head, Jamie rolled on the ground. He saw two pairs of shoes greeting him at eye level, each pair firmly set in place. Twisting his head upward, he could feel the blood warming his chin as it spurted from a large gash in his lower lip. The two upright bodies appeared mammoth and grotesque in size as his vision alternately blurred and cleared. A foot descended coming down hard on his outstretched ankle. Another foot grazed his face as it pinned his opposite shoulder to the ground.

Two sets of eyes stared down a long, vertical tunnel at him. A large forearm extended itself outright, while at the same time imparting a snapping motion to its attached wrist. Even in his dazed condition, Jamie's muscles involuntarily tightened. He saw the gleam of the five-inch switchblade knife in the glow of the floodlight overhead. Jamie's eyes moved to catch the figure silhouetted in the doorway behind the two men.

There was no mistaking the muscular frame and quick pair of hands slightly cupped and hanging loosely at his sides. This time Father Gault's face took on the appearance of an avenging eagle. Teutonic hardness permeated every pore.

If Gault and his friends were trying to frighten him, they certainly had succeeded. Then, as Jamie saw the knife plunging downward, his worst fears were confirmed. No one was going to warn him, question him, or even torture him. He was simply going to be murdered here and now, not for what he already knew but for what he might find out.

Gathering all the remaining strength his body could muster, Jamie rolled away from the two men. His head came round again to gain his bearings before he sprang to his feet. He thought his eyes were playing tricks on him. Overhead, he saw the switchblade spiral off into the night like an errant rocket misfiring over Cape Canaveral.

He had jumped to his feet to ward off what he believed to be a fatal attack. His vision cleared just in time to see the second of the two men leave the ground, lifting upward as if hit by a two-ton truck head on. The other man standing just to Jamie's right hadn't even had the good sense to fall down even when it had become apparent that the arm that had held the switchblade was broken at the elbow.

"Don't just stand there, Jamie, help me bind up these two," said Father Joe.

Glancing down, Jamie saw the short piece of rope tossed at his feet. It reminded him of the type poor priests use to hold large crucifixes dangling from their waists. The last thing he remembered before passing out, as the pain from getting up exploded inside his head, was the splotches of blood along the spotless piece of white rope.

When he woke up, Jamie was lying on the couch in his suite in the Villa of Pius VI. Father Gault was hovering over him protectively. He removed an ice pack from Jamie's swollen mouth and lips.

Jokingly, Joe said, "'Jamie, it is a bad idea to lead with your head."

Jamie grimaced from the ill-timed advice. He sat upright, and the priest placed a large cushion behind his back. Taking the ice pack in his hand, Jamie alternately questioned Father Joe and applied the ice to his lips. Without answering his questions, Father Joe insisted Jamie sit still. The priest checked to see if his pupils were dilated, indicating a concussion.

Joe encouraged Jamie to move certain fingers on command. Satisfied no internal damage had been done, the priest helped Jamie into the bedroom and laid him down for the night. Jamie protested, but Joe said he would be back first thing in the morning along with Father Rene to explain everything. No sooner had the priest covered Jamie with a heavy blanket, then he fell off to sleep. Father Joe switched out the light and left the suite. He rubbed his right elbow and bicep as he walked out of the villa toward the waiting car.

After all, he thought, it had been several years since he had executed that particular attack movement reserved for disabling two unsuspecting opponents simultaneously. As a priest, Joe abhorred the application of violence. As a man skilled in the art of self-defense, as taught by the Shinto priests of ancient Japan, he was elated that the passage of time had not dulled his reflexes

Joe's car pulled away from the villa. The two men sat in the back seat, securely bound. One man's arm was in a makeshift splint. Father Gault, sitting in front, next to the driver, recalled in dreamlike fashion his movements during the attack sequence. Such vivid stop-action flash-backs permitted analysis of any flaws in technique. He gave himself an "A" minus.

Joe pictured himself coming through the emergency exit door. He had followed Jamie to the radio station. He had amused himself at Jamie's cloak and dagger activities. Joe had intended to catch up with him outside and convince Jamie to return to America before he was seriously injured or murdered. Then he saw the two men standing over Jamie, one with a knife poised to kill. Automatically, he came to the defense of the helpless prey lying on the ground.

Reflexively taking two precisely measured steps, Joe sank down on his right leg and locked his left knee. He moved his left leg in an exaggerated extended arc. The terminal velocity of his foot generated so much force as it contacted the forearm holding the knife, that the blow not only propelled the knife upward and free of the man's hand, but shattered the man's elbow upon impact. Joe's Left foot had returned to the ground, and the priest dipped forward on the balls of both feet. He cocked his right elbow in the manner of a defensive lineman, just as the second man turned toward him. At precisely that instant, the priest generated maximum velocity in his compressed calves and thighs. His elbow caught the man squarely under the chin and drove him upward, knocking him senseless. Had Joe thrust his elbow inward at the same time, the man would have died instantly of a broken neck. The priest only intended to disable not kill.

Tomorrow, Father Joe would tell Jamie everything he knew about the death of Pope John Paul. Just now he wanted to get some sleep. His driver dropped him at his residence and then headed out of Vatican City towards Rome.

XI. THE VATICAN GUARDIANS

Jamie barely heard the phone ringing in his ear. He reached up out of the soft blanket and fumbled for the receiver.

"Uh, who is this?"

"Oh! Joe, can't you call back, I'm feeling very groggy."

"What time is it? Seven AM. What day? That urgent?"

"All right, give me half an hour and I'll be ready. Joe, about yesterday . . ."

Jamie heard a soft click, then the disconnect. Tenty minutes later, he let Father Joe and Father Rene into the suite and waved them over to the nearby couch.

"Really have a terrible headache; just let me sit down for a moment. I'll be just fine. Joe, how can I ever thank you for saving my life last night? I feel like a perfect ass."

"Nobody's perfect, Jamie."

"Oh! Please Father; spare me your wit this morning. I feel terrible."

"We know Jamie. Much of the fault is our own. Let's order some breakfast, and then we can talk," said Father Rene.

By the time breakfast arrived; Jamie felt much better but looked like hell. His mouth and chin were severely bruised and lacerated. Fortunately, no teeth had been broken. His chin was already discolored. His left eye was almost swollen shut." Hope you don't mind, Jamie, but I ordered you cream of wheat, honey and tea. I doubt if you can swallow much else," Joe said very sympathetically.

"That's just fine, Joe, but what happened to those two guys?"

"Father Rene, you should have been there. This man moved like lightning. I never saw anything like it."

Jamie was about to continue when he observed the priest's embarassment and thought better of it.

"Jamie, that incident last night created a very real dilemma here at the Vatican. Those two men were going to murder you. If we had jailed them here, it would have forced the Vatican Prosecutor's office to become involved. Only once in the last fifty years has anyone even been put in our jail overnight."

"So what did you do with them, Joe?"

"We rushed them to the hospital for emergency treatment and called ahead to the Italian police in Rome. A car met us at St. Anne's Gate, and on the way to the airport, the police confiscated their passports. Those hoodlums were escorted to a private jet and flown out of the country. I assure you, Jamie, they will never return to Italy, let alone Vatican City:" the priest was very emphatic."

"Joe, will you and Father Rene tell me what in God`s name is going on?"

"Yesterday I all but accused you of being part of a grand conspiracy. Then last night . . ." Sheepishly, Jamie's voice trailed off.

"Jamie, I'm not only a Jesuit. I'm also a member of the Papal Security Force, a group of specially trained clergy and laymen who dedicate their lives to one single solitary purpose, the protection of the Holy Father. As an international organization, we have almost unlimited discretionary powers to take whatever measures necessary to fulfill our sworn duty. We are bound, however, by oaths of poverty and use of reasonable force."

"The enemies of the Church are beyond number. Constant vigilance is necessary. Trusted Catholics highly placed in security forces and police departments around the world provide us with complete cooperation. No questions asked; no matter what the cost to themselves personally. It all comes down to a matter of absolute faith. What I have just disclosed to you must not be repeated, but both Rene and I thought we owed you that much. Agreed, Jamie?"

"Yes, of course Joe."

“I understand how difficult it is for you to trust me with such information."

"What is the current situation? Can you fill in the missing pieces?"

Jamie grimaced as he spoke through swollen lips.

"Rene, why don't you tell him as much as we know," said Father Gault, "while I finish my breakfast."

"Jamie, it's a mixed bag. We are really working on a jigsaw puzzle. That's why you were approached, to flush out the quail so to speak."

"You mean I'm the bait!" groaned Jamie as he realized what a patsy he had been.

"Afraid so. We are absolutely desperate. You were our last chance at stabilizing a situation that is totally out of control. Things had been fairly quiet for the last several years until near the end of the reign of Pope Paul VI. In Africa, several key bishops were murdered by terrorists. In South America, a number of young priests were tortured by local dictators. No one was concerned when Pope Paul VI died until, as of course you know now, Jamie, a Chinese cardinal and then a Russian cardinal died, and then Pope John Paul . . . all from heart attacks."

"The statistical likelihood of heart failure in all four cases was astronomically small. We have been on twenty-four hour alert, seven days a week since the death of Pope John Paul. We believe he was murdered along with the Chinese and Russian cardinals. About Pope Paul VI, we're not too sure. We know what killed them, but not how it was done, particularly in the case of Pope John Paul, whom we were already guarding very closely."

"Do you recall the recent flap in Great Britain about the methods employed by the Bulgarians in executing defectors who were causing them problems in the West? By penetrating their skin, usually with the tip of an umbrella or some other device, such as a syringe type fountain pen, they injected their victim with a deadly new poison causing heart failure. Even an autopsy cannot determine the type of poison used. Recently, one man survived long enough for Western scientists to get a culture of the poison from the welt area on the body where it had been injected. We believe this same technique is being employed on the victims here at the Vatican."

"It would have been a simple matter to inject the visiting cardinals, but not the Pope; he was guarded too closely at all times by at least a dozen men."

As Father Rene hesitated in his story, Jamie interrupted.

"I think I know how the Pope was murdered. It is only a theory and probably will remain that way. I don't believe the weapon will ever be found. The Pope was killed by his own papal ring."

"What! How could that be, Jamie?"

Both Joe and Rene asked the question at the same time. Astonishment was written all over their faces.

"The papal ring was a large golden one on which was impressed the papal seal."

Jamie reached into his coat pocket and withdrew his Cross pencil. On a napkin, he sketched an outline of the ring and its inner details.

"Hollowed out, it was perfectly capable of concealing a small solenoid powered by a button battery. The core rod in the center of the solenoid would have a hollow, stainless steel, surgical tip that fit flush with the outside wall of the ring."

"Anyone within a hundred yards of the Pope could activate the miniature electronic circuit Thereby triggering the button battery to energize the micro-size solenoid. The needle-like end would momentarily shoot out of the ring and inject the inserted finger with the poison. A compressed spring in the solenoid would return the needle safely inside the ring. Unbelievably clever, because examination of the ring finger would reveal nothing improper."

"But at the last minute, somebody remembered something and a new plan had to be devised! When a Pope dies, his ring remains on his finger. During the funeral mass, a cardinal smashes its seal with a little silver hammer. The guts of the assassination device would be exposed to fifty-thousand live witnesses and one-hundred million more via satellite television transmissions,"

The two priests were thunderstruck as Jamie concluded.

"Sometime between Thursday evening at I0 PM. and 7:00 AM the next morning, the Pope was murdered. Then the ring was stolen. Probably disassembled by now. Its gold content melted down and sold. You could start with the Vatican jeweler, but undoubtedly the switch was made without his knowledge."

Father Gault stood up, pounding both fists against his forehead, admonishing himself for not being more technically oriented. He acknowledged that if the Pope was murdered, Jamie had figured out how it was done. All three men were thinking the same thing. *Who? And why?* It was decided it would be better if Father Rene attempted to answer that question.

"We really don't know, but we have narrowed it down somewhat, and you, Jamie, have helped us do that, even if you aren't fully aware of it yet."

Rene went on to explain how Jamie's assignment had corresponded with their need for a decoy. That's why they provided him with so much information, hoping that someone would get nervous and make a mistake. "No one realized you might get killed over the affair. After the bombing of your apartments at the hotel, Father Joe thought it more than coincidental. He suggested we had gone too far in revealing Vatican information to you. When you became so hostile yesterday, Joe decided to convince you to leave Italy. The attempt on your life last night, however, confirmed all our suspicions. So, whatever it is you've discovered, it's having its desired effect."

"Joe, how did you know I'd be at the radio station last night?"

Joe admitted that he had Jamie followed ever since the bombing.

"The radio station was a different matter. I saw you immobilize the lock on the emergency door and knew you would attempt a break-in. You were getting the idea that the Vatican was one big financial conspiracy and all of us were part of it, isn't that true, Jamie?"

"Something like that, Joe."

The priest then went on to say there were only three basic motives he felt would justify the assassination of the Pope at this time. "Right-wing members of the Church and/or multi-national corporations could fear that the Pope was going to appease the Communists. The Communists might be afraid the Pope would bring the power of the papacy to bear in Africa and stifle the growth of Marxism.

The third possibility was that the Pope decided to instigate some radical new policy. Such as divesting the Church of its wealth and giving it to the poor. Thus hoping for a total reformation. Such a papal gesture was suggested a number of years ago, as you might recall, in a novel, The Shoes of the Fisherman, by Morris L. West. This would not be acceptable to the conservative members of the Curia."

Father Joe sat down and spoke about the Church's financial prudence.

"The third motive was ruled out, because Pope John Paul was a responsible fiscal manager. He knew that in the long run the Church could do more by being financially strong than insolvent. There has always been a running theological battle over the Church being either rich or poor. The winning argument always goes something like this:

If the Church could sell everything it owned, perhaps it could generate up to 200 billion dollars. At least one and a half billion people in the world are starving. Therefore, the Church could give the world's poor at most, and the priest stressed the words at most, "$133.00 each. But, if the Church, through its investments, could encourage industrial development in the poorest of countries, then the poor in time would prosper.

There is no practical argument that can be mustered in opposition to this line of reasoning. There is, however, a very theologically strong argument. It requires total risk. No sane pope would ever take that risk. No matter how charitable he might be. As for which one of the two remaining conspiracy theories is correct, we may never know."

Rene then said to Jamie, "Finish your assignment, Jamie, and make your report."

"Someone will watch over you the next day or two. Father Gault is fairly certain that last night's failure to kill you has tipped the hand of the conspirators. Killing you now would only intensify efforts to investigate further. Joe will call you tomorrow night to get your opinion as to the direction of the conspiracy, but no matter what the outcome, no one is likely to be brought to justice over the previous assassinations, because without the killer and the Pope's ring, our evidence is purely circumstantial."

Father Joe added, "So far, Jamie, you have been getting a lopsided view of Pope John Paul's intended actions. You should know that at least until 1977, the Pope was violently anti-Communistic. His stance was reflected in a speech when he, as Patriarch of Venice, firmly stated "Catholics absolutely cannot give their vote to the Italian Communist ticket or to that part of the Socialist Party who go hand-in-hand with them."

Furthermore, Jamie, "On more than one occasion, he expressed deep regret over the loss of Catholics in Europe and America."

"Joe," said Father Rene, "that's enough for now. Let's leave. Jamie has another appointment."

Jamie again thanked Father Joe for last night. Never again would he be quite so cynical of the clergy; appearances were very deceiving.

Putting on the best face he could, Jamie made his way to the Academy of Sciences building. It was just northwest of the Villa of Pius VI. Three people were to meet him there. The topics to be discussed were the upcoming Latin American Bishop's Conference; African Catholicism as covered by the Pope's audience of September 19 with Eduardo Pironia and the Pope's briefings at the two staff meetings of September 16 and 23.

The conference room was a bare bones affair. It had no windows, one entry door and an old oblong oak table with a seating capacity of sixteen. On the rear wall hung an antique blackboard. Three low-hanging chandeliers lighted the room. The place looked more like a mortuary than a conference room. Its furnishings had been purloined from other Vatican offices that have been renovated and re-equipped over the years.

Jamie visualized several old priests retrieving the discarded conference table and chairs from the back of a trash truck. *Their probably grumbling to themselves about not having enough money in the budget for a conference room on the third floor of the Science building.* Actually for ten years it had been stricken from their budget, and now they would take matters into their own hands.

Why, wondered Jamie, *had Father Joe arranged for this meeting in such dire old surroundings?* As it turned out, the building happened to be a central location from the offices of the three staff members, who themselves were none too pleased with the facilities. Upon entering the room, Jamie met Father Anselm, Brother Michael and Sister Anna Maria all young people, very scholarly and somber. Jamie decided on a direct approach.

"I would appreciate it very much if you would first of all review with me what had been discussed in the staff meeting with Pope John Paul I concerning African Catholicism on September 23."

It was Sister Anna Maria who spoke first. Beginning with a brief historical and geographical sketch of Africa, she said, "Africa is the second largest continent in the World. It may have been the birthplace of mankind. Except for the north and northeastern parts of the continent comprising the peoples of Algeria, Libya, Egypt, Sudan and Ethiopia, who in one form or another are followers of Mohammed, the remainder of Africa, at the beginning of the eighteenth century, was completely tribal in nature.

Any consolidated kingdoms would have been ancient and predated the rise of the Egyptian Empire. Early in the seventeenth century, explorers from the West reached the coastal shores of Africa. Penetration of the interior was almost impossible because access from the north over land from the Middle East was denied them by the Arabic nations after Roman legions no longer existed. By the early eighteenth century, slave trading began to develop into an enormous export business between Africa and America."

"And England?" asked Jamie.

"England was involved to a lesser extent because her majesty found a great deal more profit in opium runs between Europe, India and China. England operated a shipping cartel of enormous wealth. The mainland of England required no import of foreign labor. In fact, the English were busy shipping unwanted convicts to their Australian penal colony and unwanted Puritans and other hardcore fanatics to their American colonies. The colonies desperately needed great hordes of manual laborers for land and crop development."

“It must be remembered, Father Bolin, Africa consisted of thousands of tribes, each speaking a different dialect and having their own religious beliefs. Tribes began selling their captured enemies and probably their criminals to slave traders.

Jamie, startled by the priestly reference, sat bolt upright in his chair. He was almost tempted to look around to see who Father Bolin was when he caught himself.

"Yes, Sister Anna, please continue."

The nun confirmed the information Jamie had already obtained from his discussion yesterday afternoon with Father Jack Richards. "African tribes dominated and controlled the western, southern, and eastern coastlines. White ships were permitted to dock. Unless invited by Africans to join the slave hunting parties, whites did not dare move into the interior. If Africans had not wanted to rid themselves of their enemies and convicts for profit, there would have been no slave trade.

Unless the Arabs swept south, no armies in the world at that time were equipped to successfully lay siege to the coast of Africa and penetrate its interior. Slavery was a profitable export of black Africans and a profitable import for white colonialists. Black slavery, in its flourishing years, was the product of black greed and white need. The cruelty of whites to blacks on board ship, a matter of poor judgement in an attempt to maximize profits, was unforgivable as was slavery itself.

But, one must ask how many more blacks would have been murdered or indentured by other black tribes in Africa if there had been no profit in the slave trade. Would the current generation of American Negroes have even existed? Let alone prospered by comparison, if their ancestors had not been forcibly shipped to America?"

Jamie interrupted, "Why was it necessary that the Pope be briefed on the historical background of Africa, particularly the true nature of the origins and profits of slave trading with America, which at that time was a British colony?"

Sister Anna Maria deferred to Brother Michael who, dressed in brown robes and slightly portly, reminded Jamie of the little monk in the IBM television commercials. Only Brother Michael was not, however, a laughable little fellow. He was rather stern and tense. There was a note of urgency in his voice as he spoke.

"The slavery issue in Africa and America has been used to bolster the ideological premises of Marxists. They urge the black population of both continents to foment revolutionary warfare. If successful, in the end they will create massive civil wars throughout Africa. Not black against white, but black against black."

Brother Michael then spoke about America.

"American Negroes have already lost sight of their goals of integration. They accept more government jobs and big city subsidies. Their vocal complaints increase. Radicals harass and intimidate their communities. The black American social structure is now much weaker than it was fifty years ago. Holy Mother Church wants black Americans to succeed as an example of a superhuman effort of self-fulfillment in a white world. Now, Marxists, who grow stronger every day, hold up American Negroes to ridicule."

"Only because of the tenacity of the Catholic Church and its grass roots endeavors in certain African tribes, is Marxist philosophy being held in check. Black America is soft, very soft. What was needed in the fifties and sixties was a massive effort by black families to form a coalition with truly enlightened concerned whites."

"They need to develop the same determination as the Jews, Irish, Poles, Chinese, and especially Japanese, who became model achievers. Achievers, Waspish America grudgingly came to respect with their clean cities, crimeless streets and well-educated children. Heaven knows, Father Bolin, this is what the Negro families want and what I believe they pray for. Their politicians and their radicals have let them down."

"In turn, Africa will suffer a thousand times over. The Church has completely lost faith in the American government and in the average American's preoccupation with self, be it black or white. Mother Church is being trapped into making alliances and decisions that no one dreamed possible ten years ago. Even the young priests are succumbing to "Marxist's theory."

Jamie interrupted, "What positive action was recommended to the Pope? What alternatives were suggested?"

Father Anselm very patiently waited his turn to summarize the African paradox. He was very succinct in his analysis.

"The alternatives are few. Stand fast and psychologically slug it out with the communists, bible vs. guns and terrorism. Use financial leverage to encourage multi-nationals to create a consumer economy, or reach an accommodation with the Marxists. The recommendation to Pope John Paul I was quite straightforward and simple."

"If South Africa could be made into a model Christian democratic republic, Western governments and multi-national companies with the assistance of both the Catholic Church and, believe it or not, the Jews and Arabs could sweep Communism from the continent within twenty years. If, however, South Africa falls to Marxist doctrinaires and if the white minority is exiled, imprisoned or murdered, then the Church, for the sake of the African poor, must co-exist with the Marxists."

It was nearly time for lunch. Jamie suggested they reconvene at one in the afternoon.

Taking his leave, he walked back to the villa, ordered a soup and sandwich. Looking in the mirror before he returned to the Academy of Sciences building, he wondered what the nun, brother and priest thought about the ugly, bruised, black and blue appearance of his lower face. Odd no one had mentioned it at all. Jamie dabbed a small amount of talcum on the worse abrasions and left the suite.

When he arrived back at the conference room, only Father Anselm was present. Pulling up a chair, Jamie asked about Sister Anna Maria and Brother Michael.

The priest replied, "Only I was present at the Latin American Conference of Bishops' briefing held for the Pope on September 23. Therefore, it wasn't necessary to include the sister and Brother Michael in our meeting this afternoon."

Jamie agreed and commented, "Sister Anna Maria is obviously a very bright and intelligent woman."

The priest responded by saying to Jamie, "If the Pope ever approved priesthood for women, which is inevitable, Sister Anna Maria would be most assuredly very high on the list of acceptable candidates."

Jamie was then briefed on the Latin American Conference. The conference has been indefinitely postponed until such time as a new pope can be elected and approves the agenda. The conference is a means for extracting the viewpoints of all South and Central American priests concerning the status of the Church and its future programs in Latin America.

The conference could turn into a gut level fight between conservatives, Liberals and out-and-out Marxists. The latter two groups represent by far the majority of the priests, but their bishops might hold other views. The Pope wanted to know which bishops were in conflict with their parish priests and why. He also expected to find the bishops very disgruntled and testy over such issues as birth control, divorce and finances.

Father Anselm smiled as he recalled the Pope, in jest, responding with, “Well then, it will be just like being at home in the Papal Palace where I am surrounded by controversy. It probably is more pleasant to the ear when spoken in Spanish than gestured in Italian!"

Jamie raised a new question.

"What, if anything, Father Anselm, do you know about the Pope's audience with Argentina's Pironia, who is the prefect of the Sacred Congregation for Religious and Secular Institutes and head of the Latin American Conference of Bishops?"

"Only that Pironia had pleaded with the Pope to attend the conference, denounce Marxism and reaffirm the basic obligations of parish priests in ministering to their flocks. After our staff meeting on September 23, the Pope still had not committed himself to attend."

Another question mark, thought Jamie. *Which way had the Pope been leaning and why*?

Jamie turning to the priest saying, "You have been very helpful. Unfortunately, I am pressed for time and am due in Father Rene's office shortly. I believe I have all the information I need. Very much appreciate your taking the time to brief me."

The priest understood, and that ended the meeting. Jamie left the Academy of Sciences. Father Anselm gathered up his notes, returning to his office just long enough to pick up Sister Anna Maria and head for a small house on the outskirts of Rome.

Jamie found a mini-bike station nearby, grabbed one and headed for Rene's office in the Belvedere Palace. Jamie was just about to enter the portico leading to the Belvedere courtyard when he spotted Father Anselm with Sister Anna Maria. Their car was turning into the Stradone di Giardinni road, apparently in somewhat of a hurry. Jamie smiled knowingly. Little wonder that the priest had seemed preoccupied with the striking but austere nun all through their meeting this morning. Sins of the flesh were not just a preoccupation of laymen.

Suddenly, for no reason, Jamie's thoughts wistfully reached out for the sight and smell of Carol. Tonight he must try to reach her in London. In all the confusion last night, he had made no attempt to call Carol and, Good Lord, Katie was due in Rome tomorrow! What would his eldest daughter think when she caught sight of her old man with his battered face? Katie was his pet name for her, christened though she was Katherine Ann, a spectacular Irish beauty. Not yet twenty-one, majoring in English Literature at Stanford, she always looked for an excuse to fly off and be with him; at least when he was in Europe, where she loved to visit and meet new friends.

Jamie had no way of contacting his daughter until she arrived at his hotel tomorrow. He had not wired her about changing rooms. Surely she would check at the desk. He hoped no one would mention the explosion to her. Awakening from a daydream about misbegotten things to do, he found himself almost running down several tourists crossing the road as he pulled up to the Belvedere Palace. Entering the office, Jamie noticed the young novitiate, Laurent, had not returned to his duties, or he had been sent on an errand.

Walking through the open inner office door, he was greeted very warmly by Father Rene, who introduced him to the Undersecretary of Foreign Affairs from South Africa, Hans Beakman.

"How did your morning briefing by the younger members of the Pope`s staff go?"

Jamie answered, "It was a rehash of my interview with Father Richards except for the reference to the Latin American Bishops' Conference."

Father Rene said, "Jamie, I would like you to remain after our talk with Mr. Beakman. I want to hear what you thought of the memorandum on seminarian discipline."

Puzzled, Jamie shrugged his shoulders in ignorant compliance. The business at hand dealt with reviewing for Jamie the Pope's audiences of September 15 and September 25, both of which had been held in the evenings. The audiences concerned the present state of affairs in South Africa.

Jamie and Hans were comfortably seated. Father Rene sat back in his own chair behind the large oak desk and said to Jamie, "Cardinal Willebrand's audience with Pope John Paul concerned the general conditions existing in Western Europe and in particular Holland's concern over the outcome of South Africa's move towards integration. The Cardinal had urged the Pope to grant a special audience to the foreign minister of South Africa, which the Pope did. They met secretly on Monday evening at 8:30 in the Pope's living quarters. Hans happened to be in Rome this week. I asked him to join us this afternoon and give his unofficial, off-the-record summary of what Pik Roelof discussed with His Holiness that evening."

Father Rene made the sign of the cross. It obviously pained him to think of the dead Pope. Gesturing with a gracious sweep of his hand, he asked Hans Beakman to begin.

"Let me explain, Father Bolin, that South Africa is not proud of its civil rights record with regard to the majority population. There never was an easy way. No matter what the outside world may think. There is also the colored minority, part white and part black. And the Zulus are apart from everyone else. Then there are the white Afrikaners like myself. The Zulus came and conquered all the tribes in southern Africa. Our great-grandfathers fought them for the right to rule South Africa. We are as much a part of modern Africa as any tribe on the continent."

"We just happen to be the only white tribe. Rhodesian whites do not hold the same status or property rights as we Afrikaners. By the end of this century, our families will have been on the continent for 400 years. 180 years longer than America has been a nation. The problems facing South Africa are enormous."

"If whites and blacks and colored can't live peacefully, while forming a democratic republic, then South Africa will be lost to Communism. The domino effect will cause all of Africa to return to tribal warfare. The Russians see the 400 million Africans as a pool of mercenary military forces to be used in the Middle East and other parts of Asia."

Beakman then described Africa's wealth. "Africa contains almost one-half of the world's gold supply, nearly one-hundred percent of the world's diamonds, and great supplies of uranium. It just so happens that South Africa controls the mining and refining of most of these precious metals. Even more key to Western steelmakers is Africa's supply of rarer medals such as chromium, used to make special steel alloys, critical material in the production of tool steel."

"Russia's rape of these resources would make the multi-national companies look like good tooth fairies in comparison. Over the past twenty years, the United Nations has, by economic sanction and quasi endorsement of revolutionaries, brought South Africa to its present precarious position. This forced us to move rapidly toward integration and majority rule. It is not only morally right, but economically sensible. We cannot in good conscience quarrel with the supposed objective of that august body."

"I stress the UN's supposed objective." Hans Beakman became angry as he continued. "Today, as we sit here talking of freedom, fairness and morality, the present intent of the United Nations is to turn my country over to the bloody radicals, the Marxist terrorists. Sheepishly, the United States and Western Europe have gone along with the idea. The South African government made an agreement with the United Nations to permit five thousand UN troops to supervise free elections in the trust territory of Namibia."

"The UN now wants to send in seventy-five hundred troops in violation of the agreement and insists on having the terrorist leaders participate in the election process. It isn't only the white leadership of South Africa who is violently opposed to the high-handed methods of the U.N. The black moderate leaders are equally opposed and are in constant fear of their lives. It is reported that the United States, through its ambassador to the UN approves of including the terrorists in the election process."

"It is also common knowledge that the Communists recruited four thousand South African blacks after the staged Soweto riot of 1976. These recruits have been trained by Soviet backed guerillas in Tanzania, Angola and even the Soviet Union. If the full diplomatic weight of the Roman Catholic Church is not brought to bear on all moderate nations in Africa, South America, Western Europe, and the United. States, then all of Africa will be lost. The United States, after sixty years, still doesn't believe in the reality of a Communist dominated world."

"Even while it is taking place before their very eyes, your countrymen have learned nothing from World War II, the Korean War, the Cuban Missile Crisis, the Vietnam War, the Middle East mini-wars, and soon it will be the African Wars. Even if the Soviet Union relinquishes its world leadership role as a Communist superpower, China, Vietnam, North Korea, some Middle East and South American leaders are avowed Communists bent on overthrowing democratic institutions."

It was obvious that Hans Beakman was a sincere and utterly frustrated diplomat who knew the truth, but nobody wanted to hear it. Even the thought of another series of wars chilled Jamie to the bone.

Americans could sit comfortably in their homes and watch live news broadcasts of the wars on TV, via satellite.

If the cameramen didn't shoot any scenes of a sexual nature, the programs would be rated PG. That way, the kids could watch too, especially the six o'clock news. While this ugly little scenario was running through Jamie's mind, Hans Beakman was asking if either of the two men, Father Rene or Jamie, had any questions. Both men shook their heads negatively.

After a few minutes of silence, Rene and Jamie walked with Hans Beakman to his car in the parking lot. Silently, the two of them retraced their steps to Father Rene's office. Rene turned to Jamie as they reentered the office.

"At times like these when one crisis after another appears on the horizon, even a priest can become quite depressed."

In an effort to shake off his dreary mood, Rene told Jamie he wanted to discuss some important aspects of Pope John Paul's last meeting.

"It was early in the evening of September 27, and present were the Pope and Cardinals Baggio and Villot. I didn't say anything this morning because I wanted you to understand first the problems in Latin America so you could properly interpret the memorandum on the subject of seminarian regulations."

"What memorandum?" asked Jamie.

"Why, the one Father Anselm told you about today."

"Father Joe instructed him to disclose the seriousness of the report to you. It seems that in his staff meeting on Saturday, September 16, the Pope expressed concern about the selection and training of young seminarians in Latin America. He requested that a complete analysis be in his hands within ten days. It was the last memorandum he ever received. It was handed to him late Thursday afternoon, the day before he died."

Jamie asked, "Had the Pope been reading the document when he died?"

Rene replied, "The Pope had told the cardinals that evening that he was going to read the report before he went to sleep that night."

Rene went on to tell Jamie about the urgent business the two cardinals discussed with the Pope. It seemed both cardinals had spoken of the necessity of the Pope attending the Latin American Bishops' Conference. Before doing so, he was to sign into Papal Law the sweeping reform program affecting seminarians all over the world.

"You know, Jamie, I just realized another funny coincidence. Pope Paul VI was to have signed that same edict just before he died. Now the Pope has died before he could sign it. It must now wait upon another new pope, whoever that might be; and he could choose not to put it into effect."

Rene went on to divulge that the quality and type of seminarians being accepted today and their educational background left much to be desired.

He further stated, "In fact, rumors have been circulating over the last few years that due to laxity in vigilance, many Marxist revolutionary-type students have been infiltrating the Church and receiving the Sacrament of Holy Orders. The new reform program would greatly reduce their chances of being accepted. Furthermore, the change in emphasis of teaching within the seminaries themselves would either weed out those who slipped in or truly convert them."

"You mean, father, that in fact, the Church has designed a screening and educational program that could in effect create a double agent."

"I never quite thought of it that way, Jamie, but let us say we would indeed create an extraordinary soldier for Christ! Over the years, the Church has become lax in the educational requirements for priesthood. Priests are no longer scholars and molders of men. They have become sociologists, psychologists and purveyors of causes espousing the same kind of, I believe the Americans would say 'crappy' watered-down intellectualism that has almost destroyed your American educational system."

"Almost overnight, the Church finds Herself with an army of young priests who are extremely vocal and articulate in this jargon of educational mediocrity, but they can't lead, think or do. This is particularly true throughout all of the Americas. The entire Curia is adamant about the reform program, the sooner the better. The Latin American Conference had been set for the second week in October.The cardinals were urging the Pope to, in effect, go and lay down the law."

The priest moved his chair very close to the desk, and clasping his hands, he stretched his arms out on the desktop, leaned his whole body in Jamie's direction. His body language intimating that his next statement was very important and it certainly was. First, he recited verbatim a quotation made by Archbishop Manuel Menendez, head of Caritas in Argentina.

"It seems Jamie, that on a recent trip to Rome, prior to the Pope's death, the Archbishop stopped to speak with a small boy. Menendez asked the boy if he loved the new Pope."

"The child answered, 'Yes'. When asked why, the boy replied, 'Because I understand what he says."

Father Rene then asked Jamie, "Do you know why the last conclave was so short?"

Jamie replied, "No, other than a lot of agreements had possibly been reached beforehand."

Rene acknowledged that in many elections that was undoubtedly true; but the reasons for the selection of the Patriarch of Venice, Cardinal Luciani, the now late Pope John Paul I, were numerous.

The third world cardinals trusted him for his sincerity and his abiding love of the poor. The Curia cardinals, the old Italians, knew him as a doctrinal conservative in matters of faith. The European cardinals saw him as an implacable foe of Communism and the liberal cardinals knew he was an articulate and brilliant speaker, who could capture the hearts of Christians and non-Christians alike.

There was then a long pause by Father Rene . . . "Jamie, the night before he died, the Pope was also asked to postpone the Latin American Bishops' Conference for a month so that he might make a personal goodwill tour of Africa. South Africa was to be his very first stop."

XII. CHURCH AND STATE COLLIDE

"Jamie, I'm sorry Father Joe couldn't join us this afternoon. He's gone to investigate a lead that might be of help to us. He plans to contact you tomorrow at the hotel."

"As you know, Father Rene, my instructions are to complete my assignment by tomorrow evening. I plan on being in my room all day tomorrow completing the report. Tell Joe he can come over anytime."

"Jamie, we'd like you out of the country as soon as possible. You have been of great assistance to the Church, and Joe doesn't want you taking any more risks."

"I'll strike a. bargain with you, Father. Let me finish the report, and I'll leave Italy on the first available plane to London on Wednesday, after my daughter arrives from America."

"Your daughter! Contact her and have her meet you in London?"

"Look Father, one more day, and I'll be gone. By the way, how much latitude do I have in writing publicly about the Pope's assassination?"

"That subject has been thoroughly discussed Jamie, and strongly suggested you publish any information or speculation in the form of popular fiction rather than as historical fact. A mystery novel perhaps?"

"You mean cops and robbers stuff, Rene?"

"More like international intrigue, Jamie. It could contain the essential elements concerning the rapid escalation of world dangers. Whereas an unsubstantiated historical summary of the past ninety days would be lacking in proof and ignored by the public."

"What do you say?"

"I'll give it some thought, Father. But for now let's call it a day."

"Good luck, Jamie, and please be careful," shouted the priest as Jamie left Father Rene's office. He meandered for almost an hour down the streets of Rome.

Feeling the painful reminders of his beating last night, hailing a cab, Jamie sat silently, husbanding his little remaining energy. He very much wanted to speak to Carol before falling asleep from exhaustion.He wanted to look presentable by tomorrow when Katie arrived. From the hotel, he tried to call Carol at her flat in London but got no answer. Jamie fell into a sound asleep; sprawled upon the quilted bedspread, facedown. His arms lay alongside his head atop the fluffy pillows.

It was six o'clock, Tuesday night, the tenth of October. Had Jamie known the events taking place at that very moment, he would not have slept so soundly. Events that by tomorrow would make it mandatory he be in full command of all his physical and mental capacities.

At 7:23 the next morning, he opened his eyes, stretched and sat up in bed. A glance at his watch told Jamie he had slept over thirteen hours. The psychological lift of that fact propelled him toward the bathroom. He examined the remaining bruises on his face, shaved and vigorously brushed his teeth. He returned to the bedroom and for fifteen minutes meditated in a full lotus position, arms wrapped around his back, his fingers resting on the upturned soles of his feet. The meditation would help clear his mind for the busy day ahead.

Picking up the bedside phone he called Carol's London office. He was told she was on assignment in France and wasn't expected back until tomorrow. Before re-cradling the phone, Jamie called the hotel barbershop for an appointment. Then he ordered breakfast. By 9:30 he had showered, dressed and polished off a breakfast of eggs, sausage, orange juice, tea and toast.

For several hours, Jamie laboriously cross-indexed, collated and correlated an array of facts, suppositions, rumors and outright prejudiced opinions. He added a number of his own observations which by now were biased by two known attempts on his life and the possibility of a third which had been aborted.

One piece of random news he had gathered from his visit to the Vatican library needed further clarification. Jamie placed a call to the New York Times editorial offices. He spoke with an old friend concerning a news item about the tragic death of an ex-CIA man who was believed to have committed suicide on September 24. The only significant piece of additional information Jamie gleaned from the phone call was the fact that the ex-official had been living in the same building that also housed many members of the Russian embassy staff.

Could the man have overheard either accidentally or through the use of bugging devices something relating to either the Latin American Bishops' Conference or espionage activities inside the Vatican, itself? It was the date of the incident that had originally caught Jamie's eye.

The incident occurred shortly after the death of the Russian cardinal and just prior to the death of the Pope. Jamie could not link the man's death to the Pope's assassination. One thing was certain. From the news description of the manner of death, it was anything but suicide.

Jamie boiled down his basic information to several pages of concise notes. He called the hotel concierge to acquire a rental typewriter and asked that it be brought to his room by two o'clock today. A few minutes later, the phone rang. The muffled voice of a woman asked Jamie to be at the Swiss Guard station at the Gate of St. Anne in thirty minutes. He was to leave immediately. His daughter's life would be forfeited if he didn't come or if he made any attempt to contact anyone.

The voice further instructed, "Bring with you all of your notes. from your interviews. Check out of your hotel and be ready to leave the country with your daughter when our business transaction is completed:"

"Wait just a minute:" Jamie shouted into the receiver.

There was a loud click in his ear as the phone at the other end was silenced. In the brief conversation, the woman had described his daughter and had given her name, ominously stating, "Katherine is with us now."

Jamie decided to somewhat deviate from the instructions of his mysterious caller. Just maybe, he thought, someone would take the several pages of notes to which he would attach the priest's name and telephone number to Father Gault. From those notes, perhaps, Joe might decipher who had killed the Pope and why. Realizing he might not live another day, Jamie hurriedly scribbled down Joe's name and phone number attaching the information to his concise notes. He placed the notes on the desktop under the large glowing Italian colonnade lamp; perhaps as a silent testimony to his last unfinished work.

Jamie gathered up his belongings, everything except for the notes. He Checked out and hailed a taxi.

"The Vatican, and hurry, the Gate of St. Anne's entrance:"

Under the lighted lamp, atop the ornate desk lay Jamie's concise summary of his investigation.

Vatican Affair - Condensed Notes - J. Bolin October 11, 1978

- The Papal Ring and the Seminarian Report are missing.
- Pope Paul VI, the Chinese Cardinal, the Russian Cardinal and Pope John Paul I are all dead of apparent heart attacks within 45 days.
- Vatican phones monitored by LED displays called ANGEL.
- Vatican radio station with cryptographic devices and scramblers.
- Novitiate Laurent monitoring Rene's calls and has disappeared.
- Intruder dressed as priest observed when Pope's body discovered.
- Vatican a 200 billion dollar empire aligned with multi-nationals.
- Three attempts on my life by a car, by dynamite and the latest by two assassins.
- Latern Treaty, Benito Mussolini, six billion dollar Italian investment.
- Carol plagued by ringing phone, her apartment rifled, nothing missing.
- Marxists were infiltrating Catholic Church as young seminarians.
- John Paul I knew US greater military power, but soviets more devious.
- John Paul I anti-Communist bent on ecumenical reconciliation, loved the poor; dogmatic in matters of faith and morals.
- All Africa could be a communist satellite if Church doesn't intervene.
- American Negro political element Marxist biased. African leaders and terrorists are Soviet trained.
- Pope John Paul I was very intelligent, trusted by the third world, articulate and makes sense to the average man in the street.
- World Council of Churches split over financing terrorists in Africa.
- Pope John Paul I very capable, selfless, knows the needs of the poor.
- Father Anselm neglected to disclose nature of seminarian dispute.
- Afghanistan & Iran are keys to communist Middle East domination;
  South Africa key to African domination.
- The Church in Europe is being surrounded by communism.
- The Church is concerned about the United States and Western

Europe, but not committed to rapidly changing its position on dogma

- Check for long term past relationships between Vatican and USSR

Jamie stuffed a wad of bills into the hands of the driver, jumped from the taxi, and with clothes bag and attaché case in tow, walked rapidly toward the Swiss Guard on duty. The guard recognized him and accepted Jamie's letter of authority for entering the Vatican grounds, noting the date of expiration as today, October 11. The guard asked for the key to Jamie's suite and the metallic card. He did not return the letter. The Swiss Guard gave Jamie a one-day pass.

Jamie asked, "Are there any messages for me?"

As he spoke, the phone rang. The guard answered and then handed the phone to Jamie. The same muffled voice that had spoken to him less than an hour ago, this time gave final, precise instructions.

"Bring your baggage and yourself to St. Peter's Basilica. Ride the elevator to the first set of stairs leading to the dome. Go, now!"

Jamie frantically asked about Katherine, but the line went dead. He started the long walk to the Basilica. The baggage and his briefcase weighed heavily on his arms as his mind became depressed over what might happen or already had happened to his lovely daughter.

He reached the interior of St. Peter's Basilica about one o'clock in the afternoon. The sky was decidedly overcast. Looking up at the dome, he was startled by the contrast of the gray light filtering through the glass mosaics overhead and the brightly-lit ground floor interior.

Jamie went straight for the elevator. He rode it to the landing leading to the first staircase. As he walked toward the staircase the elevator door closed behind him. In the surrounding silence, Jamie listened to the sound of the elevator automatically descending.

From the shadowy recess adjacent to the staircase, a small hooded figure appeared and commanded, "Hand over the clothes bag and continue up the first flight of stairs to the next landing."

Jamie turned to go up the stairs. The head of the hooded figure rose to follow his progress. Just at that moment, the hood fell away. There looking up at him was Sister Anna Maria. A malevolent smile distorted her face.

Jamie ended his climb up the first staircase only to stare directly into the muzzle of an Italian Berreta, semi-automatic pistol. His eyes met those of Father Anselm. Anselm motioned him to sit down on the first step of the second staircase. That staircase led to the balcony platform that ominously hung 235 feet above the floor of the Basilica.

Several steps up from him, Jamie saw Katherine. Her wrists were bound and a gag was in her mouth. She appeared to be frightened but unharmed. Upon seeing her father, she managed a slight smile and a glimmer of hope settled in her big hazel-brown eyes.

Father Anselm instructed, "Put the attaché case next to you on the floor of the landing. Extend your legs straight out and place your hands behind your head."

Father Anselm or whomever he was, actually explained that it was up to Jamie whether or not he and his daughter left the Vatican alive.

"You, it seems, have already disobeyed the first set of instructions given you over the phone by Comrade Roiter."

"By who?" asked Jamie?

"Sister Anna Maria to you, idiot," spoke the priest sharply as he reached out and gave Jamie a vicious blow to the side of the head with the back of his hand.

"She called you from a room just down the hall from yours at the Hilton."

Oh, Christ sake, thought Jamie, *she must have searched his suite and found his note to Father Joe. She must have given them to Anselm before he hauled Katherine up the stairs.*

"Don't try anything foolish, Bolin."

"If no copies of your notes and source material are hidden on your person or in your belongings, you will be allowed to leave the Vatican; provided your attaché case contains all of your other interview notes and reference materials."

From below came the distinct sound of footsteps running up the staircase. The priest's eyes never shifted from their attention on Jamie. Several moments later, the nun appeared on the landing. Jamie was given a further order by the priest

"Slowly stand up. Turn around. Spread-eagle your legs and lean your body forward. Put your arms on the railing of the staircase."

Jamie looked into the eyes of his daughter. She sat only a few feet away, on the steps near him. Jamie felt the hard, efficient hands of the nun run over his clothing and diligently search through his coat pockets. Her hands plunged into his trouser pockets and then withdrew. She felt the inside of his thighs through the cloth of his pants. Jamie sensed a wave of revulsion that usually was experienced only by female rape victims.

"He's clean."

She knelt down between Jamie's spread-eagled legs and hurriedly examined the contents of the attaché case while holding a pencil flashlight in one fist and flipping through the material with her free hand. The "nun" nodded approval to the priest of what she had found.

Anselm curtly ordered Jamie to seat himself just below his daughter on the stairway. In changing positions, Jamie felt the close, clammy presence of the nun. He sat down, hands behind his head. The notes taken from his room by the nun lay on top of the rest of the material in the now open attaché case. The "nun" squirted lighter fluid all over the case and set it ablaze.

She stepped back. Then came a shocking disclosure from Sister Anna Marie, alias Comrade Roiter.

"If you wish Jamie", sneeringly regurgitating his name in familiar terms, "You can call me Madge, as I might possibly become your future sister-in-law!"

Laughing cruelly she continued, "Give my best to Carol. I haven't laid eyes on her for years, until seeing her with you on more than one occasion in Rome."

"Oh, and why the Comrade Roiter and not Livingston? Carl Roiter was my lover and then husband. He was murdered by your CIA several years ago."

Below, on the floor of the Basilica, a pair of eyes caught sight of the small flickering flame way up on one side of the dome. Had anyone cared to notice, they would have seen a man make swift, sure movements toward a waiting elevator. On the landing, the tiny fire blazed while Jamie, his daughter Katherine, and the so-called priest and nun created a bizarre setting by the light of that flickering flame in the dome of St. Peter's Basilica.

Flames played unevenly across the faces of Jamie and his adversaries.

The "priest" said, "You are to leave Italy immediately; take the next available plane for London. Contact no one. Go directly to the flat of Carol Livingston. There you will learn what is expected of you. Your daughter will be held here in Rome until word is received from London that you have arrived and everything is all right."

Anselm waved the gun, indicating Jamie should head back down the stairs and be on his way. Jamie turned to utter a few comforting words to his daughter and give her a loving hug. The nun stepped forward and drove her straightened fingers, like a well-formed spear, directly into one of his kidneys, indicating that he was not following instructions.

Out of sheer animal response, Jamie whipped his open hand around with lightning like speed. The impact of the blow lifted the nun up and flung her backwards, almost throwing her off the small landing, over the side of the railing. The priest's arm holding the Berreta swung around, anticipating a possible continuing attack by Jamie. A figure leapt forward out of the darkness of the stair well. No sooner had he appeared on the landing than one of his feet flew upward with all the fluidity of an avenging angel and sent the pistol flying through mid-air.

Father Anselm set himself to meet his attacker head on. The nun, recovered from Jamie's blow, appeared at the side of the priest with something clutched desperately in her steely small fingers.

In the eerie light of the burning papers, Jamie was aware of the powerful physical presence of Father Joe and the glint of a steel blade in the hand of the nun. Circling around Father Joe She darted in front of Jamie, bent on burying the steel blade to the hilt in Father Joe's chest. Without hesitation, Jamie dove from a half-standing position on the stair step. The force of his trajectory sent him and the nun tumbling down the first staircase. As the two bodies hurled past, Anselm turned and ran up the second flight of stairs. Jamie's daughter, Katherine, just rising to her feet, was knocked flat by the escaping priest.

Exerting a super-human effort, Jamie dislodged his arms from around the nun, and twisted his body sideways, halting his painful slide down the staircase. Gingerly, checking for broken bones, he stood. Father Joe had followed behind Jamie and stooped over to help him up.

"Are you okay?"

"I think so," groaned Jamie.

Joe checked on the nun, who, some ten feet farther down the stairs, had caught her leg in a set of upright stanchions supporting the railing. She lay there grotesquely, face up, arms flung backwards, stone dead! Her neck was broken.

Jamie raced back up the stairs and embraced his daughter on the landing above. It took him several seconds to realize she stood there gagged, hands tied behind her back. Looking down on the floor of the landing, he picked up the knife that had fallen there when he had tackled the nun.

Jamie cut the gag and freed his daughter's hands. They held each other tightly in gratitude for their mutual safety. Father Joe came back up the stairs toward them.

"Joe, you're simply an amazing man. But this time your quick actions in my defense may lead to very sad consequences."

Jamie told Joe what had happened.

"Could you take care of Katherine while I hurry to London?"

"What about the priest, Father Anselm? And, how did you know where to find us, Joe?"

The multiple questions came rapidly tumbling out of Jamie's mouth. He knew he had to leave immediately for Carol's sake. He had to be certain Katherine would be safe and wondered what Joe was going to do. Father Joe asked Jamie and Katherine to sit down a. moment on the stairs while he made it clear to Jamie what must be done next.

"First of all, Jamie, we don't have time for me to explain how I knew where to find you. Next, there is a Vatican Lear jet standing by at the airport outside Rome to fly both you and Katherine to London. I suggest when you're on the plane, the pilot radio ahead and confirm a commercial airline ticket to the United States for your daughter. You can perhaps see her off before you go to Miss Livingston's."

"After what you have just told me, I'm afraid our own plans have gone awry. Make yourself very conspicuous at the London airport. If you aren't met by one of our people at the airport, walk around outside your Miss Livingston's flat for awhile before entering".

"Remember the young blond novitiate, Laurent, secretary to Father Rene? Well, he's not. He is one of my young priests and was only there that day in the office to meet you. I sent him on ahead to London Sunday afternoon. I was certain Miss Livingston would be used somehow to get at you. Now run along, it's getting late. Go to the Vatican hangar number thirty-eight at the airport. You are expected."

"Hopefully, you and Laurent will find each other in London, or he has already rescued Miss Livingston. In either case, when you and he meet, everything will be explained. I will see to Father Anselm. Maybe we can get him to talk. If everything goes well, I'll be in London myself by tomorrow morning. I'm very anxious that you should be out of Italy as soon as possible."

Jamie took Katherine's hand and started down the first staircase. Father Joe turned to let them pass, and both men gripped each other's hand. Joe lost no time starting up the second stairway. Somewhere, 235 feet above the floor of the Basilica, Father Anselm waited for him on the open balcony platform. There was no other way down, except back down the same stairs they had all earlier ascended.

The Lear jet taxied down the runway. Jamie sat back and breathed a sigh of relief. He told Katie what had been happening to him and how relieved he was that she was safe and sound. It was most important to Jamie that she immediately returned safely to Stanford. He would make up for the loss of her European holiday when he rejoined her in the States.

The co-pilot came back into the cabin.

"We have a confirmed reservation for your daughter on a Concorde flight direct from London to San Francisco. Departure time is twenty minutes after your E.T.A. in London. There won't be any Customs problems for either of you since you're traveling on a Vatican plane.
A special Custom's officer will meet the plane as it lands and clear your passports without delay."

Before they knew it, London's Heathrow airport was looming up as Jamie stared out the window. Sure enough, the Customs official was there. With hardly a minute's delay, the official allowed Jamie to escort Katie to her waiting flight.

Jamie watched as she boarded the plane and then briskly walked to the main terminal. He made a general nuisance of himself by loudly asking directions to various points of interest around London. He stopped at the bar in the airport lounge for two drinks. The first one was for his nerves, and the second one he left untouched. After thirty minutes and no sign of any contact, he went outside and hailed a taxi.

"Number 116 Hartford Road, Piccadilly, and hurry, please."

Climbing into the back of the high-ceilinged cab, Jamie realized, as the driver turned around to address him, that she was a pretty girl in her early twenties.

"Now listen, Guv, the traffic is very heavy tonight, so if you don't mind, I'll take my sweet time about getting you there," she shouted back at Jamie between smacks of her lips as she alternately chewed and blew bubbles with the gum in her mouth.

How ribald, thought Jamie, remembering that London at one time had the greatest and most polite taxi drivers anywhere in the world. Those cabbies had represented the ultimate in civility to an outside world of tourists visiting the British Isles every year. It was getting dark. Jamie was exhausted from his rigors. His body ached all over. He leaned his head against the sidewall of the taxi and dozed off into a deep sleep. An hour later, he heard the cab door unceremoniously yanked open.

"That will be eight pounds sixpence, Guv."

The cabby reached inside and shoved hard on his shoulder to wake him. Jamie jerked upright as she shoved him and asked for payment. Without another word, he handed her a twenty in American money and stepped out of the taxi. Before him stood a row of buildings, all middle-income apartments now lodged in once-stately homes. It was easy enough to spot Carol's building. Outside, on the lawn, was a large, white, wooden sign with 116 Hartford Rd. imprinted in big bold black letters on its face. A modest amount of traffic was passing by.

Jamie carefully made his way between onrushing cars. Crossing the street, he moved in the direction of her building. He traversed the block several times before entering. It began to rain, and by the time he reached the door, there was a veritable downpour. Scanning the mailboxes, he found her name and flat location.

Number twenty-six; that would be on the second floor, sixth set of rooms. Realizing how close he was to her, Jamie raced up the main stairwell and ran down the hall. Throwing all caution aside on coming to flat number twenty-six, he grabbed the doorknob and turned it expectantly. The door swung open. There, before his eyes, sat Carol and Laurent, talking as if two, old, long lost friends.

"Jamie!" she shouted, jumping up and running to him.

Carol literally threw her body and arms around him and hung on with all her strength. For a moment, the love and force of her embrace almost made him forget what had brought him there. Taking hold of Carol around the waist, he led her back into the sitting room and shook hands with Laurent, who arose to greet him.

Jamie began to relax, knowing that Carol was safe. He looked around the room and surveyed the obvious damage. It looked like a barroom brawl had ensued. There was an overturned bookshelf in a corner; a broken lamp still lit, its bulb undamaged as its porcelain base lay broken. A shade laid half smashed. A general clutter of odds and ends were strewn around the room. In their midst, an overturned chair.

"Would anyone care to explain all this?" asked Jamie.

Laurent suggested that the three of them sit down. He told Jamie how he had been sent ahead to protect Carol when Father Gault had realized she might be in danger. Laurent had tried to reach her at home, but she didn't answer the phone. When he called her office, he was told she was in France and would return on Wednesday.

"I kept watch on her flat until about three hours before you arrived."

"Then I decided to break into the apartment. I had received a communication from Father Gault to expect you and possibly Joe himself sometime this evening at Miss Livingston's address."

"I started to jimmy the door of her flat when it suddenly opened. The next thing I knew, I was engaged in a fight for my life. I was gaining the upper hand, when the guy went for his gun. Luckily, I managed to tackle him and yelled for Carol to pick up the gun. The intruder, realizing he was going to be caught, broke my grip and bolted for the door. He had been holding Carol hostage since she arrived at her flat on Sunday afternoon. The intruder locked her in the bathroom during most of the days and tied her up in the evenings. I thought it was more important to protect her and wait for you, so I didn't pursue him when he ran from the apartment."

For the first time, Jamie took a really good look at Laurent. He was almost six feet tall, blond hair closely cropped and groomed. He possessed a very trim and taut, muscular body, with large hands and powerful wrists.

"Boy," said Jamie, "the Jesuits certainly know how to build 'em. No wonder the guy scurried out of here, after tangling with you."

All three of them started talking at once. It was the first time in days they could allow themselves the luxury of a simultaneous nervous breakdown. The babble continued unabated for several minutes until Jamie, shouting over the voices of the other two, said to Laurent, "Tell me all you know about the death of the Pope, the attempts on my life and the events and circumstances surrounding this entire affair."

Laurent pleaded exhaustion and suggested they all get a good night's rest and start off fresh tomorrow morning.

Carol agreed, and adamantly insisted, "Jamie, please wait until tomorrow,"

Whereupon she rose and went into the kitchen, returning with a round of cold beers, motioning the two men to drink up, as she began consuming her own. A little while later, she got a pillow and blanket from the closet for Laurent and encouraged him to lie back on the sofa. Removing his shoes, Carol covered him with the blanket.

Taking Jamie by the hand, Carol went around and turned off all the lights, making certain the door to the flat was securely locked. For good measure, Jamie propped a kitchen chair under the knob. Going to her bedroom, they undressed, and lying naked in each other's arms, slept the night away, the covers drawn tightly about them.

At eleven o'clock the next morning, Carol crawled out from within Jamie's encircling arms. She thought she had heard someone conversing in the next room. Donning a robe and slippers and brushing back her hair, she stepped out of her bedroom door to find Laurent talking on the phone. She walked by him on her way to the kitchen. He smiled and gave her a small wave of his hand. Apparently, his conversation had been going on for some time and was about completed.

While waiting for Jamie to get up, she busied herself making a pot of tea and setting the table for a late breakfast. Laurent came into the kitchen a few minutes later asking if he could be of any help.

"Well," said Carol, "if you'll watch the eggs and ham, I'll wake up the 'ol leprechaun, himself, so he and I can both hear what news you have for us."

Moving to the bedroom, she sat down on the bed next to Jamie. Brushing back his hair with her hands, she kissed his face and neck while gently urging him to get up; telling him how much she loved him and that shortly, breakfast would be ready. Slipping her hands beneath the covers, she slapped him on the behind yelling out as she exited the room.

"Eggs up in two minutes!"

Jamie stretched lazily. Taking his own good time, he made it to the breakfast table. In the bright morning light streaming through the kitchen windows, he looked like a case for emergency war relief. He had hurriedly dressed in the clothes he had taken off last night. His bearded stubble was flecked with lots of gray. His chin was still severely bruised. His hands looked as though he had used them for chopping glass, all scarred and bruised from his tumble down the stairs. Worse yet, pain and stiffness were settling in upon his bones and muscles from all the beatings he had taken over the past several days.

Emotionally, he was in high spirits. Jamie kidded Laurent about his seedy appearance and admonished Carol for her bedraggled look. Following his last remark, she gave him 'the raspberries'.

"If you don't behave, I'll make you finish your breakfast in the corner," at which point they all burst out laughing, knowing full well how miserable all three of them looked.

Laurent said he had heard from Father Gault that morning. He told Jamie, they had a rather extended telephone conversation. He thought it best, if after breakfast, they adjourned to the sitting room with their tea, and he would explain to Carol and Jamie everything that had happened.

"Joe will not be joining us in London. It seems the new conclave is to begin two days from now, on Saturday, October 14, and Father Joe will be extremely busy. He asked that you call him on Monday at the Vatican."

Jamie remembered he no longer had his attaché case or his note material. He had failed to mail his report to the general delivery box number as instructed, no later than Wednesday evening, the eleventh of October. Jamie mentioned this to Laurent, who responded.

"Father Gault knows all about who is to receive the report and why. It is no longer necessary, because Father Anselm has talked his head off to save his own neck."

Laurent asked Jamie's indulgence, explaining that he was getting ahead of his story and would like to start from the beginning.

"The Guardians of the Vatican, as we are called among those who know us, were told you were going to investigate the rumor that Pope John Paul I was murdered. It was decided you should be given as much assistance as was necessary to flush out any conspirators who might be involved. Ranking members of the Curia were already very disturbed over the triple deaths of Pope Paul, the Chinese and the Russian cardinals."

"Those same members of the Curia knew that the Chinese cardinal had warned Pope Paul VI that the Russian KGB was behind the takeover attempt in South Africa. It seems the Chinese wish to become allies of the West, because they fear a pre-emptive nuclear strike by the Russians. Their contacts among African terrorists have known about the planned Marxist takeover of South Africa for years."

"Just recently, this summer to be exact, the Chinese government pasted this information along to the CIA, as well as to its Vatican source, the Chinese cardinal. The Russian prelate was probably assassinated because of the information he passed on to Pope John Paul I. When his

Holy Eminence informed the Curia of what was discussed, if you'll excuse the expression, all hell broke loose! The Russian prelate had learned that there were a great number of moles buried deep within the Church's clergy."

"Come again, Laurent?" Jamie exhorted.

"There are nests of well-trained Soviet espionage agents who are priests in the Holy Roman Catholic Church," explained Laurent, "You, yourself, encountered one yesterday in Father Anselm and the nun, Sister Anna Maria, who was his female counterpart."

These agents, known as 'moles', infiltrate an organization and do absolutely nothing subversive for years until they are ordered to do so. Some agents trained by the Soviets have been known to remain dormant for thirty years before being used to carry out one single act of espionage."

Carol, who had been sitting there quietly listening, turned to Laurent incredulously and told him he must be joking.

"It's like something on the telly. Surely, no sane governments actually indulge in that kind of trashy behavior, now really,"

Jamie broke up laughing at her remark and said, “the key word was 'sane', and there were no such things as 'sane ' governments."

"Go on with your story, Laurent." Jamie was, by now, hanging on every word.

"The KGB is no longer satisfied with a number of mole nests within the Church and the Vatican itself. There is a major effort underway in Latin America to massively infiltrate the seminaries. Marxist agents are winning young, inexperienced Catholic priests over to their way of thinking because of the absolute poverty of the poor in their parishes. The Church realizes She is being outflanked by the Soviet long-range strategy and must decide whether or not to go along at the risk of completely alienating the government of the United States and many other countries in Western Europe."

"If necessary, the Vatican could play its trump card. Its own massive financial position in multi-national companies could be used to silence politicians in Western governments who might criticize the Church if She makes a sharp turn toward the left. Make no mistake, the Church has set Her sights on conversion of the poor in Africa and Latin America, and She cherishes the faithful ultra-conservative Catholics behind the Iron Curtain."

Laurent continued, "The Vatican communications network receives information instantaneously from around the world. In fact, every bishop in Europe is expected to make a full written report to the Pope every five years, including a personal audience. Every bishop in the world is expected to do the same every ten years. The Vatican receives and transmits coded messages daily, as you now know, Jamie."

Father Joe apparently had told Laurent it was all right to disclose all this information to Jamie since he had nearly gotten himself killed trying to find out about it.

"Through its worldwide sources, the Church alone has clearly discerned the Soviet master strategy."

Laurent added, "And, Jamie, we believe you were very close to solving it based on the authoritative information you have amassed."

Laurent continued, "Russia has established an offensive base in the Americas, Cuba to be exact. She can launch not only ideological warfare on Latin America, but from Cuba, she can successfully mount a first strike nuclear attack with conventional aircraft on the United States. With the exception of West Germany, there is no doubt in the Vatican that Russia could overrun Europe in thirty-six hours with her 40,000 tanks fully supported by infantry. Having gained these advantages, Russia distracts the Western allies with all manner of feints and bluffs."

"'What are her immediate goals?" asked Jamie

"Her immediate goal is to overthrow the Iranian and South African governments and take complete control of Africa and the Middle East. Then, economically, she can squeeze Western Europe dry, and it will simply fall into her lap. Presently, everything is slightly ahead of schedule. As far as Russia is concerned, Western governments are idiotic, and since Franklin Delano Roosevelt gave them Eastern Europe, they have lost all respect for the United States except for it technological skills and industrial, military and agricultural productivity."

Secretly, John F. Kennedy pledged not to invade Cuba. He appeared as a hero to the American public. Russia obtained what she never dreamed possible, a Marxist dominated country in the Americas protected by the United States. There are only two organizations that the Russians fear, the Catholic Church and the Peoples Republic of China. When they have secured Europe, Africa and the Middle East, all of Russia's efforts will be turned militarily and politically toward China."

"That chess game has been underway for about thirty years, starting with Ho Chi Min and Mao. Eventually, North Korea, Cambodia and Vietnam will begin to eat away at the borders of China, militarily supplied by the Russians. The long-range problem for the Soviets is the Church. They have known this since the early days of the Revolution."

"How long have the Church and Russia been at this game, Laurent?"

"In 1933, the United States recognized the Bolshevik government of Soviet Russia. Between 1917 and 1940, it is believed that the Russians murdered millions of their own people. Thousands of priests and nuns were murdered, and by 1935, the Russians had destroyed or otherwise converted to other purposes 24,000 Catholic churches."

There is on record in the Vatican a report filed by a Jesuit, Monsignor d'Herbigny, which completely summarizes the long range Soviet objectives and their fear of the Catholic Church."

Jamie was familiar with the generalities of that historic meeting.

It seems the priest had been sent on a diplomatic mission in 1925 to meet with the then Russian Foreign Minister, Chickerin. Who, in the course of their meeting stated, 'We communists feel pretty sure we can triumph over London capitalism. But, Rome will prove a harder nut to crack. If Rome did not exist, we would be able to deal with all the various other brands of Christianity. They would all finally capitulate before us. Without Rome, the Christian religion would die. But Rome sends out, for the service of her religion, propagandists of every nationality. They are more effective than guns or armies."

Chickerin had been quoted as stating, "The result of the struggle, my friend, is uncertain. What is certain is that it will be long."[1]

Laurent continued, "No power on earth now stands against the next successful stage of the Russian Master Plan for world domination except the Holy Roman Catholic Church. In all probability, Pope John Paul I was murdered as you, yourself, Jamie, described to Father Gault. Without the ring, no proof exists. The cardinals were assassinated to make certain they would not be around to convince Pope John Paul I to personally intervene in Africa and Latin America. Russia now controls the third world countries' voting strength in the United Nations and gains additional votes every year as Marxist regimes multiply."

Laurent went on to explain that the Pope was going to make a personal tour of Africa. When he arrived in South Africa, he was going to lend his support to the moderate blacks and the white government to swing the free elections favorably toward democratic objectives. Furthermore, he was instructing all his governmental emissaries to influence Western governments toward reaching an accommodation with South Africa, thus wrecking that portion of the Soviet strategy. Finally, he was going to address the Latin American Bishops' Conference, signing into Canon Law the strict new seminary requirements.

"The Marxists understood the persuasive magnetic personality of Pope John Paul I and knew he had behind his folksy exterior a brilliant intellect. Thus this one man could wreak havoc within ninety days on the most crucial next phase of Russia's plan for world domination."

[1] A. A. Bezcehungen des Vatikans Zu Russland, Vol. I; and its English translation can be found in "The Vatican in the Age of the Dictators - 1922-1945", p. 135

Laurent continued to spellbind Jamie and Carol with the unfolding of this historic and now tragic confrontation between one holy man and a cancerous world philosophy. The Church is theologically opposed to Judaism and Islam but only on an intellectual level.

For the last one hundred years, the Church has done everything possible to withdraw from even the hint of encouraging holy wars. In the 1930's and 1940's, it correctly realized that Russian Marxist theory and the Soviet Union were much more of a long-range threat to humanity than Nazi Germany.

The Church fervently hoped that Germany would defeat Russia. In turn be beaten by England and the United States. Insuring the survival of Western ideals and Christianity. The unforgivable slaughter of Jews and gentiles alike by Germany in World War II completely obscured democratic Germany's extreme dilemma in the late 1920's and 1930's. Only the Church and her princes correctly understood what happened.

The Germans were absolutely paranoid concerning a communist takeover and for good reason. The horror stories coming out of Bolshevik Russia were almost unimaginable. As the German economy collapsed, it was either Hitler or Communism. The Germans did, in fact, choose the lesser of two great evils.

It was unfortunate that at the time, many Jewish professors and intellectuals and artists inside Germany were openly in favor of Communism. Hitler cleverly used this against them in a maniacal fashion. Sadly, for entirely different, mistakenly humanitarian ideals, liberal-thinking Jews throughout the Western world supported Marxism for almost fifty years.

Only in recent times have they come to realize the truth. The Zionists in Israel have no such illusions and are passionate anti-Communists. The Church and its popes would never abandon the Jews and the Islamic peoples who believe in the same God, in order to reach an accommodation with Marxist atheists.

The Russians know this, and there has never been any doubt in their minds about what action Pope John Paul I would take. What was important was the charisma of this particular Pope and the critical time at which he chose to speak out.

"Who was the assassin, Laurent?" Jamie had finally asked the $64,000 question.

"It seems that Father Anselm has confirmed enough of the modern portion of the scenario I have just described that the Vatican now knows who was behind the murder of Pope John Paul and why Jamie, you completed your assignment by forcing the actual assassin out into the open. He was afraid of what you might find out. Your mysterious employers are more than pleased with your efforts, even though they couldn't receive a copy of your analysis. The Vatican, thanks to your investigation, now knows the truth. The assassin is of course, Father Anselm."

Jamie interrupted at this point and inquired about the other attempts on his life and how Father Joe had known where he, Jamie, was yesterday in the Basilica.

Laurent replied, "Father Anselm was aided in his conspiracy by members of the Italian Red Brigade. Anselm, remember, was a professional. He had no intention of killing you unless it became absolutely necessary. By tapping various telephone lines and bugging certain offices, he was able to know what you were up to at all times and how far you were progressing in your investigation. He was in a car with several members of the Red Brigade, whom he wanted to keep an eye on you in Rome, because he himself would be too conspicuous. When he spotted you crossing the street and pointed you out, the idiot driving the car thought Anselm wanted you killed and on that instantaneous assumption attempted to run you down. Fortunately, you were too quick for them."

Carol gripped Jamie's arm as Laurent told about the explosion. Apparently the Red Brigade occupied a room in the hotel next to Jamie's original suite on the sixth floor of the Hilton. Anselm wanted them to install another device besides the setup they already had to monitor your phone and bug your room. He took the risk of going up to bring them the new equipment. After all, Jamie hadn't met him yet, and at the time, Anselm never expected to meet him, let alone brief Jamie on African Catholicism.

When he arrived at the room, Anselm found one member of the Brigade manning a bugging device and a telephone tap. Anselm began explaining why the young man should drill a small hole in the bedroom wall, in order to install a wide-angle lens and photograph Jamie in bed with Miss Livingston or anyone else.

Anselm hoped that somehow Jamie could be blackmailed. If that failed, Anselm could release photographs that might reflect unfavorably on Jamie. Anselm and the young, high-strung Red Brigade kid got into a violent argument over practically nothing. Anselm left, slamming the door in disgust with having to deal with such an undisciplined and motley group. Anselm told Father Joe he was so upset at the time that he had accidentally knocked down an old lady upon departing the hotel lobby.

Apparently, the young man in the room said to hell with all the blackmail nonsense as a means of silencing Jamie. He drilled the hole in the wall all right, but instead of installing the special optical device, he chucked in a stick of dynamite and ran out of the building. He was shot by an Italian policeman just after the explosion. Anselm terminated his use of the Red Brigade after that escapade.

"What made them come after me?" asked Carol.

"Well," said Laurent, "last Sunday morning, Father Joe realized that you might be used as a hostage. The whole time you and Jamie were in Rome together, the Vatican had you followed and monitored, including, I believe, as you would say, your 'roll in the hay' on Saturday afternoon."

"Incidentally," continued Laurent, "Joe asked me to apologize to you for all the surveillance. It was a necessary part of the Vatican's own security measures."

"When Joe learned your room had been broken into, he surmised that what they wanted was your London address, so I was assigned to keep and eye on you. The Vatican simply checked with your hotel. They in turn quickly checked out your credit card reference files through a friendly banker and had your home address within fifteen minutes."

"Why did they try to kill me at the broadcast station?" asked Jamie.

Laurent smiled and said, "Father Anselm had Father Rene's office bugged. He listened in on the confrontation between you and Joe on Monday morning. That's when he conceived a brilliant plan. Anselm called on two KGB agents in Rome to almost, but not quite, kill you sometime Monday evening. He assumed that you would then be convinced that a conservative element inside the Vatican, including Father Gault and Father Rene, were involved in the Pope's assassination. The Marxist cause would be greatly assisted by your subsequent recovery and no doubt public disclosure of the facts."

"But that plan backfired," interrupted Jamie.

"Yes, Jamie," explained Laurent.

"But there was a contingency plan. Prior to Monday, Anselm asked an assigned KGB agent in London to hold Carol prisoner in her apartment for several days. He did not want you to mail your report Wednesday evening, if between Friday of last week and yesterday, you uncovered information that would expose the true assassination plot.

By Tuesday, Father Gault and several other members of the Vatican Guardians were watching you too closely. Anselm decided to kidnap your daughter as a way of getting you to give up all your documented information."

"Anselm wanted to get you out of Italy as fast as he could, before you and Joe together figured out what was really going on and who was responsible. Anselm didn't want an outsider's confirmation in writing to back up what the Vatican already suspected. Killing you would only have intensified the investigation. The Russians were more interested in destroying your papers and getting you out of Vatican City than in killing you."

Laurent concluded by telling Jamie that Father Gault told him to relax; the Church could now take care of its own. But, would Jamie be so good as to call Joe on Monday. Joe wanted personally to thank Jamie for his assistance; and, as far as saving Jamie's life, it was all just part of Father Gault's responsibilities.

The young novitiate then stood up and stretched while running his fingers across his beard, telling Carol and Jamie that he had been called back to the Vatican on another assignment and wished them both well. Carol asked if he had to leave now, and Laurent told them he would stop just long enough to pick up his belongings from a nearby rectory and be on his way, after a fast shave and shower. Looking at his watch, he estimated he had less than two hours to catch his plane. Carol walked him to the door.

Both she and Jamie thanked the young, handsome novitiate for rescuing her last night. Carol gave Laurent a grateful hug; and a sisterly kiss on the cheek, teasingly telling him he need not report either the hug or the kiss to the Vatican on his return.

Closing the door behind the young novitiate, she closed the door on Jamie's Vatican adventure. Turning around, she undid the belt to her robe and placed her hands behind her. Leaning on the doorknob, the robe fell open. Carol crossed her legs. A seductive smile illuminated her face alluringly punctuated by her emerald green eyes.

"It seems forever, Jamie."

For the next four days, she and Jamie fell in love a thousand times. Both of them spoke with Katherine long distance as well as Jamie's other two children in America. It was agreed; Carol would resign her job and come with him to the States. First they would spend a glorious ten days in the south of France and dismiss forever from their minds politics and religion, enjoying the solitude of their own company to the exclusion of all else.

EPILOGUE

On Monday, Oct. 16 - Out of a sense of friendship and loyalty, Jamie Bolin did call Father Gault on that very day, October the sixteenth, by which time he had learned that the Church had held one of its shortest conclaves. The Curia elected the Polish Cardinal, Karol Wojtyla, as the new Pontiff, to be known as Pope John Pau II. The very same cardinal Jamie and Carol had seen only a week earlier dining in Rome!

All calls, Jamie found out, for Father Joseph Gault had been directed to Father Rene's office. Upon hearing Father Rene's voice come on line, Jamie asked to speak to Joe, and inquired if Laurent was again occupying the outer office. As Jamie now looks back and remembers it, there was dead silence on the phone.

Father Rene told Jamie that Father Joe had been killed when he and a Father Anselm had fallen to the floor of St. Peter's Basilica from the dome balcony platform 235 feet above.

Jamie handed the phone to Carol, who was standing next to him at the time. He sat down, placed his hands to his face, and cried like a baby.

Carol talked to Father Rene for quite sometime, explaining about Laurent. Whereupon she was informed he was missing. Rene could not explain to Carol why Laurent, had told Jamie that Father Joe was alive, to say nothing of the remainder of his bizarre tale.

Father Rene said that even now the Vatican hadn't been able to put all the pieces together. Only Father Gault had known the whole story. Rene asked Carol if, at the appropriate time, Jamie might be willing to return to the Vatican and tell what he knew. Carol said she would speak with him, and later get back with Father Rene, which she never did.

Later that week, Jamie and Carol did go to the south of France. There, on a beach one day, Jamie told her he figured out what had really happened. Father Anselm was only a pawn in the game. It was Laurent, bright, young, handsome Laurent, who had tried unsuccessfully to murder Jamie. Each time, Father Anselm probably had tried to talk him out of such a foolish action. Laurent was not a mole, but an active KGB agent inside the Vatican. It was his ego that made him disclose to Jamie and Carol all those salient details last Thursday. But, no there had to be something more to it than that, and Jamie knew what that something else was.

Jamie's report was not going to be used by the Vatican to start a witch hunt for the assassin of Pope John Paul I. Jamie's report was specifically requested to be in no later than the eleventh of October, and Laurent knew that as well. Why the eleventh? Because, by the time it reached the hands of the appropriate cardinals, who could use it and have time to verify its conclusions, it would be October the thirteenth, only one day before the new conclave.

There would have been just time enough time to demand the election of yet another staunch conservative, absolutely trustworthy, Italian prelate. Such revelations would insure the election of an ultra-conservative pope regardless of any prior negotiations or agreements the Cardinals had made amongst themselves. Without documented evidence to influence the selection process at the conclave, anyone could be elected.

If a non-Italian pope were elected, the power of the Curia in the Holy Roman Catholic Church would change hands rapidly over a five-year period. It was not necessarily true that this new Pope himself be a mole or even sympathetic to the Marxists. What was important was that somehow the KGB knew with the death of Pope John Paul I, the next Pontiff would not be Italian. This would achieve a major step in undermining the ultraconservative, anti-Communist element presently in control of the Vatican.

Jamie realized that with the death of Pope John Paul I, it was no longer possible for the Church to intervene in time to affect historical events now taking place in Africa, the Middle East and Latin America.

Laurent had been, in effect, a double agent, the kind government bent spy agencies dream about. He had engineered the holding of Carol as a hostage, and then when he was ordered by Father Gault on Wednesday, just before Joe died, to fly to London and protect her at all costs, he simply telephoned the KGB agent inside the flat and set up the apparent rescue. Laurent expecting at any moment Father Gault would show up and believe him a hero.

Laurent learned Thursday morning, before Carol and Jamie awaken, that both Joe and Father Anselm were dead. He concocted the new scheme of telling Jamie just enough to make the story believable and distract Jamie from attempting to rush back to the Vatican in time to perhaps upset the planned outcome of the new conclave.

Friday, Oct. 20 - That same week, Jamie told Carol what he had now known to be the truth. It was belatedly reported that just before the convening of the conclave last Saturday, another Polish cardinal had died unexpectedly, Cardinal Filipiak of Poznam, while he was in Vatican City awaiting the beginning of the conclave.

Thursday, Nov. 9 - Several weeks later, a really bizarre item appeared in newspapers throughout the United States, one of those really grisly, little-known tales. It seemed that somewhere in the Virgin Islands, a handsome, young, blond European had been seen on the beach with a stunning Eurasian girl.

Witnesses caught sight of a gleaming metallic object that the man obviously had been showing off to his lady friend. A short time later, his body was found lying nude in a clump of nearby bushes. There were three deep stab wounds in his back and chest. The strangest part of the story was that his ring finger had been cut off, severed at the palm of his hand.

Jamie never saw the last two news items and always supposed that the Communists would eventually win in their struggle with the Holy Roman Catholic Church. But then, one never knows who the players are, and which side is really winning.

THE END!

Made in the USA
Columbia, SC
05 April 2019